THE COUNTESS
OF PRAGUE

Books by Stephen Weeks
The Countess of Prague
Awakening Avalon
Daniela
Sword of the Valiant—the Legend of
Sir Gawain and the Green Knight
Decaying Splendours—Reflections in an Indian Mirror

The Countess of Prague

Stephen Weeks

Poisoned Pen Press

Praise for the first
Countess of Prague Mystery...

"Highly entertaining, with a compelling mystery and a whirling dervish of a heroine who combines all the best traits of Elizabeth Peters' Amelia Peabody and Kerry Greenwood's Phryne Fisher, this wily, witty countess-sleuth's escapades will have readers clamoring for more."

—*Booklist* (starred review)

"...the plot is crammed as full of intrigue as a Viennese pastry is of cream. Weeks blends equal parts espionage and farce into a frothy confection..."

—*Kirkus Reviews*

"Hooray for Countess Trixie! Stephen Weeks has conjured a breath of fresh air with this colorful and memorable character. Fans of Elizabeth Peters will be charmed by the intrepid countess and her cast of valiant helpers. With its exotic setting and the promise of many more adventures to come, *The Countess of Prague* is sure to delight."

—Deanna Raybourn, bestselling author of the
Veronica Speedwell and Julia Grey mysteries

"Beatrice von Falklenburg is hands-down the most intrepid sleuth since Amelia Peabody. Stephen Weeks' deft handling of historical detail and culture mores makes *The Countess of Prague* an unforgettable read. Utterly charming!"

—Tasha Alexander, bestselling author of the
Lady Emily Mysteries

First Edition 2017

10 9 8 7 6 5 4 3 2 1

Library of Congress Catalog Card Number: 2017934131

ISBN: 9781464208423   Hardcover
       9781464208447   Trade Paperback

Poisoned Pen Press
4014 N. Goldwater Boulevard, #201
Scottsdale, Arizona 85251
www.poisonedpenpress.com
info@poisonedpenpress.com

Printed in the United States of America

to
Kateřina Z.

And thanks to
Auriol, Victoria & Lucie
for their inspiration.
Somewhere, in a mixture of these
diverse personalities, lies the Countess.

This book was written at
Skvorec Castle, Prague East, Czech Republic

I wish to thank the late
Rene Tesař
for his confidence in this work,
William Parker for proofing
and all those in Prague who helped me
find my way round the city as it was in 1904.

Prologue

It was in late February, when the melting mountain snows had swollen the banks of the Vltava. That great river normally forms a placid mirror for Prague's famous silhouette of golden-tipped spires, onion domes, and the gables and roofs of the fanciful houses of the age of the Empress Marie-Theresa — the view crowned by the old royal palace of the Castle. But presently the river had become an untameable monster. Its waters rushed like the torrents of hell through the genteel city and the ancient Charles Bridge was saved only by its stronger rebuilding after the great flood twelve years past.

For four days whilst these torrents tore through like express trains, ten or twelve or twenty abreast as if in some devilish race, those good citizens of this metropolis who ventured out had their curiosity aroused by the corpse of a man whose progress through the rushing waters had been arrested by the wooden staves stationed in the river to break winter ice and to prevent the flotsam of such a flood as this from damaging the Old Town Mills or indeed the new masonry of the Charles Bridge itself. Those on the bridge with opera-glasses could see little more than those without: his was just a gaunt shape, draped with weed from the river, in an attitude of accidental crucifixion on the staves.

And finally, on the last day of February, that is February 29th in the year of our Lord nineteen hundred and four, the anger of the waters subsided, their level dropped and the water became calm enough for the watermen to go about their business again. Dimly lit by the moon-round gaslamps on the embankment — for the Superintendent of Police did not want to excite a crowd by retrieving the body in daylight — the crucified form was pulled down and dragged on a boathook towards the shore.

An early spring mist lapped like milk on the surface of the river and was feeling its way insidiously into all the nooks and crannies of the water's edge which included the ancient slipway now bridged by the Františkovo Esplanade.

Two officers of the police were distinguishable by their stiff hats from the knot of watermen ready to pull in the boat and heave ashore the burden it was towing, a sodden heap of wet garments, barely recognisable as having once been a living being. It was dragged onto the cobbles.

Thus began the grand mystery which ended my solving of *petits mystères* as a sort of innocuous parlour game and took me into the darker nightshades of excitement — and fear — such as I had never experienced before and from which, as a woman of Society, I had been all the time protected.

In my mother's house even the tops of the piano legs were given little ruffled skirts so as not to arouse the sensibilities of polite young people in the upward mental progress of thighs to varnished wooden loins. Anything to do with Nature and the Lower Classes (a somehow inseparable combination) was completely hidden from us. 'Life' outside our Society merely came to us by way of tradesmen's tittle-tattle relayed by the servants or sensational articles in the newspapers which I had to steal from my brother. But then my mother was English, an explanation all in one. At least in Bohemia one felt nearer — according to her rather vivid imagination, at any rate — to the depravities of the luxuriant East or the wild Slavic splendours of Russia and beyond. The Turks had arrived at the walls of Vienna, after all, and even in Bohemia the coffee served in many establishments is what one would call Turkish.

Half of this exoticism flowed in my veins as the blood of an old Czech family; and half of it was purebred English, thirsting to cut the prim bonds of my stays and see…an adventure. But I must not dwell on myself. By and by I am sure the reader will learn enough — perhaps too much — of my own foibles. It is the narrative of this whole extraordinary affair which is of interest, hardly me. The corpse with its disfigured face pulled from the flood, seemingly without an identity, was just the beginning…

Chapter One
Life's Lottery

"A Count without a bank account, doesn't count" — thus spake my husband, who by his own words, should have been countless, an unaccountable Count. By the turn of a card, aided by the great agricultural depression which had gripped most of Europe for nearly a decade, his father had managed to lose the country estates with the fine castle that bore the family name, Falklenburg. They said he had died of a broken heart at his folly, leaving my husband with a worthless title, the breweries, some parcels of land in an unspeakable country town, a large pile of Brazilian railway shares and a huge social obligation.

His wisdom should also have included "Once a Count, always a Count" — for he felt bound to keep up appearances. For a time, and that included the time directly following our marriage, we lived well. Income seemed to be increasing and whilst we were not rich, I easily persuaded my husband that we should rent the old palace of the Counts of Harrach in Jindřišská Street. At least it was a proper palace, with two carriage entrances (an "in" and an "out") onto the street and all the rooms — the decent rooms, that is — on the first floor over the domestic offices. However, I have to admit that this was no longer the smartest part of the city, no Mayfair or Belgravia. Commercial concerns were now being built all along the thoroughfare and I understood that until our offer, old Count Harrach had been considering selling the building to a shoe manufacturer to 'sell shoes to the people'. I didn't realise that 'the people' were in need of shoes, such was my snobbery then. In the villages it was common to see young women going to the well, or children almost grown, unshod. But one cannot call prejudice ignorance.

In fact, almost as an insult, or so it had seemed, a new hotel had opened practically opposite our palace only the year before: The Palace Hotel — designed not to receive members of the upper classes who might have need of such an establishment in the capital, but mere 'commercial travellers and sales representatives'. The result of this was that I had given standing instructions to the coachman always to turn right on leaving our "out" entranceway, thus avoiding having to pass this upstart that was no more a palace than was the railway station.

Suddenly two years ago the income which had supported our almost modest household — thant is, modest for those with aristocratic obligations — appeared to stop. My husband told me that the decline in the fortunes of our breweries had caused this. We had managed to keep the brewery next to our old castle in the country and another in the nearby town.

Here I should point out that almost every castle in Bohemia has its own brewery. Beer is the national staple — as desirable, but more abundant than water in the Sahara Desert. To have the building's chimney visible from the drawing room windows is *de rigeur*. In England, I don't have to say that to have any associations with trade, or certainly to admit to any, is instant death in Society. Drawing room windows in country houses there must only overlook lawns, parterres or avenues cut through one's own woods. Livestock must be kept at a distance, beyond a ha-ha. Human livestock, and the habitations thereof, must not be visible. Several great English houses had moved whole villages to prove this point. In Bohemia, castles are nearer to villages and towns, and in fact are part of them, and the scent of toasting hops and roasting malt pervading the air in garden or house is proof enough of ancestral lineage and financial stability.

But now the Count was telling me that the rise of the great factory breweries in Pilsen and Budweis was threatening feudal brewing, and hence we were poor. We were rescued by the modest inheritance of my mother-in-law, who had died that summer. But we were living off capital, the banks offering too low an interest for us to scrape by. We were facing the prospect of having to rent our carriages by the hour and dismissing our stables. Monsieur Yves, our chef from Paris, had already gone (well, he was actually poached by the brand new Hotel Paris, but a stoneware bowl's throw away). At least I insisted on keeping Sabine, my maid. How could a lady do without a French maid?

So it was time to improvise, and somehow I managed to keep our heads held high enough in Prague and Vienna, and my Drawing Room Evenings were just as respected as those of greater palaces — and perhaps harboured a few more of the more interesting artists, writers, and musicians than some of the stuffier establishments of Austo-Hungarian Imperial Society.

I had heard nothing of the corpse retrieved from the river. Sensational news of that kind was usually relayed to me by Sabine, she having heard it from Müller, the butler. But of late Müller had taken to insisting on having Saturday nights off unless it was a Drawing Room or a dinner party, and I had missed the reporting of this find from the river. Real news — and by that I mean news of new milliners setting up, who is flirting with whom, or which captains from the Újezd Barracks have now been posted to what regiments in the Imperial provinces — I would hear, of course, from my friends. Gossip is a far stronger medium than flimsy broadsheets with ink that can so easily stain a satin bodice or ruin a good pair of gloves just by opening the things — unless they'd been ironed first.

In the end it was the telephone which conveyed the news. It was Sunday afternoon, and Müller's discreet cough made me turn from my writing bureau. Müller, a man of middle age, was just over medium height, from a family in one of the German cities of North Bohemia, had his hair swept back in the manner of clerks, servants, and petty officials and sported mutton-chop side whiskers. As usual, his eyebrows were lifted as he spoke, as if to give some expression to his flat, unruffled speech.

"The General is on the telephone," he said, opening the door of my boudoir a little wider so that I could follow him to the little *cabinet* at the head of the stairs where the apparatus was installed.

General Albrecht Schönburg-Hartenstein was my great aunt's husband. Uncle Berty, as we all called him, was now retired. He spent much of his time at his clubs — the Deutscher Klub and the Wiener Cercle — and considered himself an upright Austrian, totally humiliated in war but loyal and correct nevertheless. Naturally, he patronised the theatre and the opera but no-one would have thought him artistic in any sense; he was far too conventional. He considered the Czechs in the family he had married into to be mildly seditious, which amused him rather than giving him concern. For this sweeping racial generalisation my half-Czech origins counted as full.

The copper wires crackled.

"Trixie," he said without any social foreplay, as was his manner, "the Police Commissioner has been round to see me. The body of a man was pulled out of the Vltava yesterday. He is hardly identifiable, having met with a terrible death, and there were no possessions of any kind with him — but his underwear bore a distinctive laundry number."

The line crackled again.

"Are you there?"

"Yes," I replied. "You were telling me a laundry number?"

"Yes, it transpires that an astute member of the Police Department recognised the mark as an army number. The corpse was that of an old man, far beyond military service, so they checked with The Invalides Hospital, and it is they who must have put the police in touch with me — for, you see, it's old Alois. They still use the old veterans' army numbers there. From the time one first follows The Colours right to the grave, so it seems, a soldier is a number."

Alois had been Uncle Berty's batman all through his army career. He had retired with my uncle more than twenty years ago, spent ten years as a valet for a German gentleman living in the city, and for the last seven or eight years had been living at the army veterans home, in the fields on the edge of Karlín. Uncle then went on to tell me that he had been asked to go to the City Morgue to see if he could identify him. Knowing my penchant for adventure, he asked if I had the strength to accompany him. It was his not-so-subtle way of ensuring I would say yes. Strong? Of course!

Uncle Berty had been the subject of my solving the very first of my little mysteries, as I liked to call them. How simple that had been to solve, or rather to prevent from happening — a simple little party trick!

I had found myself at a dinner party given in the Kolowrat Palace on the other side of the river, directly below the Castle in more gentlemanly Malá Strana. It was a smallish party, only twelve of us, and I noticed between the serving of the fish and the meat that Uncle Berty, sitting almost opposite me, had pocketed two of the crested silver dessert spoons that formed part of the elaborate service of cutlery and solid silver salvers on which we were being served. Now I knew of his penchant for removing items like this. He just couldn't help himself. Whether it was the thrill of the chase, the risk to life and limb now that there was no cavalry in his life to chase him, or quite simply some disease of the mind which creates such compulsions, I do not know. However, I was certain that he had them tucked into his waistcoat.

He always returned what he had taken. It was usually a few days later: "Look here old man, I seem to have come away with your cigarette case. I am so sorry…" But tonight, I was surprised he hadn't realised that the irascible old Count Kolowrat always gave his butler strict instructions for the courtyard doors of the palace to be locked until all the silver plate was accounted for and securely back again in the strong-room next to the butler's pantry. This could cause such a very embarrassing scene, very bad for Family.

Before I withdrew with the other ladies I carefully secreted two other spoons in my evening bag. When the gentlemen had had their cigars and liquor and joined us in the Drawing Room, I took a brave step, one which had dominated my thoughts fully for the previous thirty-five minutes. I didn't usually do this kind of thing. I was no shrinking violet, but also no noisy hussy. "Ladies and gentlemen," I announced like some kind of fairground barker, "I have a new conjuring trick to delight you — if you will allow me, Count."

I turned to old Kolowrat, who nodded approvingly.

"Here I have in my hand, a pair of silver spoons," I went on. Both my hands, I might add, were sweating. I had never done any kind of public display like this before. I was not an exhibitionist and it was before I was married. The spoons I held aloft, so that everyone could see them.

"Uncle Berty, will you step forward, please?"

Looking a little surprised, he did so.

"So here you see the spoons…and now you don't!" and I passed my hands quickly behind my back, dropping the spoons into a convenient fold of my bustle, an indication in itself that this was a few years ago. My hands returned to the front, and I opened my empty palms to this very select audience. There was a brief second of absolute silence.

"Now Uncle Berty, if you please, allow me, " and I reached into his waistcoat and produced the identical pair of crested spoons.

I raised the spoons into the air. "Bravo" and hearty applause was the universal response to my apparent sleight of hand.

As the tumult died down I quietly passed the four spoons to Countess Kolowrat who winked at me — whether from admiration for the trick, or in acknowledgment of the truth, I shall never know. "Beatrice, my dear," she said in a confidential manner, "you are so clever."

Uncle Berty was pacing up and down the pavement outside the Morgue when I arrived. He turned to me immediately: "Damn bad business if it is old Alois," he was saying. One couldn't quite make out his expression underneath his copious moustaches and side-whiskers which seemed to unite in one continuous fur mat. But his eyes were fiery — a sign I knew of old.

I had taken a fiacre from outside St. Jindřich's churchyard, where there were always one or two waiting, rather than hang around for my brougham to be made ready. The fiacre's single and singularly unattractive horse had made swift work of the journey of only a few minutes.

The Morgue was a new building, replacing the rat-infested structure that had adjoined the old ghetto down in Josefov. But at any hour, like its predecessor, it attracted the potentially bereaved and the curious to view the unclaimed bodies of the day. Fortunately, I had never had occasion to visit the place before.

"But why, Uncle?" I asked. "Why such a 'bad business'?" For all I was aware, Uncle Berty hadn't visited old Alois in ages — although I had heard he had been very solicitous in paying the extra for him to have a single room in The Invalides with special rations — meat on Sundays and Wednesdays, fish on Fridays, and five large jugs of beer daily.

"I'll have to explain later," he replied. "Didn't Karel ever tell you about the Tontine?"

Karel is my husband.

"The what?" I asked.

"Then obviously he didn't. As I said, damn bad business all round if old Alois is on parade at this moment in front of the Almighty."

Even allowing for an early March day it was chilly inside. New electrically driven refrigeration devices had been installed, which I was informed, were far more efficient than the running water, cold from the Vltava, that had served the previous establishment. Uncle Berty was soon shaking hands with the Police Commissioner, who introduced Inspector Schneider, who was handling this case personally under the direct supervision of the Departmental Superintendent.

We passed through a long chamber, bounded from the public by a series of plate-glass windows at which the morbid, the nosey, and the genuinely concerned were pressing their faces to get better views of the current crop of corpses laid on the slabs before them. Our man was in an adjoining room, a dormitory — if Sleep Eternal could be described thus — for just four departed souls.

The sheet was removed and the scene revealed was one of utter horror. Something terrible had happened to the face of what was clearly an old man, now stripped of his clothes and whatever dignity he deserved in death. His features were really quite unrecognisable. Uncle Berty nodded for the sheet to be replaced, then shook his head. "I can't say it was or wasn't him," was all he said at first — then he added, "And was it murder?"

Inspector Schneider produced a type-written report. "The doctor completed this but an hour ago. Together with the police observations, it makes interesting reading. You see, it might not have been murder at all. The injuries to the man's face were made sometime after death, which could well have been from natural causes — he was, after all, of advanced age. They could have been made as he was dashed against the staves in the river, for example — or some other accident."

"So he might have simply had heart failure and toppled into the river?" I asked. If I was brought here, without even being offered smelling salts, then I should at least put in my two-kreutzers'-worth.

"Now that's the curious thing," Schneider went on, "for that's impossible. You see his pockets were weighted with stones, and there was some form of cord about his ankles. Whoever dumped him into the river wanted him to stay there. It was only this flood that has meant his body couldn't settle."

"But I don't understand," queried Uncle Berty. "If he had died of natural causes, why couldn't he have been buried quite normally?"

"That's what we have to find out," replied Schneider, "and there's another even more curious aspect to this case. The matron at The Invalides says that Alois Tager is, allowing for his age, quite well and alive. In fact, you can go and visit him yourselves."

Uncle Berty seemed highly agitated at this revelation and we were very soon bound for The Invalides Hospital by the river in the suburb of Karlín. It was a large building trumpeting eighteenth-century military grandeur, home to several hundred pensioners of the Austrian army. The gravel drive was lined with cannons on wooden carriages that appeared to date from the Napoleonic Wars — but if it looked like a palace from the outside, the inside was quite different. Perhaps the inmates would have felt uncomfortable without the familiar Spartan surroundings of a barracks.

The matron and warden, who were apparently a married couple, were anxious to give Uncle Berty the full treatment that a famous general deserved, although obviously somewhat put-out that no notice at all of his intended visit appeared to have been given. Employing a matron and a warden who could share the same bed, and who between them could take any leave that was necessary whilst requiring no outside help, with one always there in charge, was indicative of the spirit of meanness that pervaded the place. These two employees had caught the mood of the governors to perfection.

It was soon clear that old Alois, dead or alive, did however get his extra allowances that Uncle Berty generously provided — but no doubt to the nearest gram of meat and centilitre of beer.

The corridors were full of these old soldiers of the Empire, wearing the military-style tunics peculiar to The Invalides, relaxing in the weak afternoon sun by playing cards or smoking their long pipes. We were shown into a bare white-washed room with a plain pine floor and four simple wooden chairs. "Mr. Tager will be here in a moment," we were told.

"*Mr.* Tager?" asked Uncle Berty.

"After working as a valet for some years, Tager sees himself as a servant rather than a sergeant. In fact he is allowed not to wear the military tunic. Others like to keep the old discipline, but it is really up to them. They find the blue tunic affords them better gratuities in the city, if the truth be told," answered the matron.

In less than a minute a door at the far end of the room opened and an old man, bent with age and seated on a wooden wheeled chair was pushed into the room. His head lolled onto his chest, and when he did finally look up his eyes seemed weak and watery and there was no recognition in them.

"He's like that, I'm afraid. He'll not know you," offered the warden.

"And how long has he been…well, insensible?"

"He had an unfortunate fall a few weeks ago. We thought he was dead. But we had the card and sent word to those people of his to come for him. They came within the hour and he was taken to hospital. When he came back, about a week ago, he was much reduced in his abilities." It was the matron who replied this time.

"But why wasn't I informed?" Uncle Berty's voice was rising. I could feel the pressure in that well-known steam boiler of his, behind his lined forehead, increasing. "And who do you mean, 'those people of his'?" He seemed quite indignant.

"Why, The Union of Servants, of course. His years as a valet had earned him entry," said the matron.

"But Uncle," I interjected — and not just to calm him down — "is this old Alois or is it not?"

It looked as if a sudden thought had struck Uncle Berty. Then he turned from looking in the direction of the old man and looked me straight in the eye: "Of course it is he. Who else could it be?"

I was about to ask "then who is it in the Morgue?", but for some reason I decided not to say anything. Uncle Berty, after all, must be able to recognise the man if anyone could.

I shared Uncle Berty's carriage back to Jindřišská Street.

"I'd better tell you why Alois is so important to me. Besides being old comrades — we had survived the slaughter of the Battle of Königgrätz and many another scrape I can tell you, and never a day passed without my belt and boots being polished to perfection, decorations all in order and my coffee just as I like it — besides all that, there is the Tontine. And that's a matter of real importance."

"You said you'd explain…"

"And so I shall. I'm still surprised your husband hasn't — I mean, you must have noticed."

"What, Uncle Berty?"

"That your income suddenly dried up a year or two back. That was because of the Tontine. He never explained?"

"I am only his wife, remember. But I shall be totally exasperated if you don't this minute explain it to me."

Uncle Berty raised a bushy eyebrow. I think he would have rather liked to see his pretty Countess great niece have a temper tantrum. It might stir his blood. However, for a quieter life he proceeded to explain:

"A Tontine is a lottery of sorts. It is a way of raising finance, and it is named after an Italian banker by the name of Tonti, who started such a scheme in France two hundred or so years ago. Twenty years ago a Tontine was proposed and raised here in Prague."

"Wasn't there once a Tontine Theatre up near Vinohrady some-where? The building would be about twenty years old, surely? It's called something else now, I think."

"Precisely. The promoters of the theatre raised two hundred shares of one thousand guilders each to build the theatre, and then signed a lease to the management for forty thousand guilders a year. It was solidly built — not like these wooden arenas which have sprung up around the city in recent years. The rent from the theatre was distributed to the shareholders equally, but on the following basis — and this is where the Tontine idea comes in — each shareholder has to nominate a person over sixty years of age in order to join the syndicate. Then, as each of these nominees dies, the shareholder loses his stake, and the dividend to the remainder increases accordingly. When there is only one left — secured on the last surviving nominee — then that shareholder reaps all the benefits."

"And are you a member?"

"Yes. The Tontine Theatre was indeed the investment, and I was persuaded to join by your husband. A thousand guilders was not a huge sum to put down, and the potential reward is enormous. Your husband —"

"Don't tell me — the great gambling Falklenburgs. He had a share, I suppose?"

"He did."

"And he lost it?"

"Unfortunately, yes. You see, he secured it on his mother's life. She seemed a person in very good health for her age, able to live long, very long indeed. Věra had a strong constitution."

"But she met with my mother, and they began hunting together…"

"The English. How reckless they are when they are around horses. And this 'side-saddle' — how could she be expected to survive jumps over hedges and streams perched up there like that?"

"My dear Uncle, I am sure I could stay mounted through The Charge of the Light Brigade. Mother-in-law's horse stumbled, that's all."

"But the point is she died, and Karel lost his investment — the annual income together with the chance for the big dividend at the end. At the time we were down to three — Karel's stake, mine, and a Jewish banker in Josefov."

"And who is your nominee?"

"Trixie, you must have guessed —"

"Of course. That's why you have been so solicitous about paying for his extra comforts."

"My old batman, Alois. A man of iron. As tough as —"

I cut him off: "But I saw you hesitate when trying to identify him. Did I not?"

"My dear niece, I don't really know if that is him or isn't. It looks like him, but then I have to guess how he would look if he couldn't recognise me. It was that mischievous glint in his eye which I missed. I have often found on the battlefield that corpses are quite difficult to identify — it is the animation in the faces of the living that counts for half the ease of recognition. But you understand I had to acknowledge him. Did you think I would possibly risk losing my share now too — the Tontine having got down to just two lives?"

"You are an old scoundrel, Uncle — but why really did you invite me along for the visit to that chamber of horrors?"

"There is more to this business than meets the eye. It is clear that dirty work is afoot — but why on Earth should someone else want to keep old Alois alive in this way?"

I thought for a moment. "I agree. I should have thought that the problem with Tontines is the temptation to bump people off when it gets down to such ridiculous odds. This is just the opposite, and yet there is no such thing as a Good Fairy. I have had a sheltered existence, but that I do know."

"Precisely."

"And why me? I am good at solving the little mysteries in our own social circle, I grant you. Apart from a pair of silver spoons, I have repatriated an entire wallet containing no less than a thousand krone."

"I would have returned it. I had no wish to take the money — it's just that the wallet was so very tempting, left in a jacket draped over a chair so near the billiard table. You understand?"

"Quite so, Uncle. But this is a mystery in a very different class, surely. Which is precisely why it intrigues me already."

"I have the half dividend of the Tontine — that's twenty thousand krone a year — coming in, so there's enough to pay whatever your expenses might be. I see this being more complex than it may look. It needs looking into."

"And dangerous, Uncle? Have you thought of that? I wouldn't like to end up at the bottom of the Vltava, of that you can be sure."

"I somehow feel that no-one will suspect a perfectly respectable Countess doing a little delving. It is the perfect disguise. I would not be surprised if the famous Sherlock Holmes himself does not adopt such a ruse."

"He would never get into the shoes, Uncle. Or tolerate the forty-five minutes it takes Sabine sometimes to sew me into my dress — but then the great Mr. Holmes would probably not be attending any balls."

By this time the coach had arrived outside the Harrach Palace in Jindřišská Street and had been standing for some minutes. The coachman was too well-disciplined to interrupt, and my footman was waiting patiently to open the door of the carriage. I put my gloved hand on the rail of the door, just under the window — the signal for my servant.

"Where do you think you will start, Trixie?"

"With this," I said, and with my other hand proffered the card of The Union of Servants which I had removed from the matron's desk at The Invalides. My first act in this saga, and the beginning of my new life — as a lady who does something.

On such a high note, as if ending a scene in a cheap melodrama, I stepped out of Uncle Berty's carriage which sped off towards the hustle and bustle of Wenceslas Square at the end of the street, and out of my sight.

Chapter Two

The Theatre of the Absurd

The address given for The Union of Servants turned out to be a single door in a narrow side-street where the New Town meets Vinohrady. For centuries Vinohrady had been the site of the King's vineyards, but over the last fifty years it had gradually been built over with apartment houses for the bourgoisie as Prague expanded up the hill beyond the limits of its old fortifications, rendered redundant by modern cannons. Indeed it was from Vinohrady's commanding heights that the city had been bombarded by those wretched warlike Prussians first in the 1750s and then again in the 1860s.

The door had no doorbell and no letterbox, and over it — in paint which had faded and begun to peel — was a sign which could still be made out: 'The Tontine Theatre Stage Door' and over part of this was a much newer black-and-white sign proclaiming "The Union of Servants." On the door was painted: "In attendance, Mondays and Wednesdays, 8am to 11am." Round the corner, The Fenix Theatre — as it was now called — stood in a distinguished square, the model of propriety. It was temporarily closed, awaiting a new production in the spring which would shortly be announced and which would be produced by the theatre's manager, a Mr. Gerard Duvalier.

I stepped back to where my carriage was drawn up outside that dingy side doorway and got back inside. "There must be some mistake," I said to the coachman. "Drive me home." Actually I thought otherwise: I knew I was onto something.

It was as I was awaiting luncheon at home that I began to take stock of the situation and my preparedness to deal with it. I came into the dining room and found an unopened telegram awaiting me by my place, which was the only one laid. It was from Karel announcing that he would not be home for luncheon as he had promised — for I thought he would be alighting from the train arriving at 11 a.m. — but that he would in fact be delayed for several more days in Vienna. I was annoyed because this meant that he must also have sent another telegram to the butler or the cook. Normally I resented anything which undermined my position as mistress of the house. How I would dwell on such petty affronts, but today I didn't care a jot!

My mind was being nourished by more important matters and the first thing on it was this Inspector Schneider. Should his investigations find that the man in The Invalides is not Alois Tager, but an impostor, then Uncle Berty's finances would be in ruins. On the other hand, Schneider might well come across interesting evidence of what lay behind the fraud — for perhaps there was something worse in store for Uncle Berty if he were simply to ignore what was going on. But that was why he asked me to unmask the mystery, surely? Uncle Berty was to be found somewhere between the goading devil and the ocean's deep. Whatever happened, I decided, I should keep in touch with this Schneider, if only to divert him away from the extraordinary truth which was staring us in the face, resolving that instant to invite him for English tea the following afternoon. Having called for pen and paper I hastily wrote a note which I had sent by pneumatic. The telephone was still an instrument of intimacy, like whispering in someone's ear, whilst the pneumatic post literally flew one's letters on a blast of air under the streets of Prague — the epitome of efficiency and modernity.

But the usual tiresome day, that normally would have stretched forth listlessly until some amusement or another was destined to occur, seemed today filled with thoughts of things that had to be done. I summoned Sabine.

"I want four or five plain dresses, just like the one you are wearing," I asked her. "And I want hooks-and-eyes. I won't have time for you to sew them on."

"But, Madame," cried Sabine, "my dresses have buttons."

"Yes, of course." How out of touch I was. Common buttons, of course.

"And the colours?"

"Plain, dull — mustn't stand out. Brown, grey, dark colours."

"Very well, Madame."

Sabine turned to leave, but I had another thought. I opened my bag and handed her the card for The Union of Servants. "Have you heard of this organisation?"

She shook her head. "Maybe I can ask Müller?"

"Is this another one of his days off?"

Sabine nodded. "Then I will ask him myself when he returns," I said.

Once the table had been cleared I went into the library. Most of the books had been inherited and thus never opened. On those few occasions when I did look more closely at them, I found many of the volumes still had their pages uncut. But on the shelves near my husband's desk were his books, the ones he actually used. Soon I found what I was looking for, a general encyclopedia and also a Prague Almanac for the current year.

I made myself familiar with the general principles of trades unions and of course disturbed myself with the thought that my servants were, according to modern thought, treated appallingly. All except Müller, that is. I just hoped that The Union of Servants was indeed a fake. I couldn't deal with strikes, lock-outs, and negotiations with Workers' Committees — Heaven forbid! Certainly there was no reference to this Union in the Almanac, whereas every other body active in Czech or Austrian affairs seemed to be represented.

Next, I decided to take practical steps to become a detective, for that — surely — was what I was to become, even if only for the duration of this peculiar affair. Downstairs, on the ground floor, was a room my husband used to receive tradesmen and conduct such business as would not be appropriate upstairs. This, I decided, would become my office. I had the footman and the kitchen boy rearrange the furniture, what there was of it, and I knew that all this would infuriate Müller — but then he shouldn't have taken the day off, should he?

Then, on the table I arranged some blank slips of paper. These I began to fill in with what few facts were available to date. When, as a newly married lady, I had first taken on the responsibility of running a household, I had found this method of putting tasks on slips of paper to be invaluable. It quickly became clear to me from the scanty information adorning the scraps of paper that there was an open gap — through which my theories could fly. Surely the 'Alois' at The Invalides should be watched? Maybe then I would be able to discover his true identity.

St Jindřich's churchyard was but a few steps away. Outside its low boundary wall was the place where the public fiacres loitered, waiting for passengers. There was a drinking trough for the horses and usually there were feed-bags too. In the winter there would be a stall selling hot *klobásy* — the common sausages of Prague. Behind the wall, in the old churchyard, were some large blocks of stone which had remained there after the architect Josef Mocker, having re-gothicised St. Jindřich's Church, had then turned his hand to the tall belfry tower by adding a fanciful, spiked gothic roof. Over the past generation or so all Prague has been turned into a rendering from some fairy-tale picture-book.

Amongst these odd stones was always a knot of urchins who would be available to run errands, fetch and carry, hold the cabbies' horses, and generally do anything that would earn them a few kreutzers. If the shoe manufacturer had wished to sell shoes to the people, then this would have been a very good place for him to start.

I summoned the footman, since Müller was not available, and told him I wanted him to go and select four of these urchins, ones that looked of better character at least, including one who must be about my size — and that I wanted to interview them. In an hour or two my new office was filled with the youngsters, causing me to open the window for somewhat fresher air. I managed to do all this as if I were born to the job. I had to keep going at this frantic pace, for if the music stopped, so to speak, perhaps I'd never recover my nerve.

I had the urchins lined up and first asked them their names. Two were called Honza and two Jirka. So the two large Honzas and Jirkas I called Honza Major and Jirka Major, and the two smaller, Honza Minor and Jirka Minor. I told Sabine to get my purse, and I treated each of them to the price of a new pair of shoes. I really couldn't have my new employees going about barefoot. Then I asked Honza Major, the boy who was about my size — and maybe he was fifteen or sixteen years of age — if he would go and buy a complete new outfit for himself, on condition that he return quickly with his old clothes and give them to the housekeeper here for washing.

I could see my footman looking aghast as I paid out the money, but I assumed he had been a good judge of faces and of character and that these fresh-faced boys of the streets could, within certain limits, be trusted. I told them all to be back at my new office by seven o'clock in the evening, sharp — for we had work to do.

At six-thirty I told Sabine to go down to the kitchens and retrieve the boy's outfit, which should have been washed and dried by that time. A moment after she left my boudoir I decided to go after her. There was something I needed to insist upon, and anyway I was beginning to enjoy visiting the bowels of my palace. I confess that I had hardly ever seen the kitchens or the other service rooms. Beyond the green baize door was a whole world virtually unknown to me, and isn't it the unknown which is always exciting?

Down in the room next to the stone-floored kitchen I found the boy's few clothes draped over one of the big ceramic stoves. A laundry maid was heating irons on the fire, ready to press them.

"No, no — don't do that," I cried, making it clear I meant to take the garments away with me.

"So it's for fancy-dress, Madame?" asked Sabine. "You want the authentic look?" She smiled.

Sabine was fast on the uptake. Then and there I began to try the things on.

"Sabine, where is the shirt?"

"Shirt, Madame? There is only this ragged coat and the trousers."

Poor boy, I thought. How little I knew or understood. How little he wore.

"Also," she added contemptuously, "these — socks." These last objects seemed more holes than wool.

"Sabine, go to my husband's dressing room. Find that thick white flannel shirt of his — the one he wears for shooting. We might have to cut the sleeves. And some socks."

"*Oui*, Madame."

Very soon the Countess of Falklenburg was transformed into a regular urchin of Prague. This naturally caused much merriment amongst the servants and I realised I had to ask them to tell no-one outside the household. "Otherwise my little surprise will be spoiled" I thought to add. I wondered if they believed my little fib about fancy-dress, but what else were they to think?

I went upstairs to my dressing *cabinet*, and stood in front of the cheval mirror.

'Bold steps, Trixie — you must take bold steps…' I said to myself, 'You'll get nowhere without bold steps…just stuck where you are.'

It hadn't occurred to me before that I was "stuck" — but that was indeed the case: not enough money to go further up in Society, and yet not having the ability to enjoy life without feeling guilty about the obligations of *noblesse*. How free I would be as an urchin! I winked at the disreputable creature looking back at me from my mirror.

⌇

By seven-thirty my modest force of four urchins had arrived at The Invalides Hospital. There were thus five of us all told. One was conspicuous for the newness of his clothes, another by the cleanliness of hers…I mean his — and also by that person's rather delicate ankles, had they been visible. Thick woollen socks, itchy and coarse to the touch, did supposedly cover them, except of course for my silk stockings underneath, which I would certainly not do without. I did not forgo my silk drawers either — there are limits! Four of the band walked most uneasily in stiff, new shoes. For two of them they were the first shoes they had ever worn. To the observant my bespoke boots with their neat pointed toes would have been a ready giveaway.

I felt curiously vulnerable, as if in one of those nightmares where one finds oneself naked in the street or at some grand social occasion. It was my gloves — or, rather, the lack of them. I couldn't remember ever going out without gloves, winter or summer. I was abroad in the world, bare-handed.

Müller had returned before we had set out. I had explained to him the new development. Naturally he was disappointed not to have been involved from the start, showing it by even turning up his nose at the odour of poverty still lingering in my husband's Business Room.

"How do we get them washed?" I had asked him.

"Quite simple, Milady. We give them the money and they go to the Vltava bath-house on Na Struze Street. Once a week should be entirely sufficient."

By "we" he meant that he would dip into his pocket for the cash and that I would eventually reimburse him with his monthly wages. Despite his meagre servant's earnings he always managed to have a wallet full of banknotes and pockets jingling with change. I, for my part, never seemed to be able to lay my hands on a single krone when I needed it.

By seven-thirty-six we were all gathered beneath a window. It was now almost completely dark and the only light we could see was that spilling from the lamp inside the room which was nominally that of Alois Tager. For the moment I didn't know my little urchins as individual personalities, but I did know that some necessary familiarity would occur sooner or later. I had briefed them well before setting out. Once we had identified our man, they were to watch him in shifts, follow him if he went out, and daily report his movements to me. The paltry salary I offered for this work seemed like fairy gold to them and it made them very anxious to please. Besides, I think they were rather intrigued by this Countess in *mufti*. But the lure of gold was also to buy their silence. And since I had trusted them, I believed they could be trusted as their way of repaying my confidence in them.

In a few moments we could just see that the door of the room opened and the creaking wheeled chair was trundled in. The old man sat there in it, alone in the room, staring at the door for some while. Each of the urchins clambered up to the sill to take a look. They had marked their target. It was time for me to go and leave them to their nocturnal vigil.

I'd had my brougham parked out of the way, down by the river. Shaking my hair loose from under the cap that had lately been Honza Major's and pulling a dark cloak over me, I jumped in, startling the drowsing coachman, and soon we were heading up through Karlín and towards the Old Town along the old Königgrätz highway, or perhaps I had better refer to Königgrätz by its Czech name, Hradec Králové. Having a bit of Irish blood in me as part of my English roots, of course I sympathised with a culture that had been suppressed by a rude invader.

The moon faintly illuminated a string of barges on the river and the carts of perhaps the last of this year's ice-breakers, which were already lumbering along to await their dawn start by the riverbanks. The ice was for the beerhouses and butchers. Winter was about to give way to spring with only a modest frost and the ice-breakers' transparent harvest was rapidly diminishing. But, you see, I was already beginning to realise there was another world out there, beyond the salons of the rich, the bored, and the jaded.

In the city proper, as we were rattling down Hybernská Street, accordion music spilled out from the gaslit interior of a still-crowded *hostinec* by the old Staatsbahnhof, Prague's first railway station. And I was happy.

The next morning, following my breakfast tray, I was to be found seated as usual in front of the dressing mirror as Sabine brushed my hair. Although this normally took anything up to an hour-and-a-half, today I instructed her to be brief: twenty minutes at the most, despite more tangles than usual. I could not conceive how many hours I had wasted in front of this particular mirror — how I debated with myself whether to use "Beatrice" more or "Trixie" less. Today was certainly a Trixie day. Trixie, I felt, was more a name for an adventuress. Perhaps, as in the novel of *Dr. Jekyll and Mr. Hyde* that I had finished reading only last week, I could be two people: Beatrice by day and Trixie by night!

But this was a time for changed attitudes. As I had been getting into bed last night I had noticed a black speck on my ankle. I raised my leg to brush it off — and the speck had jumped away. A flea. That in itself did not shock me: I had often come across the things from my mother's dogs, although never in my bed-room. It had made me think of my responsibility to the poor boys, whose orbit of existence was so totally different from mine. I would ensure Müller pressed the right money in their hands and sent them regularly to the Na Struze Street Baths.

I stared hard at myself in that mirror wondering how this face — so familiar to me that I felt it couldn't fool anyone — would handle this Inspector Schneider when he called. Maybe I should flirt with him, seduce him into not pursuing the old man in The Invalides. In any event, unless he was so very smart, he would never make the connection with The Union of Servants. Never. And this so-called Union must hold the key to the mystery, I felt sure. Yes, I literally reflected again on the matter, this face was capable of fooling at least Inspector Schneider! Bold steps… don't forget!

With my hair loose, my robe *décolletée*, I found I was also staring at the new Trixie — who had, even for just a few hours the night before — tasted emancipation. I had felt what it was like to be unconstrained: to be able, if I so chose, to run or to climb. I could do anything, go anywhere — just like a man. How wonderfully free it must feel to be, for example, Karel — who can simply send off a telegram to dear wifey, just like that, to state that he would be a few more days in Vienna or wherever. And what would he be *doing* in Vienna? It was not my place — or shall I say Beatrice's place? — to deign to ask.

On the other hand, it is a woman's place — her duty — to seduce. Once my hair was reasonably brushed from its tangles of the night before, I stood up, which was Sabine's signal to put me into my corsets. The Inspector would be distracted by such a dainty waist as mine, I felt sure.

After she had finished lacing me, pulling me down into a wasp-like fifty-two centimetres with which — despite my little bid for emancipation — I was most satisfied, I completed dressing and sent for Müller.

"Milady…?"

"Tell me, Müller, what do you know of The Union of Servants?"

His faced flushed red. "It is a social club, Milady. It meets on Saturday evenings."

"And does it offer other benefits to its members?"

"How do you mean, Milady?"

"If you were ill, for example — would they take you to hospital?"

"Not that I know of, Milady. I can make enquiries, if that would be Your Ladyship's wish."

"No. I was just curious." I was certainly curious as to why he'd flushed so red at the mere mention of the Union, but I went on: "Now, about the cucumber sandwiches for the English tea this afternoon…"

My mother had been very punctilious about teaching me how to instruct staff in the preparation of cucumber sandwiches. The bread must be that white, anaemic stuff of English nurseries; the crusts must be cut off each slice before making them into tiny triangles; the cucumber too must have its peel removed. A little sprinkling of pepper can be used, a pinch of salt, and lastly, the tiniest pinch of refined sugar. They should be made no more than fifteen minutes before serving.

"Are they to be prepared as usual, Milady?"

I had been hoping to spend at least a quarter of an hour at this chore, and now the wretched man had denied me of it. This was the way I realised I was used to passing my days, in the exaggerated pursuit of small things. At that moment the footman ran upstairs and whispered in Müller's ear.

"There are two young men to see you, Milady. Well, one of them is but a child. I understand it is Your Ladyship's wish to interview them in His Lordship's Business Room?"

It was Jirka Major this time, accompanied by Honza Minor — half my force. Jirka Major recounted how, after the old man had stared at the door for some thirty minutes — seemingly waiting for someone to come — he had boldly stood up, climbed out of the window, nearly discovering the watchers, and had calmly walked down to the street, turned left, and walked to the end of the electric tramway line. There he had boarded the city tram, closely followed at this point by the two of them — Jirka Major and Honza Minor. As the tram passed down Na Poříčí Street it crossed with another, going in the opposite direction. One second he was there, and suddenly, the next second he wasn't. The urchins did not know if he had managed to jump onto the other tram or whether he had simply jumped down into the street. In any event, he had vanished. The two lads got down and wandered about the streets for a while, but they did not catch sight of him again.

"Do you mind, Missus, if we went in his room?" said Jirka Major rather sheepishly after he had finished his report.

"Well, it's not strictly legal, but what did you find?"

"Nothing really. The man has no papers, unless they are in an old locked box. But we did find out something, didn't we, Honza?"

Honza Minor, tiny, swarthy with a mop of black hair and bright-eyed, piped up: "Yes, he likes onions. Has a whole cupboard full of them."

I thanked the two for their vigilance and got Müller to pay all of them in advance for a further twenty-four hours. Now at least it was clear to me that the man in Alois Tager's room was indeed an impostor. However, if anything, that made matters worse. The Tontine would be lost to Uncle Berty if this were to be found out, and now it might be said that I — and perhaps Uncle Berty, if I told him — were deliberately holding back the truth. I spent a moment examining my morals. Bold steps won out. With Inspector Schneider I would have to be even more circumspect. That would be fun.

"Tell me, Inspector, is there any more news about the dead man?"

We were in the drawing room. Tea had been served and Müller had withdrawn. Inspector Schneider was making heavy weather of balancing a china plate laden with too many sandwiches for one helping, a napkin, a bread fork, and a cup and saucer. He needed practice for these English tea-time gymnastics on laps and tiny side tables of the most unstable design. I hoped I would be putting him at a distinct disadvantage.

I quietly observed him as he struggled. Not so old, considering he was an Inspector — perhaps only thirty-five or six. A mere boy compared with the usual types one saw as senior officers in any Austrian Imperial service. Dark-haired, but I liked that. No moustaches but a well-defined strip of beard that gave him the feel of an artist more than a policeman — I liked that especially. And grey eyes — not the "steel grey" of cliché, but the grey-blue of a wintry sky.

Swallowing down the last of a sandwich he was able to answer my question: "News? Only that your great uncle wants to give the found man a decent burial. He says no matter who he is, he deserves a wooden box and grave that can be recognised, even though it will have no name."

"How very peculiar," I added. Uncle Berty could very nearly give the whole game away by showing too much care for this "unknown" corpse.

"Your great uncle has suggested the grave be identified by the only mark we have — the laundry number."

Uncle, I thought, that is far too near the truth for comfort. He'll be ordering the regimental band to turn up next.

And then he slipped it in, the shell from his personal Howitzer: "And may I ask what is your interest in The Union of Servants?"

Good God! How could he know that? Had he traced the card from The Invalides? Should I bluff this out? But perhaps he could trap me. Then a brainwave:

"My butler is, I believe, a member. I went there the other day. I wanted to check that they do have social evenings on Saturdays — otherwise I am concerned that my staff may be having nocturnal rendezvous on a far too regular basis."

"Well, that explains it. You see we're keeping the place watched. Your carriage was noted; you were noted. Our man there is very thorough."

"And in what connection?"

"Oh, nothing to do with our case. No, this is something else entirely. For the last few months — in fact from about November of last year — coinciding with the sudden arrival of this 'Union,' there have been a spate of thefts all over the city. Nothing very large taken at any one time — a jewelled tie-pin, a watch and chain, gold cuff-links, ladies' adornments of various kinds including a complete set of jewels which were only paste, and I cannot believe the thieves would be so ignorant. These are all things servants could so easily purloin themselves."

"So the 'Union'?"

"It crossed our minds that the Union might be the fence for all this stuff. It certainly wasn't coming into the regular places — the pawnshops and the shadier dealers down on Dlouhá Street."

I was thinking of a panic Karel had got into a couple of weeks ago. Now that was a watch-chain, with a particularly valuable emerald fob. But it somehow reappeared or he managed to find it again, so it certainly wasn't one of these mysterious disappearances.

He went on: "We turned the Union offices over a few days ago. It was done carefully so it should not have been noticed — but there was nothing there. Just the records of their members and the usual correspondence."

"You impress me," I said only half jokingly, "with all the vocabulary of crime, I mean — 'fence', 'turning somewhere over'. So I assume what you are looking for must be — in your parlance — a 'snitch', no?"

Schneider laughed. "Well, we couldn't get one of our own men in there — that is, as a member. These Union fellows checked his credentials and found, of course, that he wasn't engaged at the address he'd given. He was refused membership, turned away."

I was feeling more relaxed now. I didn't think his pursuit of the Union had anything to do with old Alois. I shifted my position in my chair quite deliberately. He would have caught a flash of stockinged shin if he was sharp, or eager.

"There's another curious feature about the place," he went on. "At the Fenix Theatre, in the square — and as you've noticed, the Union's offices were once part of the theatre and despite the fact that it's closed at present, once a week a very grand crowd arrives."

"That's hardly odd, is it? It is simple to find out who is organising private concert parties or the like."

"No. It's not that. Our chap stationed in a room overlooking the office entrance couldn't help noticing that so many of these distinguished people arrive by tram. Not one in a carriage."

"And the evening is a Saturday, I suppose." I was already having an idea about this.

"Yes. It is. So it is." Schneider looked at me in that condescending way men do when a woman dares to have a thought of her own, especially one a step ahead of his thinking. So to even the score I tapped my cheek very gently in the social semaphore that indicates to the viewer that he has an enormous eyesore of a crumb in the corner of his mouth. He quickly dispatched his napkin to mend the offence while I smiled benignly with what I hoped was coquettish menace. I decided to end the interview while I was on the high ground, so to speak.

I rang the bell and Müller appeared to show the young Inspector out whilst we exchanged the usual meaningless pleasantries.

"You will see on my card I have written my private telephone number. If ever the need arises —"

I cut him off politely: "Oh, I am sure I shall not feature in any of your investigations again. But do let me know if there are any more developments in the matter of the dead man. It must have been a mix-up with his laundry, of course — but then that means —"

"That we still don't know who the gentleman is. Only one of them can be Alois Tager. Good day, Your Ladyship."

I had nearly four days to wait until Saturday evening, for then I was sure I would find out something of great interest about this

Servants' Union; it must be connected to the balls or concerts that were held on Saturday evenings in the theatre. There were just too many odd events happening that led back to this one place, once called The Tontine Theatre.

Hold the apparatus for me, will you, Müller?" Müller dutifully held the part like a candlestick and proffered the earpiece to my ear. "That's a good man."

After what seemed an eternity, Uncle Berty was brought to the telephone at the other end.

"Good Lord, Trixie. I thought it must be an emergency — or my wife. Nobody telephones one at one's club." I could sense Uncle's mild apoplexy.

"Uncle, will you still be there in an hour?"

"Well, yes — of course. I'll be having luncheon at…"

"Thank you. Good-bye, Uncle."

Müller replaced the earpiece on its rest. "Be so good as to send Sabine to me again, will you?" I said. Servants at least give women some opportunity for ordering men about. Common courtesans have that chance, too, I supposed. Men turn to jelly at the hands of a woman who will — well, I can't say "give" exactly. We all have our price of one kind or another.

I had hardly got back to my boudoir before Sabine was once again there. It hadn't been many minutes previously that she had been occupied on the new reduced-time hair-brushing regime and pulling the corsets back only to fifty-four centimetres — just a little more comfortable for a woman of adventure.

"Sabine," I announced, "I want to see my husband's wardrobe."

Due to our economies, Karel's valet had had to go. The butler
and the maid attended to his dressing requirements between
them. Men's attire is, after all, so simple to put on compared
to that of a lady of fashion. And he looks well in whatever he
wears. He's slightly built, so clothes hang well — and not too
much taller than I. "The best gifts come in the smaller packages"
he was always reassuring me, before we were married. It wasn't
his vanity which precluded him from ever saying "the smallest
packages," for he knew very well the size of the minute box
that might contain a ring with a very fine diamond, or a pair
of ear-rings to match, for that matter. As I had reflected earlier,
we all have our price.

In a short time I stared at the mirror: Could I possibly get away
with this? — I wondered. But I knew this was a time of change
for me…change and challenge, and I was ready for both!

The Deutscher Club was on Na Příkopě — the grand street
that once ran along the moat of the Old Town's fortifications,
and faced the town walls. During the last century, following the
demolition of the walls, the other side of Na Příkopě has been
built up with grand commercial and institutional buildings,
such as Uncle Berty's club.

Karel was a member but rarely went there, and on the one occasion I was invited, being a woman — although a Countess — I
had to use the side entrance, very much like some woman of the
night, and visit Karel for coffee in the Stranger's Salon. "Stranger"
was, I presumed, the club's euphemism for the female sex.
That attitude was certainly never conducive to introducing any
intimacy into the cold, arranged marriages of the high-ranking
military staff and politicians who were the club's mainstay.

The club's entrance hall was lined with tall, grime-dulled eques-
trian portraits — old men on young horses; surely there was
some metaphor there? There were few paintings of the battles
these warriors had fought, for the Austrians had had a run of
losing most of them over the last hundred years. To make the
club member feel illustrious and the visitor tiny, the rooms were
as tall as cathedrals.

The head porter eyed me suspiciously. I could feel his eyes
searching out various items of my apparel with disapproval.
They lighted first on the carnation I had bought from the flower-
seller on the corner of Panská Street — I thought one of these
new colours so much more fetching than the normal red that
Karel wore. Then the eyes travelled across to the rather jaunty
way that I (and Sabine) had tied the silk cravat. I felt my heart
pounding — so loudly, I imagined, that the man behind the
desk must have heard it.

I was hesitating, expecting him to initiate the conversation, such
as it should be. Women should not be so forward…except that
I wasn't a woman at this moment. I started to ask for "General
Schönbur…" and suddenly I stopped. My voice…I simply
hadn't thought of it, having devoted all my attention to looking
like a man. Now I would be giving myself away. I converted my
first utterance into a coughing fit, while preparing my voice to
descend to the lowest octaves I could reach…

The head porter finally deigned to look up at me, at my face, and
took off his pince-nez. "So you're another one of these theatricals?" he asked, but he did not wait for a reply, nor even asked
my name. "I shall have the General informed of your presence.
He will be found in the Reading Room."

I walked as boldly as my timidity would propel me, hoping not
to see myself in a mirror — for surely then I would have given
up this nonsense. One male booted foot, filled out with two

socks, boldly stepping out, followed by its companion. Where on Earth did I get this ludicrous bravado? If I were unmasked, it would be the biggest scandal to hit Prague since the morganatic marriage of Archduke Ferdinand. But on the other hand, this was a test — if I could get away with this, then I could get away with murder…but, on second thought, that wasn't such a good analogy.

At last — and the ten or twenty seconds had seemed to last an age — I could see him from behind. I recognised that distinguished head of grey-white hair, in front of which was the daily from Vienna, the *Wiener Zeitung.* In one move he folded the paper, rose and turned. There was a look of excited anticipation on his face, I swear it. He was not actually disappointed as he got closer, but it certainly wasn't the same expression — like a dog salivating before a huge bone — that he had worn for that brief moment before. Who on Earth was he expecting?

"Good Heavens! Trixie, I shall call the authorities. You just can't do this. It's never been done."

"Uncle, the Tontine, remember — and your late batman? It's very serious, you must know that. I need to see you."

"God, Trixie, I suppose you're right. In prison, having broken club etiquette will hardly seem relevant."

"We are in this together, remember? I have some news."

"Well, you'd better stay for some lunch. Only club food, I'm afraid. We men rough it when the distaff side isn't around. Makes us feel like hunter-gatherers rather than affected French boudoir chasers."

"Talking of which, Uncle, who are these 'theatricals' who visit you here?"

Uncle Berty went crimson — no, beetroot red. He skillfully fielded the question:

"Remember the Tontine, Trixie. As you said, we are in it together."

As we made our way to the Dining Room, Uncle Berty bent forward and whispered in my ear: "By the way, I think that is more of a summer suit. You should wear a black frock-coat in the winter. Karel knows the form, of course."

I said neither of the two rejoinders that crossed my mind — not 'But Karel is the last person on Earth I would confide in', nor 'And do your theatricals only wear black?' Uncle Berty was known — and feared — as a once ferocious old warrior, so I chose not to antagonise him any more than I had already. I ran my hand through my hair, trying to smooth down the newly cut ends which I felt were sticking out like the quills of a porcupine. Of course this was a risk, but it was sort of on home turf. If I could get away with this, then perhaps I did have what it would take to be the detective needed for this mystery. And it would keep all the money in the family — no strangers dipping into it.

When we were seated he leant across in a very confidential manner: "Trixie, for God's sake, keep your voice down."

I determined to speak a whole octave lower.

"So there's news from The Invalides. I got it just this morning. Our patient spent yesterday until darkness sitting and staring at the door to his room. This morning — and he doesn't sleep there — he resumed his watch. At about ten-thirty two gentlemen, escorted by the warden, entered his room. They asked the inmate if he was Alois Tager, to which, after a moment or two, he gave a cursory nod. At this the two gentlemen left. After ten minutes, by which time the two gentlemen had left the establishment, our inmate stood up, took another coat, put on a hat, and simply marched out of the place."

Uncle Berty had an explanation:

"As is customary at this time of year, and again in another six months, I get a letter by pneumatic from the directors of the Tontine Financial Association to say that a certain number of nominees are still alive, and my share is therefore…well, now it's just two lives and half shares. Those were the doctors doing their twice yearly visit. Judging by the speed of the communication, they must have already done old Pinkerstein's nominee."

"Pinkerstein?"

"He's now the only other shareholder in the game. Banker fellow, lives opposite the Jewish Town Hall — owns the whole block, the one they have been rebuilding on the site of a corner of the old ghetto. I shouldn't think he gives a damn. In the last twenty years his fortune has, I am told, increased twenty times over."

"By owning a bank? I thought banks hadn't been doing so very well." I realised, after the event, that this gem of wisdom had been given me by Karel. It could well have been one of his stories to cover losses on horses, Tontines, or baccarat. I hoped his losses didn't include the expenses of tarts — he wasn't charismatic or wealthy enough for a high-quality mistress.

"No. He bought an invention and the company which manufactures it."

"Manufactures what?" I asked.

"The common suspender clip. Humble, but prolific."

"Yes, I read an article in some magazine only the other week. They say that the suspender will take all the romance out of underwear. Who could possibly find such complicated engineering romantic compared to simply untying the silk ribbon of a garter?"

"I think wearing men's clothing is making your tongue too loose, my dear. I am blushing at the thought."

But how wonderfully we had steered clear of his 'theatricals'. Were any as pretty as me, I pondered as finally a very ordinary meat soup with noodles was served. I had heard that such behaviour is common in the army, but I hardly expected it from — well, from somebody I knew and respected. This certainly was a time for discovery. I hadn't decided yet whether the notion — that my own uncle might be "one of those" appalled me or enthralled me.

"I suppose your attire is because you are now a detective, on the scent — eh?" he enquired, and I told him about what I had found out so far — and the police suspicions of The Union of Servants.

"There's something certainly going on," said the crusty old fellow when I'd finished. "For example, I can't find my medals at the moment. Now that's strange, isn't it?"

It was Saturday evening. My carriage went past the theatre first, at my command. The streets were slippery from the melting snows, and Tylovo Square, where the New Town meets the slopes of Vinohrady, reminded me, as so often Prague did, of the boulevards of Paris. Umbrellas were down, however, as for the moment it was not raining.

"I want to see what's happening first, before I get down. Go round once more," I called out to the coachman.

Indeed there was quite a throng around the porticoed entrance to the Fenix Theatre, and a very smartly turned-out crowd it appeared to be. There were bound to be people I knew. They could tell me all about it, surely this mystery, whatever it was, could be solved in a trice, I felt certain (the foolish optimism, of course, of the beginner). But it was strange — mine was certainly the only coach in the square; there were none outside the theatre, not even a fiacre or two. As we were again on the far side of the square a horse-tram drew up, and out came ten or twelve more guests from a common tram. What could be going on? Had Society embraced socialism without my having the faintest inkling?

It was already dark, and the great outside gasoliers cast their bluish light on fur-trimmed capes, elaborate hats, twinkling jewels, men in Ulsters, monocles, and kid gloves. Society. This was a Society "do," no mistake about it, and despite my lack of invitation (and I was wondering how on Earth I could have been missed out), I would find some mild enjoyment in it. After all, if this event is connected with The Union of Servants, then presumably there would be large numbers of them to wait on us.

So it was with a keen sense of anticipation that I stepped from my carriage, the door held open by a theatre commissionaire in a braided tailcoat with brass buttons. In a moment I was already deeply shocked: this flunky winked at me. Well, I thought, if that's the way The Union of Servants encourages its members… and then he addressed me:

"My, you do look the part."

I had a good mind to bat him about the ears with my fan, which was still in its weighty silver case. But then I had the sense to keep quiet. I was here to investigate, although I had never been insulted in this manner by such an individual before in my life. I surmised correctly that detective work would mean biting my tongue on more occasions than just this one.

Inside, the theatre foyer served as a big ante-room. Coats were being taken off and handed into a cloakroom. There was now a greater twinkling of tiaras and exposed areas of bosom, low-cut dresses being the fashion of the moment. But try as I might, I couldn't actually see anyone I knew. I put this down to the fact that we were mainly all walking towards the theatre auditorium, and so most of the company was presenting its back to me.

As we passed into the auditorium itself I could see that it had been transformed. It was no longer a theatre. A huge stage set not only filled the stage itself but projected forward on wooden platforms so that it filled the stalls to form all four walls of a huge ballroom, lit by the glow of hundreds of candles in three or four huge chandeliers. The crystal chandeliers, however, were slung on ordinary ropes from somewhere above the stage.

There were white-haired old generals bedecked with medals, even — at least I thought I saw — a flash of a Grand Duke in full dress. Their stately wives or consorts fanned themselves from the heat of so many people and so many candles. I was puzzled. Surely such an event as this should have been announced properly in the Social Calendar?

An orchestra as one might find at such a ball was playing, which had not reached lively waltzes yet. The evening was only just starting. Supper was laid out on long tables on one side of this artificial ballroom — and strangely, it was set out in the new-fangled style where one had to virtually serve oneself. The waiters, such as there were, existed merely to lift the lids of the large silver-domed chafing-dishes so that guests could poke about and furnish their own plates. That was not to my liking, but then — at twenty-eight — I was already feeling a little conservative sometimes. Tonight was to be one of those times, obviously. I felt like my mother.

There were other things which slightly annoyed me. No — they plainly attacked my sensibilities. Maybe it was the way one or two of the guests held their forks, or the way one blew her nose, or perhaps the way a couple seemed to share a joke with too loud a laughter. I was beginning to bristle. My innate feelings of Class, that sense when the dignity of my proper station in life seems threatened, when…when I had the shock of my life.

Standing in front of me, not more than six metres away, was my husband. Karel was supposed to be in Vienna. How dare he be here? And with whom? Luckily for him he was talking to another gentleman, or else I would have made a scene. I had always imagined myself in a jealous rage — but Karel had never even provided the stimulus for that. Now I was to be disappointed again.

I strode purposely towards him. He was turned away from me. I spoke clearly so that he could not avoid the clarion call of his own wife:

"Karel. Karel?"

My commanding tone was instantly recognised, for he immediately turned round. And I was confronted by Müller, Müller my own butler dressed from head to toe in Karel's clothes and wearing Karel's decorations. And he flushed the colour of my husband after a good session with the schnapps.

"Milady. I can explain," was all he could find to utter.

Even pulled in to only fifty-four centimetres, all I could find to do was to faint: a fine thing for even a novice detective.

Chapter Three

Into the Breach

I awoke alone in a stuffy, airless room with a window of obscured glass. It appeared to be a dressing room for an actress, although it was certainly tawdry enough to take the allure of the stage from me in an instant. On one wall was a large mirror surrounded by electric light globes which were not illuminated. Around its perimeter were various *carte de visite*-sized photographs of actors and actresses, perhaps those in the most recent production. There was that distinctive smell of greasepaint, despite there being none in evidence. In fact, the only evidence of human occupation was feathers which had dropped from an ostrich boa near to the door. The gas mantle lighting the room itself needed changing so it was hissing, while some very distant voices were coming from somewhere outside.

It was a depressing place. Collecting my thoughts together I wondered if I had only dreamt that I had seen Müller, dressed as my husband. But the fact that I was obviously still in the theatre gave that nightmare some credence. I was still in the pink organza dress which I had worn to this peculiar ball, although it had been loosened around my bosom…yes, yes, I had fainted. How stupid of me to put myself at their mercy…whoever "they" were. Perhaps I wasn't cut out to be a detective, after all.

I quickly got up, straightened the folds of the dress, making sure it was sitting correctly behind, did up the braids at the front and went to open the door. It was locked. I tried it again — perhaps the lock was stiff…but no! I was being held prisoner. The room which up to that point had merely been depressing suddenly took on the aspect of a frightful tomb. If only it had been my husband, and how was Müller connected to all this?

But the voices I was hearing — they didn't seem to come from outside at all. They were in the room, or at least that's how they sounded. Looking up I could see just over the door a metal funnel-like object — that's where the voices were coming from. Of course, it was a kind of speaking tube, presumably connected to the Stage in order to call performers. There was a conversation going on, its tone in raised voices, near to the far end of this appliance. There were two men, rough men of low rank, arguing — and what's more, what set my ears tingling, was that they were speaking in English, that is if the accent of the east side of London could be described by the same adjective as Shakespeare's tongue. I recognised the accent because my mother used to imitate it when she used to read *Oliver Twist* to us in the nursery. Cockney, she had called the brogue.

"So she's a real Countess, is she, you say?" said the first man.

"But I can't think what she was doing 'ere. Must've been some kind of mistake. One of her own servants recognised her," replied the other.

"And didn't no-one stop her? You had a man at the door, didn't-cha?"

"'E just thought she was a good 'un — well done up for the party — not a *real* one."

"Blundering fools. Now she knows. Knows too much. You realise what you'll have to do?"

"When the others come back, eh?"

I too realised, only too well, I was in imminent danger of my life. It seemed impossible that such low deeds could be done to a fine woman in a beautiful evening gown. Would I be pulled from the Vltava, too? It was simply too disgusting to contemplate.

A moment's pause was what I needed first, so as not to panic my thinking. After that I must concentrate on getting out. To deflect my mind my eyes wandered over the photographs of these thespians tucked into the frame of the mirror. One or two of them looked vaguely familiar; perhaps I had seen them on the stage myself, or perhaps most of those engaged in the acting profession tilted their heads in that fashion, smiled so falsely and with darkly made-up eyes, male or female. But then one of them made a different impression. He looked familiar in another way — hadn't I seen this man recently? But I didn't want to excite my brain over this, especially when there was work to be done in seeing if I could escape.

Ninety seconds later two thoughts came. The first was, having surveyed the room, I could not think of any way I could let myself out of it. The second was about that actor…in this photograph — certainly I had seen him recently at The Invalides: the bleary-eyed man playing the role of old Alois! That was him; I felt sure of it. Obviously he looked here a little younger and very much more cheerful — but it was his thin features and soulful eyes, even when dry, that gave him away. I quickly plucked out all the photographs from around the mirror and hid them in my little evening bag, miraculously still with me. Perhaps they would turn out to be an entire rogues' gallery, if ever I lived to identify them.

With that last action I knew that a deep gloom would soon settle upon me. How long would I have to await my fate from these rascals? And if only I did know more than I did. I still couldn't work out these villains' scheme and what it was all for. I also realised that I didn't know how long I'd already been here — or even what time of night it was, or if it was day and the windows were shuttered. I hadn't taken a watch nor, of course, any money — what need have Countesses for such things at a party?

At the very instant my heart had begun to sink in earnest, about to gravitate to the very depths of despair, there was a tap at the windowpane. I tried to open it, but to no avail. Whoever it was on the other side could see me struggling. A darker shape got near to the window casement, darker than the deep grey that was sufficing as either lamplight or moonlight. "Stand back," a man's voice was saying — and a booted leg came smashing through the glass with jagged fragments shattering to the floor. The alarm must soon be given by these sounds, I thought — and then there was a hand outstretched. I gave myself to it, and was pulled towards its owner.

He gave a startled cry: "But what have they done to you? Your hair, Milady," and for the second time in one night I was staring incredulously at Müller, now balanced on top of a ladder. I felt a chill breeze. As he manhandled me down the precipitous slope of this swaying thing, I realised he had been shocked by the fact that my hair had been cut short. But that I had done yesterday. After Sabine had spent such a time brushing it and I had dismissed her, I had chopped a fair measure of it off myself. The untangled tresses I put in a box to remind me one day of former graceful Countess Beatrice. Then I had dressed in a suit of Karel's and marched with a broad, mannish step to Uncle's club. It all seemed like an age ago.

The wig my milliner had loaned me must have become abandoned somewhere in the Fenix Theatre. "Please don't concern yourself on that score, Müller — I am unharmed by them." As I said this I made the mistake of looking down, and this made me feel quite... No. I had fainted for the last time this evening — or rather Beatrice had. All I had to do now was to close my eyes and rely on the strong grip of my rescuer. But my nerves were further shaken by a shudder — the ladder had slipped a few centimetres on the icy surface of the pavement so far below. I could see some others running to the base of it to save it from toppling. I gritted my teeth as heroines do in cheap novelettes and soon I was gliding gently to Earth...

As my feet touched the pavement, Müller realised that his arms were still around my waist. I hadn't had that reassuring grasp for a long while! He quickly moved his hands away as if my whale-boned form had given him an electric shock. "I am as pleased to see you now as I was surprised earlier," I heard myself saying, somewhat imperiously. Then I uttered these words for the first time since he had entered my employment: "Thank you."

Standing by were four familiar figures, two taller and two shorter. My urchins! And there was one other — the recognisable figure of a lamplighter of Prague, doubtless glad to have his ladder returned.

But my bag — what of my bag, with the photographs? Müller had correctly read the anxiety on my face, and drew from behind his back the very article. "I retrieved this from the sill, Milady."

Müller summoned my coach which was waiting round the corner, and soon I was on my way back to Jindřišská Street. I recognised the side entrance to the theatre, that purporting to be The Union of Servants' office, as we passed by. Two men were running out, running in different directions — not realising that one of their birds was flying from under their very noses. I couldn't get a proper glimpse of them, but one of them at least seemed a large, rough shape — a person I would not like to have handled me, or to have sent me to the bottom of the river, if that had been their purpose. The other seemed thinner, his legs slightly bowed, perhaps — but I had hardly a chance to see.

In my newly familiar kitchen with its big stoves that are alight and warm all day and all night and with so many bright copper pans on big shelves, Müller and the hall-boy who let us in, made hot *grog* for all. I felt as if I were merely recovering from some ill-conceived practical joke and not from an experience which had quite possibly threatened my life. I was heartened only by the fact that I seemed able to brush off such fright on the basis that I had recovered intact from it all — and that, as if it had affected some other person's life, was simply connected with the business upon which I was engaged. Or perhaps it was a little more sinister — that the world of my Mr. Hyde couldn't really threaten that of my Dr. Jekyll?

The urchins looked with wonder at the hall-boy's blue velvet coat with gold frogging and at his white stockings, buckled shoes, and gleaming heraldic buttons, blue and gold being the livery colours of the Falklenburgs.

"Can you have a flag?" I was asked directly by young Jirka Minor, with his hands cupped round his steaming grog and between noisy slurps. But how was I going to stand on manners now, with my life-savers?

"Do you have cannons and a real castle?" asked Honza Major, the tall fair-haired youth who was the leader of this little band.

I decided not to tell them that, whilst my husband is indeed entitled to a flag, he really has no flagstaff from which to fly it. And as for the castle, a mere game of cards had rendered it sold to a manufacturer of pianofortes. Nothing very feudal in that, and all the cannons in our armoury had been powerless to stop it!

It came time to turn the youngsters out. It seemed such a natural thing to do — people have bedrooms, don't they? They must go to sleep? But I caught the reproving glance of Müller. Only just stop and think for a moment, Trixie — I found myself saying to that haughty, insensitive Beatrice still inhabiting a good proportion my brain. That corner of St Jindřich's churchyard is probably all the home they have; there are no beds with patchwork quilts, nor tender mothers to tuck them up.

"Müller, a moment, if you please."

"Yes, Milady."

"When we had stable lads, where did they sleep?"

"Over the horses, of course. Nice and warm up there — even though we've only the pair of bays at present."

"Then you know what to do."

Müller, smiling, led the little troop out, each tugging at his woollen cap as he passed. Never mind that it was bad-mannered to wear hats indoors. My little army was now resident. I had a garrison.

I was still in the palace's kitchen when Müller came back a few minutes later. It would have seemed wrong to address him in the formality of the upstairs rooms, and the stove in the Business Room had not been lit today. I had children staying, I was thinking. There was no accounting why Karel and I hadn't had any. Perhaps it was the insecurity of knowing he was, at heart, a gambler or perhaps I, in my vanity, wanted to preserve my youthful figure. But the thought that four souls were in my charge for the moment warmed my heart more than I could have imagined.

The hall-boy would normally sit in a chair by the kitchen stove, drowsing all night in his livery and in attendance in case a caller rang the bell. Since no-one was expected, and I wanted a quiet word with Müller, I dismissed him. He was just leaving the room when I called him back:

"And what's your name?"

"Tomáš, Milady."

"Thank you, Tomáš. Good night."

On closer inspection I noticed that his stockings were darned and wrinkled and his knee-breeches were too baggy. His coat had seen better days. His shoes were a bit scuffed too. I would ask Karel to deal with this. It wouldn't have surprised me to learn that these costumes were fifty years old — maybe more.

Müller raised an eyebrow but said nothing as the boy left. Perhaps he was annoyed I had dissolved the value of his personal "Thank you" by giving out another. Two in one evening. The first two ever to servants.

"Now Müller, I want some explanations — but it is for information, not recriminations. So tell me — who were all those people?"

"At the ball, you mean, Milady?"

"Yes. Of course, I have a fair idea by now — but it is only a theory, a rather fantastic theory."

"Well, they were all servants. Every week we are invited to come dressed as our masters or mistresses. I think we do a great job."

He was on the point of saying "Don't you?" — but quickly realised that it might not be something I'd be very pleased with.

"They fooled me, didn't they? That must be fine enough praise? But tell me, for what purpose is all this?"

"Enjoyment, Milady. We have a good social evening of it. There's plenty to eat and drink. It feels agreeable to some to get their own back on the airs and graces of their employers. I mean, can you imagine what it must feel like to be on the other side for an evening or two? Then there's the rewards too."

"Rewards?"

"Yes, every week there's a handsome cash prize for the best turned-out "master" or "mistress." And in a few weeks' time there's to be an outing for all of us — a special excursion train to a spa where we will all have a very good time. All we have to do for that is to attend at least six of the party evenings. Anyway, that's what's organised, nothing more." He stopped suddenly.

"And…?" I encouraged him to go on.

"So I cannot understand why the managers got so upset that you were a real Countess. I mean, what's it to them? The only ones who'd get into trouble would be us servants for borrowing all the clothes and wearing the jewelry."

I now understood all about the rash of thefts the Inspector had described, and why the more conscience-burdened servants had returned the items after use. Perhaps there had been someone there at the ball wearing Uncle Berty's medals.

The photographs were in my bag, I remembered. I went through them until I found the one of our impostor. I handed it to Müller.

"This man. Do you recognise him?"

"Yes. He's one of the actors at the Fenix. Before that he played at the Variety Theatre on Na Příkopě Street. Does a wonderful impersonation of the German Kaiser. And funny, my word! You know, when he does 'Give me a woman who loves beer and I will conquer the world' — he is just so very funny."

"But isn't the Kaiser only in his late thirties? This actor..."

"Hans Grübbe is his name."

"Isn't he somewhat older?"

"A little perhaps, but look at the photograph. That's him playing the part of an old man in *The Brecht Family Chronicles* last year. They say he has wonderful makeup. And that tearful look, that's his speciality. They say it's simply onions."

Another explanation. So many in one evening.

"And do you intend to go again?"

Müller hesitated. "Well, I can't really —"

"Oh, don't mind about the clothes. I am sure my husband won't regard it." (I would tell him not to regard it.)

"Well, no. I don't really like the way they treated you, Milady. It has soured my appetite for what I thought was a little piece of innocent enjoyment."

"But my dear, Müller, I want you to go. And I want you to tell me all about this excursion when it is announced. All about it."

The whole of the following day, Sunday, I kept to my room. It had been such an ordeal and I needed to rest. I came out of my room briefly for lunch, having missed Mass, and had tea served in my boudoir. In the evening I started to read a new novel, *The Sham Prince*, but I put it down in the end. Reality was beginning to be far more exciting to me than fiction.

With my breakfast tray the next morning, served at ten (I was still recovering), there was a telegram. It was from Karel, that wretched husband of mine. I just knew it would be something inconvenient, and it was.

ARRIVING 11AM TRAIN STOP KAREL STOP
FELICITATIONS

'Felicitations' — was that all a young, spirited woman would want? He was older, of course. My mother equated wealth with rank and rank with age. How wrong she was on almost all counts — particularly *this* Count, I mumbled angrily. My anger was really directed at the circumstances, the timing. I wanted Karel to come home when I was the hero of the hour — the greatest solver of mysteries in Bohemia. However, I would have, I supposed, to accept my lot and be the dutiful Countess awaiting his arrival at the station.

Müller knocked.

"Good morning, Milady. The General has just telephoned and has asked me to relay to you a message. It is this: could you meet him at his club for lunch? Red carnation, dark suit. I presume that makes some sense to you, Milady?"

"Yes. Perfectly. You can telephone a reply that I shall certainly attend on him at 1p.m."

There must be something on Uncle Berty's mind, I was thinking.

"And the young persons, Milady?"

"For the moment, there is nothing for them to do. But don't send them away." Then I went on to tell Müller that they could have bread and soup from our kitchen, and at night they could use the stables. I was thinking of a particular task for them, but not until one or two other matters had first been resolved.

Sabine's hair-brushing ritual had virtually vanished by virtue of the vanished article, and she was at a loss to know which clothes to lay out for me. I could now be convincing as a ragamuffin, a rather suave man about town, a traditional tiara-ed Countess or, with the plain dresses she had made, an ordinary woman on a common tram. But for my husband, it had better be back to normal.

Although the Franz-Josef railway station, popularly known as the FJ1, serving the lines of the West Bohemia Railways, was only the shortest carriage drive from Jindřišská Street, it was my habit to be early and to sit in the Refreshment Room until the train was announced. I let the carriage wait outside, in front of the station, and entered the Refreshment Room directly and found a seat at the far side, overlooking the platforms under the great new double glass roof which was part of the station's rebuilding. Luckily for what was to transpire, the seating along the walls of the Refreshment Room was arranged in a series of booths. This afforded me the privacy which I preferred.

No sooner had I settled and begun to look at the menu card — although I knew it backwards as I had always been there to greet Karel as the dutiful wife that I was — than an awful, terrible feeling of *déjà vu* came over me. In this case, it was it was not something I had seen, but that I'd heard. Two distinctive, rough English voices drifted over from the next booth to assault my ears. Because it was so noisy from the throng of people within, the crowds on the platforms, the sounds of carriages squealing to a halt, the shouts of guards, and the violent chugs which precede locomotion for engines just starting out, I could not make out what they were actually saying. It was enough for me to know that they were there, only a metre or two from me. For a moment I was paralysed with fear and loathing, but then I got a firm grip on myself.

I asked the waiter if he wouldn't mind taking a note out to my carriage, waiting outside. Quickly I scribbled a message to Müller to get Sabine to put the urchin's guise in a bag and if Müller knew where my husband kept his revolver, to put that in too. I didn't think to ask for any bullets! These things to be sent round as soon as could be.

In a few moments a conductor walked through the room with a bell and blackboard announcing the imminent departure of the Spas Express — to Karlsbad. I could hear the scraping of chairs behind me and when I thought it was safe to look, I saw the two distinctive shapes of the men I had last seen by the Fenix Theatre's stage door. Perhaps it was because I was half English, but I reckoned I could probably recognise an English villain anywhere — and now there was a world full of them. One of these particular villains had distinctive red hair.

The train to the spas was due to leave at five minutes past eleven. This would give me little time. Fortune was smiling on me when at eleven o'clock exactly the train from Vienna steamed into the station perfectly on time.

My husband stepped out of one of the leading carriages and was quickly embraced by his loving wife. He took his pipe out of his mouth and lifted his soft hat a little — both of which gestures were to make him think his appearance was by this means somehow improved.

"My dear — your hair…it is — is it different?" were his first words.

He was wearing, I noticed, the *Duc d'Orleans* with the brim turned up, from Čekans the hatters in Wenceslas Square, which I had bought him for Christmas last year — or was it the year before?

"Dearest, it is only a wig," I answered, "Don't trouble yourself about it. Now, come over here a moment."

"A wig? But why, for Heavens' sake?"

I was pulling him to one side of the throng, "Do you have any money on you?"

"Well, yes. I think I have two hundred. You know I usually carry —"

"Could you give it to me? I need it…" but then I hesitated. How could I explain for what purpose? Quite apart from the fact he might say no, it would take too long. "I need it…at this moment. Right now, in fact."

Mystified, but sensing my urgency and determination (and he knew better than to argue against that), he got out his wallet and handed me the money.

"Everything is perfectly well at home. There are four urchins lodging in the stables. Cook will give them soup in the kitchen. Müller may need to borrow one of your suits next Saturday — oh, and your decorations, but I shall be back by then, I'm sure. I have to catch the train to the spas. I'll tell you all about it when I return."

At this point Müller appeared and ran up to us carrying a carpet bag, which he handed to me. When he had caught his breath he looked me earnestly in the eye — something a servant wouldn't normally venture to do, of course, but then I'd had very close bodily contact with Müller only the day before. Maybe he thought that gave him rights. He spoke gravely: "Do you think this is wise, Milady?"

His eyes kept nodding downwards. He was clearly thinking of what I'd asked him to pack in the bag.

"Oh, nonsense," I said, but actually not believing this was wise in the very slightest — and, looking back at Karel and Müller who did not know quite how to react, so stunned were both of them — I boarded the train just as it was about to propel itself out of the station.

Once the conductor had seated me in an empty First Class compartment — and I asked him to ensure, as far as possible, that no-one else shared it as I said I was very tired and needed to rest — I then explained to him that I would have to buy my ticket. As the transaction was taking place, I tried to find out about the two men from the theatre. The conductor said he was almost positive that there weren't two such men as I had just described to him in First Class.

The train was travelling to the great Bohemian spa of Karlsbad. But this was hardly the Season, surely?

"And can you cross the border from Karlsbad?" I was wondering if this was their plan.

"From Karlsbad there's a train which goes to Nuremberg and Munich, via Eger. Change at Munich for the Orient Express to Strasbourg and Paris. The through trains start on May 1st. You can go to the Customs House in Karlsbad to avoid the formalities on the train."

In my eagerness for hot pursuit I hadn't thought before that they might be leaving the country. And I had no passport upon my person, although these were not always deemed necessary for people of quality.

Once the conductor left, I composed myself and took stock of things. First I drew down the blinds to the corridor. These men, and I'd seen them get on the train, must have gone down to Second Class, perhaps Third. I would be far too conspicuous going to look for them in the get-up of a Countess, even in the rather dull outfit I'd chosen to meet my husband. I hadn't wanted to excite him. "Urchin" was my only other available outfit.

I looked in the carpet bag. Wrapped in Honza Major's former coat was Karel's revolver. I held it in my hand and realised I would probably never have the courage to use the thing. On the other hand, I'd been foolish to embark on this part of the adventure alone. Surely I might indeed need it? What had started out as solving a little puzzle had suddenly turned so much darker.

I looked at the thing more carefully for it was the first I had ever closely examined a revolver. I saw a catch on the side, near the trigger. The safety-catch, I supposed. I found it moved easily to the touch. I quickly moved it back — but was that on or off? I could of course squeeze the trigger — but if the catch were off, and I presumed it had bullets in it, it would fire. I didn't want to risk anything. I wrapped it up again in my clothes and forgot about it for the while.

In a couple of minutes I had transformed myself once more. Leaving my things in the compartment — the conductor would look after them — and having made sure he wasn't patrolling the corridor at that moment, I slipped out and down the two First

Class carriages to the Second Class Dining Car. The journey was due to last about three hours, but I realised I had to be on the watch. I wasn't certain there wouldn't be an intermediate stop or a long enough wait by a signal for them to descend. Firstly, I should get a proper look them: after all, I had never seen them at close quarters. Then I would find a seat in Third Class — but keep my eyes open if the train halted, and at Karlsbad I would have to be very vigilant or I could lose them altogether.

I just wished I had read some of these Sherlock Holmes novelettes that had appeared by instalments in a Prague magazine. I always felt I should wait until I could get my hands on the original English edition, but my Czech acquaintances, reading in translation, had been thrilled by *The Baskerville Dog*, as it must be titled in English. Even from detective fiction there must be plenty of tips I could have learned.

There was a swing door into the Dining Car with an oval window of etched glass. I was standing by the kitchens. Peering through the glass I thought I saw them.

I needed something to make myself inconspicuous as I walked through the car. Beside the kitchens was a small office cubicle, probably that of the Dining Car Superintendent. Piled half in the cubicle and half in the corridor was a stack of newspapers. I grabbed a bundle and strode purposefully through the Dining Car, hoping that no-one, least of all one of them, would ask me for a paper.

As I approached their table (and I was noticing how modest the fare was here compared with the First Class saloon, with which I was, naturally, completely familiar), the carriage lurched as it negotiated a curve. A waiter ahead of me stepped back to steady himself, taking a moment to regain his stance with a tray of ten full beer glasses held aloft on an upturned hand. That gave me a good second to take them in. The stockier, cruder-looking character had his back to me, so I couldn't really make out his face — although I would recognise his lumbering shape anywhere, as well as his red hair. He was leaning back in his chair, his legs straight out before him.

The other didn't look quite so rough at close quarters. He wore a large cravat tied in a loose, Parisian manner, although I thought his coat to be rather worn at the cuffs. He sported a pointed beard and a waxed moustache. The sudden lurch of the train had dislodged his eye-glass, which bounced on its cord in front of a rather faded purple velvet waistcoat. He was leaning forward, his head cradled on his elbows, as if the other had said something of great moment to him.

I squeezed slowly past the waiter who was by now bending and delivering the foaming ale glasses to an adjoining table. Three carriages later, having dumped my newspapers, I arrived at the Third Class, towards the rear of train. I had never experienced anything quite like it: wooden slatted benches, wire racks for luggage, the unupholstered boarded sides of the carriages. And it was crowded.

Travellers on a bench seat in the first compartment I ventured into automatically squeezed up to allow me room — which there was, just. I decided the only way I could endure this was to pretend to be asleep, with my cap pulled down over my eyes. I could still make out the view, and I watched a flurry of snow dusting the monotony of fields and hedges, or draping the poles and wires left for this year's growth of hops.

At first the noise of the wheels beating the joints between the rails seemed unbearably loud — louder in Third Class, I thought. But perhaps that's because I had nothing else on which to concentrate. After a while the rhythmic sound aided restfulness like Oriental monks soothed by some constant mantra.

After what still seemed an interminable period the gentleman — if that is the word to describe him — sitting on my right, and who was playing a game of *Twenty-one* with two others, resting their cards on the lid of a small suitcase, pulled out his pocket watch. The journey had only thirty minutes or so to run, and the train hadn't halted once. We were climbing through low hills now and the snow looked more intense. I began to doubt if Honza Major's coat would be up to the job. In any event, I would be very conspicuous as a well-dressed lady and I decided to stay in this disguise, at least until I reached my destination and I could find an hotel. However, I'd had enough of travelling steerage for the moment and decided to sneak back to my own compartment.

As I passed along the Second Class carriages I glanced into all the compartments, but could not see the men, through the Second Class Dining Car and still no sign of either of them. As I finally reached the First Class carriages there was quite a commotion, with people jostling and filling the corridor. I squeezed through them until I was confronted by the conductor. He barred my way:

"No Third Class passengers allowed in First," he said forcefully.

He was the same conductor I had conversed with earlier. It was obvious he didn't recognise me in the slightest. I did my best to disguise my voice too: "So what's all the fuss about then?"

"Next carriage up. There's been a terrible incident. One man shot dead and a woman missing." He leaned forward towards me. "And haven't I seen you before?"

I had already turned and made myself scarce in the crowd that jammed the corridor. In the crush I felt someone pushing past me. He was behind me, so he couldn't see my face — but as soon as he had squeezed by I could see it was the rough man of the pair. In that instant I was frozen with fear. Perhaps if I had been able to cry out I could have raised the alarm. I knew instinctively that the person who had just been pushing against me, brushing his arm past mine even, was the murderer, if that's what had happened. I turned. I could just make out a smudge of red hair under the cap which he had pulled down over much of his face.

Chapter Four

The Old Tobacco Factory

I still couldn't quite believe that this "incident" had occurred in my compartment. But supposing it had, then it would perhaps have been my gun, or rather Karel's that had been the deadly instrument. I would thus be the missing woman. But who could the dead man be? I pictured the two of them together, in the Dining Car. Only one of them had pressed by me, making an escape through the throng. Perhaps a murderer had brushed that close past me; it was too terrible to contemplate. But another thing was almost as terrible: I wouldn't be able to retrieve my bag and my clothes. Luckily I had all the money on my person — I didn't believe in leaving temptation before even an honest man like the conductor.

And there was something else. What had they been doing in my compartment? Was this murder a mistake — and I should have been the victim?

For the remaining few minutes of the journey I lurked in the corridors of Second Class, trying hard not to be noticed by anyone. Lurking, I might add, being something totally alien to my nature.

At Karlsbad I got out onto the platform and went in the direction of my compartment. There was still a slim chance I could slip in and retrieve my belongings, unless, of course…but it was. My erstwhile compartment was far from empty. My worst fears were confirmed. Already there were three policemen at the place in their grey uniforms, and two railway porters were manhandling a stretcher out the door and onto the platform. The face of the man was covered with a cloth handkerchief, but I recognised the worn cuffs of the jacket and the dangling eye-glass, now cracked and spattered with blood.

I turned and lost myself in the crowd again. Suitcases were being put on the shoulders of porters, heavier trunks and portmanteaus onto handcarts. Husbands were being greeted by wives, soldiers were returning home from far-flung Imperial duties, children were playing with hoops, dogs barking — and then I saw him. The round-shouldered, brutish one. Just one of them now. It was he.

He stepped out of the station with an eerie calmness and into a flurry of waiting cabs, porters loading private coaches, people coming and going — with the snow eddying around them all, and I lost him. I experienced a terrible feeling in the pit of my stomach. He was gone. Already the light was beginning to fail in that melancholy wintry way and some of the gaslamps were being lit.

Then suddenly I caught a glimpse of him inside a horse-drawn omnibus, which was just moving off.

I quickly asked the driver of one of the waiting cabs where the omnibus was going. He told me it was to the Lower Station, for the connection to Marienbad. Of course, it was the Spas Express — Karlsbad *and* Marienbad.

"Quick, I need to follow…"

"You got money, son?"

For a moment I couldn't guess whom he was addressing. I had to be quicker. This was ridiculous. I tried a curt — and manly — rejoinder:

"Plenty." (Such a statement was entirely relative, of course.)

At the Lower Station I had time to buy a Third Class ticket (which surprised me by its cheapness). However I still didn't know what I was doing — other than what I had been doing since eleven in the morning, following two creatures, now one. But by the time I had found a relatively empty compartment, I had worked out my immediate plan of action. I leaned from the open window.

"Porter," I shouted. The fellow didn't seem to come immediately. "Over here! At once!" It was, by stupid accident, the voice of an impatient Countess.

The porter looked confused. He couldn't see the owner of the voice anywhere. I realised my mistake. "'Ere, you," I called. And he came running, although not as fast as he would have to a First Class tipper.

"I want you to take this telegram I'm writing and have it sent at once. Here's five krone."

Over-tipping is as much a crime against Society as under-tipping. I found myself guilty of the former.

My message read:

```
SEND SABINE WITH BAG PACKED CLOTHES
TOILET ARTICLES AND PASSPORT STOP WILL
EXPLAIN ALL LATER STOP HOTEL
```

Wait. I couldn't remember the name of the best hotel — or any hotel — in Marienbad. The Grand Hotel Pupp, that's it...no it's in Karlsbad. I crossed out the word HOTEL and completed with

```
RAILWAY STATION MARIENBAD ON TOMORROWS
SPAS EXPRESS STOP I AM SAFE AND WELL
```

There seemed no need for a signature — indeed it might be prudent not to add one. But I did add

```
AND ALSO MORE MONEY
```

I had another two minutes until the train was due to depart. The engine was standing steamed-up, impatient to leave — or so it seemed, which gave everyone in its vicinity a sense of urgency. However, I was starving and the smell of hot soup emanating from a sort of mobile contraption for a moment totally seduced me. I stepped back out onto the platform.

A coin or two of low value was all that was needed to be handed a cup of absolutely scalding hot liquid. I looked at its greenish tinge, but hunger and the scent of it drove me on. I discreetly wiped the chipped rim of the cup with my handkerchief, taking pains to hide its lace edge. The liquid, which must have been at boiling temperature, immediately burned my tongue before I could withdraw the cup from my lips. I realised that whatever I might do, the heat of the soup would not reduce to drinkable temperature in two minutes, and I remembered an article I had glanced by, on my way to the fashion page, in an illustrated magazine only a few weeks previously. A similar vendor, but only one of many — it had said, had been fined in Prague. His deliberate intention had been to sell drinks so hot that nobody could drink them in time for their train.

Like the vendor in Prague, the toothless old crone running the stall here in Karlsbad quite simply tipped my soup back into her steaming vat. However, the little anger that had suddenly risen in me had reduced by an equal proportion my immediate hunger. Pseudo-satisfied and nourished by my nerves, as well as relief that I hadn't exposed my well-bred, delicate female constitution to the horrors of that witch's brew, I stepped back on board.

The fact that assistance in the form of decent clothes might eventually be at hand allowed me to endure another hour and forty-five minutes of torture in a jolting, smoke-filled, pickled-fish-reeking compartment. Nearly opposite was a large man in middle age with a bushy, drooping moustache and otherwise unshaved. His eyes were watery, his clothing worn.

Either his threshold of boredom was so limited or his craving for attention so huge that he couldn't keep still. He would screw up his face or suddenly mumble something; he would open one eye and shut the other; he would scratch himself near his fly or yawn with attendant noise. In truth, my eyes were drawn to this spectacle, if only for want of any other activity to look upon. He began vigorously to pick his left nostril, and as if feeling my critical gaze, switched to the further one. But I knew more than to allow my eyes to settle on him for more than a fraction of a second, for what he wanted was for our eyes to meet — thus giving him, no doubt, an excuse to start some drunken monologue aimed in my direction.

I had seen his sort at the railway station, when waiting occasionally for Karel. But in Prague his sort would not have dared to address me. As a low-class man I was in this instance highly vulnerable. A woman of Society, corsetted into the fashionable "S" shape and moving as stately as a galleon, somehow becomes impervious to the common world. Now I was part of it. Thus the train rattled on into the growing darkness of a very uncertain evening.

Before I finally turned off the gaslight, it had occurred to me that unless the man whom I had been following was going to be staying for at least two nights, I would have to continue watching his every move in case I lost him. For the moment he was safely lodged at Marienbad's not-so-smart Continental Hotel at the wrong end of the Haupt-Strasse. At first I thought he had chosen this hotel because it was one of the few that were open all year.

I had followed him past the great looming stuccoed palaces of the Esplanade and Imperial hotels, all shuttered up for the winter. Almost alone on the ice-cold streets I had had great difficulty following him discreetly. But then I noticed that the Continental also had its own Variety Theatre — closed, of course, until the Marienbad Season would commence on May 1st, but I knew immediately he would be headed there. The Theatre seemed to be at the root of all these mysteries, but at this moment I was unable to tell why.

Some minutes after he had gone in, I had entered the reception hall and asked the porter if the gentleman had given instructions as to when I was to return with the cab. I was getting very proficient at these little charades. "And is he only staying the one night, then?" To which I had got the answer "At least two, by his own account."

"So you'd better tell Mr...."

"Jenks."

"...that I'll be back with the cab tomorrow morning. Goodnight."

I had then walked in the perishing cold, in shoes surely not really meant for ice and snow, down to the Bahnhofs-Hotel Central, opposite the railway station. They had cheap rooms for grooms and travelling servants round in a building at the back. For three krone I had the luxury of a crude bed with a straw-filled mattress and fortunately for my modesty, the other four beds in the room were unoccupied. After such a tiring day I was glad of the simple pleasure of any bed to lie on.

How uncomplicated was this world of men. Places that were occupied only by them seemed to have a different smell, not quite as distinct as the smell of stables, but discernible nevertheless. But maybe this wasn't only the smell of men, but simply of the poorer classes. To serenade me to sleep on this hard but much-needed bedstead was the ghastly thought that I was alone here and following a man, this man Jenks, who was most undoubtedly a cold-blooded murderer.

I visualised the scene in my compartment. They must have known I was aboard the train. That could hardly have been coincidence. Perhaps they had intended to rifle my possessions or, worse still, perhaps they had intended to…to go after me — for how would they have known I was not in the compartment? I was still haunted by this thought — that the victim should have been me. Or, maybe they had had an argument, and one had shot the other. Maybe it had been the intention all along of this man Jenks to murder his colleague. But then why in a railway compartment, and the one occupied by me?

By the next morning my spirits were slightly revived. It was a Tuesday, and one should have an attitude for every day of the week. Monday, for example, is for tradesmen to call to collect their payments for the previous week. Tuesday is for discreetly seeking out what social engagements one might get invited to later in the week; Monday would seem far too pushy for this. Wednesdays I saved for correspondence, mainly with relatives;

Thursdays, the day my husband was normally absent, for writing any flirtatious notes or anything that had best be done without his knowledge (any admirer was encouraged only to send flowers on a Thursday), and so on. But I was increasingly feeling that all this was an old way of life for me — one to which, perhaps, I might not return, or not easily so. Although the adventure had taken a murderous turn, it was still devilishly exciting.

This Tuesday morning, then, found me loitering outside the Continental Hotel. A weak sun had risen, melting the snow that had fallen the afternoon and evening before. It was the sun, of course, that had done most to lighten my mood.

At eight o'clock precisely, a neatly dressed gentleman — a senior clerk or a local man of business — entered the hotel. I could see from the still open and tied-back curtains that most of the bedrooms were unoccupied. In fact only one appeared, on this side of the building at least, to have its curtains drawn open casually, as if by the occupant having risen this morning. Even its casements were open a crack for some of the fresh morning air. I guessed that this fellow could be calling on Jenks, but for what purpose I could not surmise.

I stood doing my best to look like any another of the unoccupied classes, adopting what I thought was a convincing vacancy of expression, but with my eyes fixed firmly on the entrance door-way to the hotel. More than thirty minutes passed and I imagined that Jenks and this stranger were taking breakfast together. The more I thought about it, the more I could conjure up the smell of Viennese coffee, cut sausage and smoked cheese, freshly baked bread. The sheer agony of the poor, I thought, who have to trudge constantly through city streets which are full of these pleasant odours, but the full pleasure of them — their consumption — is denied them. I made a resolution that I would go to Karel's encyclopaedia and look under "S" for Socialism when next I was in his library.

My reveries were terminated by the appearance at the hotel doorway of the caller, now with Jenks. They looked well fed, the caller even brushing crumbs from the corner of his mouth. They began walking together, back up the Haupt-Strasse, towards the centre of the spa. I let them go almost out of sight before I hurried up the street to observe their next movements, a manoeuvre I had read in a detective novel — a Czech one, a pale imitation of the great Sherlock Holmes.

The two men rounded a corner and by the time I arrived there I was just able to catch sight of them entering an estate agent's premises on the opposite side of the street. It was incumbent upon me again to have to loiter until Jenks re-emerged.

I had passed, on the Haupt-Strasse, the Ladies' Reading Room. I was thinking that I should look at the early editions of the daily newspapers, for maybe they would describe the incident on the train which I imagined had happened too late for the evening ones. Apart from the uncertainty of relying on the hope that once in the estate agent's, the two would discuss business for at least a few minutes, I suddenly realised that I could not gain admittance to this reading room: I was not even dressed as a woman, yet alone a lady. This distressed me greatly.

Further down the street where I was keeping watch, several doors beyond the estate agent's, was a tobacconist's shop. The daily papers were already on pegs outside, and already there was the morning daily from Karlsbad. Trying to make the newspaper an afterthought, I went in and asked for some cigarettes. But how do you ask for them, I wondered? "I'll have ten of those, if you please" or "One of those packets, if you please" or "Some cigarettes, any will do — if you please." I just had no idea what the working man — or lad in this case — would say when ordering his "smokes." Yes, "smokes" was a good word to use.

In the end I said something which seemed to sound convincing, and in a few moments I was able to lounge against a lamppost reading a newspaper and having a go at smoking. There was a fine art to loitering and I meant to discover its technique.

The front page of the *Karlsbader Tagblatt* was devoted to the usual advertisements, but the entire second page was devoted to the

SENSATIONAL MURDER
ON THE SPAS EXPRESS
Police Seek Mystery Woman.

My hands were trembling but my eyes quickly reached the important parts from the several columns of newsprint. The victim was…theatrical impresario and lessee of the popular Fenix Theatre in Prague, Monsieur Gerard Duvalier. Mr. Duvalier, who affected to be French, was, according to the Foreigners' Police, born Herbert Higginson in Hackney, East London, England. He had for many years been resident in Continental Europe…

A description of the murder followed:

> The police have ruled out the possibility that there were two men involved, although the mysterious lady in whose First Class compartment this outrage took place had earlier asked the Conductor, Mr. Pavel Kraválek, a thirty-four year-old father of twin girls and (my eyes jumped forward) if he knew of two men she thought might also be on the train. Both were described as English, one of stocky build and average height and the other plainly the deceased.

The worst, from my point of view, was left to the end:

> The clothing worn by the lady occupying the compartment, a plain grey dress but of this year's cut and in fine quality woollen material, was found in a carpet bag abandoned on one of the seats. There were no signs of this mysterious lady. The police are working on two theories: either she was pushed from the train in a struggle — to which end railway search parties are walking the line this morning to see if there is any

sign of the missing woman, or that she, having shot Mr. Duvalier, managed to haul herself up through the window onto the carriage roof but alighted when the train came to a halt at some point on the journey. Mr. Kraválek is adamant that he was at his post throughout the journey and that the lady cannot have left the compartment, which begs the question of how Mr. Duvalier managed to enter it.

The article ended with a fearful tone:

The police are now looking for this mystery lady and the public are warned that she might be dangerous, although the murder weapon itself was recovered at the scene of the incident.

It was reading this which then caused me to reach — almost as if by some second nature — for the packet of cigarettes. Apart from a Russian cigarette experienced at my last school in Switzerland, for which the girl donor — who is now Grand Duchess Xenia Alexandrovna of Russia — was very nearly expelled, and the one or two puffs of my husband's cigar in the early days, when love was still affected, I have never smoked. But this was, I thought, for a villain at large, an entirely appropriate moment to start in earnest.

Mr. Jenks and the estate agent, on leaving the latter's premises, were distracted for a moment by looking down the street to notice a young lad apparently having a coughing fit and in the act of setting fire to a newspaper. A more conspicuous way of drawing attention to one's self could hardly have been devised. I stamped on the singed newspaper and turned my back on them, blinking my eyes which had filled with tears — not just those from nearly choking on the acrid taste of the cheap tobacco.

Using more stealth than I had employed previously, I followed the pair to various buildings in the centre of this small but illustrious town. Each time the procedure was the same — they would stop, the estate agent would stand back and often use his arms to make sweeping gestures of praise for the particular edifice before them, then a door would be unlocked and in under five minutes they would emerge again and go on to the next. This was repeated precisely five times during the morning.

They lunched at Glocke's Wine Restaurant, one of the few open during the winter and also located on the Haupt-Strasse. You see, everything of note in Marienbad is on the Haupt-Strasse. This morning's perambulation of the town had made me aware of its peculiar geography and its popularity, even more so than Karlsbad, with the English. I had only been once before. My husband and I prefer the smaller spas, one in particular in the mountains of East Bohemia is his favourite — a choice of course made by necessity; it is far less expensive there than the grand spas of Western Bohemia.

The occasion I had had to come to Marienbad had been when I was eighteen, when I was coming out in Society, and I had to attend The Emperor's Ball here — a glittering event at which I, and a large number of other marriageable young ladies of similar breeding — had been presented to his Imperial Majesty Franz-Joseph I. The Empress had not been present. Some minor ailment was blamed, but we all had known she was terribly jealous of competition, even though His Imperial Majesty was quite content with just his one young mistress who kept him on the straight, if — how shall we say it? — double-width, path.

So I had not remembered much of Marienbad's geography, my head having then been in a whirl of excitement and painstaking preparations.

The Haupt-Strasse is like the sea-front in Brighton, Nice, Biarritz, or any other successful resort facing the ocean. It has high, ornate stuccoed buildings — hotels, apartments, restaurants, and casinos — designed with a certain lightness, a gaiety which announces pleasure and recreation, but in a grand style. The effect of Brighton, Nice, or wherever is complete in that the

Haupt-Strasse's buildings are grouped on only one side of the street. Opposite are the green lawns, glades, and walks of the park below the Humelika Mountain. So, just as at the seaside, one promenades along one huge line of buildings, or sits on terraces gazing out — but in this case not into the blue, but into the green.

The park thus becomes a focus of natural interest, just as the beach would elsewhere. And as at the beach, it is here where children play, bands in bandstands perform, women sit in the sun, but preserving their skins under parasols, and young lovers stroll together with an abandon not witnessed in Vienna, London, or even Paris. Even before his Majesty King Edward VII, emperor of most of the colonial world (except, of course, the United States), took to visiting annually, Marienbad had become a most popular resort for English visitors. Perhaps they came and looked longingly for the breaking waves which were not to be found there, for had not Shakespeare himself described (in error!) "the shores of Bohemia"? But what Marienbad lacked in undrinkable saltwater was amply made up for by the curative mineral springs with their very drinkable waters for which the spa was already world famous.

King Edward's visits were supposed to be incognito, but were known to anyone who cared to find out. He went under the pseudonyms of either "Lord Renfrew" or "The Duke of Lancaster" — a democratic and popular gesture in stuffy Austria, and for this he was quite evidently thought of as a "man of the people." (Well, Dukes are people, aren't they?) He normally came in August and stayed at the Hotel Weimar behind the Goethe-Platz.

The Goethe-Platz is itself a crescent of large hotels behind the Colonnade, the huge open building whose roof is supported on cast-iron columns of the most artistic design and which houses both the most accessible of the mineral springs, from which one can drink, and an arcade of the most luxurious shops — branches of famous stores found in London, Paris, or Rome.

Today it was still officially winter here, despite the sun which not only had melted yesterday's snow but which I could begin to feel warm upon my skin. Sun is important to the morale of the loiterer, as I was finding out. I had stationed myself in the passage just next to Ruppert's, the confectioner's not too many doors along from Glocke's. This bakery was open and my nostrils were soon filled with the scents of pastries rising and almonds roasting. I couldn't determine whether this was exquisite torture or a kind of hateful self-sacrifice, but finally — after not too many minutes — my resolve broke down.

Pretending I was collecting for gentlemanly masters, I went in and ordered three slices of ordinary strudel to be put in a box and wrapped in paper. I was working out how to open this parcel surreptitiously and enjoy some of its contents when the two emerged from Glocke's. By any standards they'd had a very short luncheon.

They walked more purposefully than before their repast. Perhaps they had discussed Mr. Jenks' requirements more thoroughly over the restaurant's board and the estate agent had had some more productive ideas. Now they walked away from the centre, towards the railway station and past The Continental Hotel, suddenly taking a sharp right turn.

This street took them uphill, behind the grand structures of Haupt-Strasse, to what looked like an old monastery or convent. The chapel was raised high, but its tall gothic windows were half bricked-up. The onion-domed spire, with its weathered green copper plating, seemed to have lost its bell. A battered, noseless statue of The Virgin Mary still gazed out with blank eyes over the main doorway, but covered in netting against pigeons. The paint was peeling from the stucco, and even the sign on the wall was beginning to lose some of its painted lettering:

DOUBLE-EAGLE BRAND
TOBAC O MANUFACTORY

The printing of an advertisement poster pasted on a board nearest the street corner of this strange building had also faded in the sun. It depicted the popular singing star Ema Destinnová: "Smoke Emmy's favourite brand — have the throat of a lark!" it declared.

All that this advertiser's message did for me was to remind me of the coughing fit which had nearly done for my whole visit here only a few hours before. However, the factory looked closed. The estate agent was fumbling with a bunch of keys to admit Mr. Jenks for a viewing. In a moment or two they were inside, the door closed behind them. I could hear no key turned in the lock.

It was now that I took a huge and frightening risk. I had sensed somehow that this was going to be a place of peculiar interest to the mysterious Mr. Jenks so I needed to be able to get into this building later, should it be the one he was — presumably — looking to rent or buy. I ran across to the main door and opened it a fraction. My heart was pumping so loudly, it seemed to me, that my listening out for the sounds of the men was quite impaired. Perhaps the very fact I couldn't hear any — no footsteps, no doors opening, no conversation — was proof enough they were in a distant part of the place. I entered a reception hall, ran to the nearest window and simply opened the casement catch.

I fumbled due to my nervousness, but in a second or two it was opened. The window itself remained closed. Just at that moment, voices and footsteps seemed to be right above me, getting closer. I looked round — I could actually see shoes on the staircase descending into the hall where I stood. I could scream, I could be paralysed with fright, or I could run. Luckily instinct guided me.

I ran. Out of the main door, across the street, and soon I saw the entranceway to the back of some of the buildings in the Haupt-Strasse. I tucked in there and was just able to observe the doorway of my escape. Judging by the coolness of the way the two men left the old tobacco manufactory, they had neither seen nor heard me. I was panting with relief. Had I been wearing a dress, I would have felt a need to have changed it — but, well, I wasn't wearing one, and a bath was only a distant dream!

The two took off down another lane which went down almost directly towards the railway station. This appeared to greatly animate the otherwise grave and expressionless Jenks. Having passed by my hotel, in the square opposite the station, they turned once again into the Haupt-Strasse and sauntered in a contented fashion up the street, once more past The Continental, to Thomas Cook's Travel Bureau — not far from Glocke's Restaurant.

Here they parted company. Jenks went into the travel bureau, and the estate agent went off in the direction of his office. After some minutes, Jenks reappeared and waited on the street a short while until joined again by the estate agent, carrying a sheaf of papers. The two then went along to Glocke's again, where presumably they would be doing business. My guess, which didn't take much genius to arrive at, was that Mr. Jenks was concluding the paperwork to rent the old factory. The mystery had by this time only deepened. Any possible explanation only posed a dozen more unanswerable questions.

I needed urgently to do two things. One was to get information from the offices of Messrs. Thomas Cook. The other was to go to the lavatory. I shall only recall the former of these two activities. The latter involved my deep embarrassment at entering a public convenience only to find a man standing relieving himself into a porcelain object I took to be a urinal in full view of any other men who might enter. I turned and left. The park was more satisfactory. Gathering the information I needed seemed easier by comparison. How all this related to the death of Alois Tager, his impersonator, and the Tontine I had only one idea — that being that it was related.

Nearly next door to the travel bureau was the post office. Without much difficulty I managed to get a booth with a telephone and a connection to an operator who rang the bureau for me. Before speaking, I wiped the receiver with my now much-soiled handkerchief; I had never before had to use a public instrument. I was hoping that this operator was far enough away not to realise that I was only a few doors from where I was telephoning. In any event I spoke in hushed tones, as if the clerks at Thomas Cook's would hear my voice and in some way know I was speaking from a lot nearer than Pilsen — which is what I said.

I had very carefully thought-out what I was going to say, but nonetheless it would have made a strange sight — an urchin with the imperious voice of a *grande dame* — but fortunately telephonic communication is merely oral.

"Thomas Cook's? I am calling from Pilsen." Here I paused momentarily, half expecting the operator to cut in and say 'You bare-faced liar!' But there was silence. I went on:

"I have been trying to call my colleague Mr. Jenks at the Continental Hotel all day. They said there that he might be calling in at your office. Would you be so kind as to give him a message?"

The reply was exactly as I expected. "He's already been in. I'm afraid you've missed him. Is there anything else we can do for you?"

"Well yes, there is, as a matter of fact. Can you simply tell me what train he is on tomorrow? I have to meet up with him, you see."

"It's the seven-thirty a.m."

"And connecting to?"

"At Eger connecting to the *Train de Luxe*. The Express to London."

I went on to tell him that I should be arriving in Marienbad later that evening and should be requiring two tickets on the *de Luxe* for myself and my maid. I asked him if he could call by the Bahnhofs-Hotel Central at eight-thirty with the tickets. Showing how light business must have been in Marienbad out-of-season, the manager — for I was told it was he I was addressing — willingly consented.

I hung up the apparatus, half absolutely satisfied with my day's work and half completely terrified that unless Sabine arrived with my proper clothes, then I would have to let Mr. Jenks slip away. By now I felt unable to keep up this ridiculous guise any longer, and for tomorrow's journey it would be impossible — *Trains de Luxe* were strictly First Class.

Mr. Jenks was either obliged to go by this method for reasons of speed, or he was treating himself as a reward for his own good work. After all, he only had one fare to pay now. Which paymaster, I wondered, would be pleased with that — for I was beginning to doubt that this Mr. Jenks could himself possibly be the mastermind behind whatever elaborate scheme was afoot.

Chapter Five

An Unexpected Stop

The train from Karlsbad arrived on time and Sabine walked straight past me on the platform, followed by a porter trundling a large steamer trunk. From the perspective of a poor urchin, how refined and wealthily-wise even a lady's maid appeared to be. I even detected she was wearing a light perfume. Hmm.

I followed her into the booking hall where she had the porter set down the luggage, paid the fellow, and then stood, looking around. She observed a shabbily dressed young man sidle up to her and wink. She nearly fainted.

"Madame!" she exclaimed, recognition having taken place in the matter of another second or two. "I can see why you wanted some clothes."

"Sabine. Thank goodness. But don't talk further here. Get a porter to take your things over to the hotel in the square straight in front of the station. Take two rooms or a suite if they have such a thing. Best rooms — it's not an expensive place. Use your own name. I shall arrive in a few minutes — but let me have that small bag you are carrying."

I held out my hand, as if for a tip — which the startled Sabine did not think to offer — and uttered a "Much obliged." I had practiced touching my cap and bowing like the best lowliest.

I was soon delivering the lady's bag to the one suite the hotel possessed on the second floor and sitting for the first time in what seemed an age in a comfortable, upholstered chair with someone — at last — at my beck and call.

Sabine was busy unpacking various things. At length she stood up and surveyed what had become of her mistress. "Now, where shall we start?" she sighed.

As the wayward Trixie was being put back into the formal appearance of Beatrice, I ventured to tell Sabine about what was happening: "Now, where shall I start?" I began.

After the shock of telling her that next morning we were going to board the train for London, I then told her everything I knew — although of course I did not tell her about the Tontine. That the Tontine had been compromised, and my Uncle and I were deeply implicated, was something I thought was not needed for our journey. And when she looked weary, both from getting me in my proper clothes and from what I had told her (oh, and I didn't say in so many words that Jenks was probably a dangerous murderer), I found myself saying "And, Sabine, for the remainder of this adventure, until we are back in Prague, your pay is doubled."

Money, although in itself is not everything — for you cannot, for example, buy class (although respectability is another matter) — it certainly does have a soothing effect on most people. Sabine, I discovered, fell easily into that category. There were more inducements too: "The Hotel Klinger, I am reliably informed, although closed until the Season starts, still maintains its restaurant. King Edward stayed there on more than one occasion, although he now prefers the Weimar. I doubt very much this Mr. Jenks will wish to dine there — but tonight we are going to have the finest dinner that the Count's money can buy."

Sabine, God bless the woman, had already smelt a rat. "And before dinner, Madame?"

"Really, Madame, was it necessary to *steal* this lamp?"

I was helping her through the window of the tobacco factory when she chose to make this observation. "It was necessary in that otherwise we would be in pitch darkness at this moment — or, if you are enquiring about the theft itself, then I believe that to purchase such a lamp, if one could be procured so late in the evening, would only serve to arouse suspicion, don't you?" I suppose I could have simply answered "Yes."

She still seemed uneasy. "But we will return it," I added.

That made her a little more comfortable as we started out on our exploration. At least she had the thought of dinner to sustain her hopes, whereas to me, the very thought of a decent supper just seemed an almost impossible dream after so much deprivation.

We wandered through many rooms. The equipment of the tobacco manufactory had all gone — long ago, judging by the dust and cobwebs. All there was of any peculiarity was the immense empty space of the former chapel — just a vast, empty room now. Religious items must have been entirely removed even before cigarette-making machines had been installed here.

"It's odd, though, isn't it," I observed, "that cigarettes were made in a former House of God?"

"Well, here, Madame, I have some knowledge of this. Mrs. Norová — she's our cook, you know — "

"Yes, of course," I cut in abruptly. Actually, since Monsieur Yves' departure I had really not taken the faintest interest in the names of our cooks — or even how many there had been.

"Anyway, Mrs. Norová comes from Kutná Hora."

"We call the place Kuttenberg — at the moment," I said — again like a prig. In any event the Czechs will have their day, eventually.

"…and she smokes Empress" — Sabine suddenly stopped short. Staff caught smoking were subject to instant dismissal, especially female staff.

"Please continue, Sabine. I shall turn a blind eye."

"Well," she continued, a little hesitantly, "she's also a Protestant…"

"Two blind eyes, then!"

"And every time she lights one she never fails to tell us that Emperor Josef the Second closed some of the monasteries and banned most of the monks and to add insult to injury had several of the places converted to tobacco factories. And there's two of them at Kutná Hora, where Empress are made."

"Well, that explains it then," I said. Oddly enough, my Catholic blood is really from the English side. Karel calls himself one, but that's only because in Austria one must. I have on occasion caught him looking longingly at the Protestant images of the chalice. But that may have been for more secular reasons!

Despite Sabine's perfectly good explanation, I was just a little annoyed that she had had the answer and I had not. If this relationship was going to work, and sharing a potentially dangerous adventure was not a time nor place to have between two people any issues of rank, then it would have to be me who changed.

"So, time for supper," I said reassuringly, as we made our way more confidently to the hall with the open window.

"Oh, thank the Lord," sighed Sabine with relief. "I was just so terrified."

But she had had the guts not to have complained before. She might well be made of sterner stuff than I, I thought.

I observed Jenks boarding the train, having made a particular point in being early. I peered through the half-drawn blind of our compartment.

"That's him," I said, pointing the fellow out to Sabine.

He therefore did not have the advantage of seeing the two of us board the train, for obviously he would have been able to recognise me. The thought of what could have happened on the train to Karlsbad made me shudder. I told Sabine that we must keep watch on the door constantly and to scream out loud if anyone so much as touches the latch. At Eger — only a relatively short journey — we would transfer to the *de Luxe*, and I knew that in the sleeping cars one could lock the doors of the compartments from the inside. Then we would be safe.

Fortune was with us. We kept watch while the *de Luxe* stopped at Nuremberg, Stuttgart, Kehl, and Strasbourg. Jenks did not step from the train. We kept together all the while, taking our meals at odd times in the Dining Car. Jenks, I had presumed correctly, liked his meat and potatoes at the more regular feeding times and was thus not seen there by us.

Eventually, late in the evening, we steamed into Paris. It was to the Gare du Nord, for the train was destined for Calais, Dover, and London. Sabine was slightly sad at having to pass through her native city without touching French soil or, as she put it, eating proper bread. She was looking dreamily out of the window, even though all she could see was a railway platform not much different from most we had seen all day. But to her, those people out there, her people, they were all eaters of "proper bread" — as well as being lovers of horseflesh and garlic-eaters *par excellence.*

I could see her eyes were moist with tears. Goodness knows how many years it had been since she was last home. She had been with me constantly for five years, taking her two-week annual holiday down in Moravia, where she helped some relatives of Karel's former valet, Klopček, with the wine harvest. So that some of those garlic fumes and the sounds of thoroughbred members of the Gallic race could at least reach her, I let down the window halfway. I thought she seemed intoxicated by the view presented her.

"Madame, Madame," she was saying urgently, "it's 'im. It's 'im!"

"*Mon Dieu,*" I cried…well, we were in France, and indeed it was Jenks — on the platform. Either he was taking a quick breath of fresh air, or he was leaving the train.

"There's no time to lose, Sabine. Pack these things at once."

I looked about the compartment. There were the dressing pins, neatly out of their box to facilitate easy use. The brushes, combs, and perfume spray correctly laid out. Underwear had been correctly unpacked for the morning. I could see the handiwork of a servant, not of the terminally untidy, helpless individual which was myself. But there was no time. I simply scooped up everything into our travelling bag.

"There are two hats and two stoles here, Sabine. We will wear one each."

"But the portmanteau, Madame? What about 'eet?"

"It will simply stay in the luggage van to Victoria. We will claim it there — but maybe he's just taking some air."

I said that, but didn't believe it. The London ticket may have been purchased to put anyone off the scent. In any event he was allowed to stop over in Paris, if he so chose. So were we. I had simply not gone through all the options. I'd had over fourteen hours to have done so, and I had been lazy. I should have made some slips of paper; they would have worked — cards, stronger and more durable than paper, marked Options 1, 2, 3, and so on.

No time for this self-reproach now, I thought. Sabine had done a remarkable job of grabbing what remained after my lightning scavenge. In what seemed like no time we were on the platform.

Jenks was still visible. He was showing his ticket to the Inspector at the barrier. Sabine had ours ready. I hoped we weren't going to have to follow him all through the impossibly busy streets of Paris — but on this score we had luck.

Once onto the station concourse, Jenks headed upstairs for the restaurant. I would certainly not be unhappy eating there, if we had to. As if in defiance of the worldwide law concerning the standard of food in the proximity of railways, the restaurants at the great termini of Paris were all first class. Of course, the French always revelled in being *au contraire*.

I soon found myself seated at a table some distance from the man, with my back to him. A waiter brought us a basket of bread to be getting on with, before ordering. Sabine smiled at me. I thought it would be appropriate to smile back — I knew what she was thinking. "Even if it is only for this, it will have been worth it!" For my part I was also enjoying the splendour of the place. Only the French could dedicate such overpowering crustaceans of architecture to the service of food; in another country such a style would be reserved for an audience hall to impress foreign ambassadors, or the throne room of a megalomaniac despot.

After swallowing her first mouthful, Sabine was able to give me a running commentary on events, small and large — reporting what was over my shoulder. Since she was of the Gallic race, then the first reports were naturally of a culinary nature.

"Madame, he has finished the plate of oysters. Now there is a plate of chops."

"And? Come on, Sabine, is he alone?"

"No, Madame. Another gentleman has just joined him."

"So tell me — what does he look like?"

"*Distingué*, you might call him. High-domed forehead, swept-back greying hair — bushy black eyebrows that almost meet. Intense. Intelligent…"

"And?" God, it was so awful to have to rely on another's sight. I began to feel how a blind man must.

"They are talking. Jenks — how you say it? — Jenks is not eating for the moment…well, just picking. He is smiling. Then he is not smiling. And now…"

"Yes, yes…?"

"The gentleman rises, and he leaves. This Monsieur Jenks is now eating another plate of oysters."

My astute detective's mind had come to the conclusion that since Jenks was eating like a madman, he hadn't ventured into the Dining Car at all since Eger. That showed he did have some element of caution — or fear.

Now it was Sabine's turn, and just as our *terrine* had arrived on the table:

"Madame, Madame —"

"Once is enough Sabine. Now quickly, what do you see?"

"Another gentleman to see the Monsieur." But she seemed rather agitated by the fact.

"And?"

"But, Madame, 'ee looks exactly like the first gentleman."

"Now, Sabine, that's because it probably is the first gentleman. I don't know as this proper bread and this paté are doing you any good. No wonder the French are so —"

"No, Madame. The first gentleman was wearing grey with a black striped waistcoat. This gentleman is wearing black with a dark red waistcoat."

"And what now?"

"Another plate of chops for the Monsieur. And he offers the gentleman a glass of wine. They talk."

The second caller looked like the first and they appeared to have the same conversation, except that — second time round — our Monsieur did not seem to smile. The second caller left.

"Another comes," announced Sabine after an interval of a few minutes. I was by this time tucking into some duck, a favourite dish of my native Bohemia — but exquisitely prepared the French way. There's no denying they know how to do things in the kitchen, though hardly on the field of battle these days. But perhaps in the bedroom.

"And I suppose you will say he looks exactly the same as gentlemen numbers one and two," I asked in a sarcastic way, annoyed that I was the secondhand recipient of the news — but circumstances could have made it no different.

"Exactly, Madame. How did you know?"

A piece of duck seemed to stick in my throat. Did they have wings, the damned things? I thought they just paddled in the water with webbed feet. "And?"

"This time he has chops with potatoes *à l'Anglais.*"

"You mean fried?"

"*Oui,* Madame."

"How disgusting!"

However, I was thinking about how to find out what any of this could mean. The interviews were lasting only a few minutes each; I didn't have much time. I had an idea.

"Now, Sabine, here's what I want you to do."

Sabine was coming back to the table. Just as she was sitting down, she leaned forward, whispering in an urgent tone:

"The Monsieur, he is going."

"You have the photograph?"

Sabine nodded.

"Then it is safe to let him go," I said. "We could never follow him discreetly now — or leave here in such a hurry. We'll just have to presume that he will go on into London, and then simply disappear into the world's biggest metropolis. Anyway, tell me what happened?"

"Well, as Madame asked me, I stopped him on the staircase and asked him if he was indeed the great Erich Munar, who so often graced the stage in Paris. He looked a little indignant at first. So I said your next line: 'But I do recognise you from the stage, don't I?' And, Madame, as you said — he smiled. And in another moment or two I had got from him his signed photo-graph — which I have 'ere for you."

There, as Sabine had described, was a man naturally blessed with the same features as the other two. His name, printed below, was Jules Lefèvre.

"What does it all mean, Madame?"

"It means, dear Sabine, that we shall proceed to London on the first train which leaves at a reasonable hour tomorrow morning. I shall stay here at the station hotel, and you have what is called, in His Imperial Majesty's Army, *furlough* for seven hours. Would that be of use to you?"

I could see a certain glint in her eye. Certainly she wasn't going to knock-up aged grandparents at this time of night.

"But before you go, I have a question for you. There were three actors interviewed by this Mr. Jenks. Which one got the part, do you think?"

"It is strange Madame, because of the three, it seems that only one left disappointed — and didn't shake this man Jenks' hand. The other two seemed pleased, and shook the hand vigorously."

Again, this only deepened the mystery — but it was such an odd clue, it had to be significant. Then I thought to ask:

"I know they all looked roughly the same, these three. But what about the two who — shall we say — got the part?"

"Madame, you always know what is in my mind. Those two, they looked so alike — like twins."

Sabine left faster than the speed of sound, before I could have the faintest possibility of calling her back and asking her any more questions, and I was left turning over the *carte de visite* photograph in my hand. *Distingué* was what she had said. She was right — far too distinguished in appearance to be a mere actor, but then I supposed that this whole mystery was all about appearances. To look like somebody is to be somebody — that thought I was turning over in my mind. "Jules Lefèvre" was this gentleman and actor — and there was another, identical. But why?

Chapter Six
Flower of Cities All

When Sabine caught up with me — and nine-thirty, as I had been at pains to point out, was quite early enough for any woman with pretensions to beauty to set out — I was at the hotel receptionist's desk busy firing off telegrams to all points of the globe.

To my husband:

```
NOT A MURDERESS EXCLAMATION STOP IN
LONDON LATER TODAY AND SEEING MAX STOP
IT'S QUITE A TALE STOP SORRY ABOUT LOSS
OF REVOLVER
```

No. I dropped the remark about the revolver. I must be cautious. Then, as an afterthought, I'm afraid, I added:

```
STOP YOUR LOVING WIFE BEATRICE
```

"No," I said to the clerk behind the desk, "change that to Trixie."

Then to *The Archivist*, *The Times*, Printing House Square, London EC:

```
URGENTLY REQUIRE CUTTINGS OF STORIES
CONCERNING THOSE WHO RESEMBLE HM KING
EDWARD STOP CALLING BY OFFICE 4PM STOP
COUNTESS VON FALKLENBURG
```

Then to my younger brother, Max (he hates being called Maximilian, but then my parents had been thinking of calling him Hyacinth, the traditional family forename of the impoverished von Morštejns):

```
IN LONDON TONIGHT STOP HOPE ALL RIGHT TO
STAY FEW DAYS LOVE TRIXIE
```

I should have pointed already out that my brother left to seek his fortune in London, blessed by having an English mother with the correct pretensions at least, if not the capital. All he would tell us is that he worked "In the City," meaning in that den of thieves, robbers, and hapless gamblers known as The Financial Institutions of the City of London. He stood a chance, so I was told, of making enough wealth to set himself up properly. Or a chance of gaining nothing. The Tontine was a safe bet compared to his chosen direction in life. I hadn't seen him in four years, but I felt quite in order imposing myself on him as he had recently moved. When I said he was my younger brother — that was so, but only by a matter of eighteen months.

Lastly, to Uncle Berty:

```
THE MYSTERY DEEPENS STOP HOWEVER AM IN
GOOD FORM STOP YOU HAVE SET ME FREE STOP
YOUR LOVING NIECE TRIXIE
```

Sabine looked somehow different when we were re-united. It took me a while to realise what it was that had caused this change.

"I am sorry it was such a short break in your native city," I began. "I'll make sure you have a longer break on our way back — would that be all right?"

"Yes, thank you, Madame. In fact I've already promised him —" She broke off suddenly, having said just a little more than she intended.

Sex can be such a great restorative, yet doctors seem never to prescribe it. Perhaps it would put them out of business if its powers were more widely perceived.

Sabine kept taking furtive glances over her shoulder. I wondered if her mysterious midnight lover was lurking somewhere in the shadows. She could recognise what I was thinking, probably by the little frown on my brow.

"Madame, I hope you don't mind me mentioning this — but I felt sure this morning that in the crowd by the ticket office I noticed the police inspector who came to visit us."

"You mean that Inspector Schneider? My dear Sabine, that's impossible. You haven't seen him again?"

"No, Madame."

"Then it was someone with a passing similarity — I feel sure."

But this little incident did serve to remind me that sooner or later I would be suspect Number One in the murder of Gerard Duvalier.

In a few hours we were destined to see the White Cliffs that were England's frontier with the sea, and in the relaxed atmosphere of our compartment — no longer worried by any Mr. Jenks — the concerns of home finally became irresistible, and so I had to ask. It was not Sabine's place to suggest them first.

"Well," she said after a little thought, "Müller was very concerned for you — and not a little jealous that I should be called upon to travel, and not him."

"That's rather flattering of him, don't you think, that he actually wanted to be by my side?"

"After what happened to you at The Servants' Union, he felt he could not return there. Besides, he could hardly ask his Lordship for the use of his cravat and tie-pin, could he? Perhaps when you are back —"

"I did warn my husband."

"But that's not the point, Madame. It would not be his place to do such a thing. As a butler you can steal half a bottle of whisky now and again — but you may never ask for it. Oh no, that would never do."

"The lads? I feel I have rather left them in the lurch."

"Not at all, Madame. Here Müller has come into his own. He has them properly organised. They are following the movements of the gentleman residing sometimes at The Invalides, and it is they who are watching every event connected with the Fenix Theatre. There were some old clothes in a trunk in the attic we found — probably from the Harrachs — and when they need to be, they can now look like proper little Lord Fauntleroys."

There was but one thing left on my mental list. "And my husband? How is the Count taking it all?"

"You can only have my opinion, Madame. I think perhaps he feels it is Divine Retribution — he leaves you too much to your own devices, and you find some amusement elsewhere. He does not believe you are a murderer, of course — any more than you would be capable of climbing onto the roof of a railway carriage, so he knows there has to be some reasonable explanation. And once he knew you were asking for me, then all seemed right with the world again. A Countess with a Lady's Maid can hardly get into trouble — or so he thinks."

Sabine waited a moment for me to say something, but I was a little lost in my own thoughts. Then she offered, softly:

"You see, I think he still loves you."

I looked up, perhaps seeming a little surprised.

She went on, choosing her words with some caution: "None of us think His Lordship has…has a mistress. That must mean something."

Yes, I had forgotten how the servants must speak of us. News of semen on the sheets, for example, must spread like the tidings of the Battle of Austerlitz. Fortunately, such discoveries could only have been in line with what was normal in the marital bed. That we had not had children was due to other factors, which concern neither servants nor readers of detective narratives. That my husband had no mistress was indeed a rarity.

The constant rhythm of the wheels had stopped. Through the window there were harbour walls, dockside cranes, sailors in their blue guernseys, and wheeling seagulls. The train was being slowly manoeuvred onto the ferry from Calais to Dover, a miracle of modern engineering. I remembered reading that it was possible to be on the sleeper and to wake up in London, entirely unaware of the crossing. In the same way, I was thinking, as some dutiful wives manage to sleep peacefully through their husbands' snoring, even though the husband sounds as if he were driving an entire herd of restless pigs to the slaughterhouse.

The train passed through Dover Station, left the seagulls behind us and in two hours was in the heart of London, at Victoria Station. Sabine would go in search of our luggage and I would go immediately on the first errand of my investigation. In the meantime, Jenks — that is, if he had continued his journey to the capital — was now lost in this metropolis of a million souls.

The archives of *The Times* of London occupied the attics of its offices in Printing House Square, in the heart of the city. Mr. Elderbridge was the chief archivist — a man of very small stature, who sat on his high stool like a gnome. He had lank hair, a high forehead, and eyes that were so shrunken-looking behind the extremely thick lenses of his round spectacles that his gaze resembled that of a reptile. To add to his striking visual appearance he had a very high-pitched voice. In short he was the kind of character that had to remain hidden in dusty vaults or low-ceilinged attics. He would never excel on a sports field, or defending some picket on the North West Frontier of Britain's Indian Empire — he had been born for this very job, and in it I would find he certainly did excel.

"If you would be so good as to sit down here, please," he said in a kindly tone, moving some piles of paper from a chair and dusting its seat. The piles were simply added to other piles perched on what must have been, underneath, a table. Evidently he rarely received guests.

"They usually just send a boy round," he went on, fussing over some files, "and what with you, from the Continent even! Would you like some cordial or some tea?"

"I'm afraid time is slightly against us, Mr. Elderbridge. I trust you understood my telegram?" I could effect a politely efficient manner *par excellence* when I chose; my mother had taught me that of English ways at least.

"Of course, of course. Now let me explain how my system works. Nine years ago I started keeping a clippings index. That means I cut from an additional copy of the paper any article I thought might interest someone at some time in the future. Don't ask me the criteria I use. All I can say is that it has been a great success. I can, for example, help you instantly."

"You can?"

"I have two clippings to hand. The first is one I have just found for you. It concerns a certain bulldog named Rex from St. Helens, Lancashire, who bears an uncanny resemblance to His Majesty —"

My heart sank. I knew this would be a waste of time. I was sure I was really no good at solving mysteries after all. I could call that feminine intuition, or just plain realism!

"— the other I laid my hands on first about six or seven weeks ago at the request of another caller. Sat right where you are now, he did. Odd that I should have had exactly the same request twice like that, isn't it?"

He reached into a box that was filled with clippings of various sizes, some of them pinned together by their corners. This was a single small piece:

EDWARDS IN A TUSSLE
A Tale of Two Kings

Two actors who both thought they had landed the part of His Majesty the King in a lampooning new production *All the King's Mistresses* came to blows outside a theatre, The Majestic Music Hall and Variety Theatre in Wilton Street, Bow, London E1, yesterday.

Both bear an uncanny resemblance to His Majesty and are in frequent demand for performances depicting the Monarch. The disagreement started after they had left the office of Mr. George Buckle, the theatre proprietor, last Tuesday at around 12.30 and 1 pm, respectively. Both understood that they would be engaged for the role and after each had retired to celebrate at The Leg of Mutton public house adjoining the theatre, trouble soon ensued. Blows were exchanged, although neither was injured.

It is a salutary lesson to Republicans and to other reformers that perhaps the country is best served with only one Monarch!

I put the cutting down. It was just what I was looking for. The fact that it had been sought before was also the evidence I needed that I was on the right track. It all fit. It was a preposterous idea — but still the main question was unanswered — why?

"This other caller, Mr. Elderbridge?" I asked, "Was he of stocky build, rough in appearance, and with red hair? Might have used the name Jenks?"

"Why yes, Countess — I mean Your Ladyship — that's him all right, but he didn't give his name. Do you know the gentleman?"

"If only he were a gentleman!" I replied.

☙

Sabine was guiding the cabby up the stairs with the portmanteau. Max, my brother, was holding the door open. The cabby was no doubt regretting the offer of his assistance as the apartment was on the fifth floor and there was no lift. Fortunately for him, Max was a good tipper.

I was taking a tour of inspection.

"When you wrote and said you'd moved to Mount Street I thought you had taken a house, Max."

"Trixie, these are some of the best apartments in Mayfair, built less than twenty years ago when the place was generally recognised as the most stylish street in London."

"But you've hardly a stick of furniture — thank God at least you've got good carpets."

I had breezed through the sitting room which opened out in the dining room. "And where are your staff? Couldn't you have sent your man down to take the box up?"

Max was silent on this one, now paying off the cab-driver. Since he was turned away from me, I could look at him dispassionately. He was a tall, handsome man — with our mother's fair hair, a moustache with a graceful wave, and if he had turned, the most piercing but somehow soft blue eyes. We looked a pair, bred from the same stock. His deep-cut brow, which gave him an air of intense concentration, was from the von Morštejns. I wondered how he would look amongst my mother's people, the de Clyffordes. They were very grand, however, even though my mother had been raised very much as the poor relation, owing to her circumstances.

Ah, here's the kitchen (I was striding about with a proprietorial air already). "And why don't they keep the place at all tidy?"

"Now I know you are going to find it hard to believe, Trixie, but I am servantless. Difficult times, the manpower shortage because of the Boer War and now the fact that I am enjoying my privacy," explained Max, coming up behind me. "I predict that the servantless household will become highly fashionable — one day."

"And anyway," he went on, "I have the latest machine for cooking — it works by electricity."

There was indeed a monstrous apparatus at one end of the room. I opened a cupboard. It was full of tins of sardines. "Max!" I exclaimed at the sheer horror of it all.

"Sweet sister, I didn't say I knew how to operate the machine."

"Cooking, like most of the wifely arts, is quite simple. It consists of mixing various ingredients and changing the temperature of the whole. You will have to learn, Max" — but not from me. I didn't have the faintest idea beyond making hardboiled eggs for painting as Easter gifts.

In one week I had now seen the interiors of two kitchens — quite remarkable, I was thinking. Next I poked into Max's bedroom. It was a very brief visit: "And how many times a year do they collect your laundry?"

Max now sat me down back in the sitting room.

"Look," he said, "the place is in a mess, and I can only agree."

"So Sabine will sort it all out for you. She will make it a habitation fit for our species. I will sleep in your room, Max. Sabine can take the small bedroom, and you may sleep on this sofa. It will only be for a few days."

I could see that, quite apart from Max's feelings, Sabine was about to protest too. These were duties for a Maid-of-All-Work, not a Lady's Maid. Servants were very particular about such distinctions — just as I would be about recognising, now that I was here again, a Baron below an Earl (whose wives respectively would be a Baroness and a Countess) and an Earl below a Duke, who would of course be lower in precedence than a Royal Duke, and so on. Interleaved between these, like tissue paper in a photographic album, were also Viscounts and Marquesses — just as there were Under Footmen and Grooms-of-Chambers in the household hierarchy.

"And, Sabine, when Mr. Max's apartment here is gleaming, I'm sending you back — and you may break your journey in Paris for a whole week."

Sabine smiled, a faraway look creeping across her face. How easy it would have been, I thought, to have ended the French Revolution thus. "Let them have holidays" was what M. Antoinette most obviously should have declared. Love would have been their food!

"Now Max, we shall go for an early dinner at the Café Royal. Fortunately I have plenty of money with me. Karel gave it to me as he believes I am a murder suspect on the run! But all this is a long story. Perhaps tonight I shall tell it you — but in the meantime, do you recognise this man?"

Max brushed off my seemingly fantastic comment in the way that brothers and sisters by force of habit rarely take each other seriously. I pulled out of my handbag the photograph of the French actor. I showed it to him, but keeping a finger over the printed name.

"There is something familiar in that face. Let me think on it for a while. But a clue?"

"He is a well-known personality in politics or of the ruling classes in Europe, I should imagine. Indeed he is most probably French. I presume not military or religious because he wears no uniform of either. One thing I can say is that he is not a personality of the theatre."

"But Trixie, that's just the kind of printed *carte de visite* an actor would have."

"Very well. I take my hand away. There is a name you haven't heard of — so instead, just tell me of whom the face reminds you. Perhaps that is fairer?"

Max stared hard at the man I had nearly seen in the restaurant of the Gare du Nord.

"So now tell me, why were you talking about such economies? That's not the von Morštejn way, surely?" I was trying to lighten the tone to give him a chance to concentrate on the face, but I didn't succeed. Max's tone seemed serious:

"There's a war brewing between Russia and Japan. It could break out in earnest any day. Russia is on the very brink. It has already attacked Port Arthur and I have invested heavily — and have advised others to invest — in Trans-Siberian Railway stock."

"Karel's family was nearly ruined by buying Brazilian railway shares. In fact the shares weren't to blame in the end. Complete ruination came about as a result of a game of cards as I don't mind telling anybody — nor need reminding you. It's a good lesson. But surely, with Russia needing to send all those troops towards Japan, then the railway will do well?"

"But everyone here believes that Japan might win!"

"You can't be serious, Max. How could that affect things? The Japanese won't try to invade St. Petersburg or anything, will they? And they're such tiny people too!"

"No, of course not. But if Russia does lose, then the word is that revolution will break out there. Then the stock will be even more worthless than those Brazilian shares of your father-in-law."

"So…?"

"I am selling, for whatever price I can get, however low."

"Then we had better cheer ourselves up, hadn't we?"

We walked just round the corner into Berkeley Square and found a hansom to take us to Regent Street. I was twenty-one when I was here in London last, when my mother had insisted she take me to "come out" and be presented at Court — to attend the traditional Queen Charlotte's Ball, just like any another debutante living on some country estate in England with well-tended acres and an enormous ivy-clad pile of a house that was either ancient, built-up over the centuries, or made to look like it, but then I supposed I was just being bitter that our ancestral castle in Bohemia had been lost. Oh, for spires and turrets of any vintage!

Again the capital of the world's largest empire — and undoubt-edly the largest there could ever be — excited me. There was the soft, but constant, clatter of the traffic and the hum of the sheer mass of humanity, day and night. Stories that were in the newspapers here had worldwide implications; there was a cer-tain *gravitas* that was missing in Austria. In Vienna and Prague the papers were filled with stories of unrest in Serbia — with Balkan revolutionaries and anarchists. But how could some story from, say, Belgrade or Sarajevo ever have any impact on the world stage? How could anything from the Austrian Empire ever affect history — whereas, here in London the tentacles of power reached from China to the frozen north of Canada, from the teeming bazaars of India to the jungles of Africa. I snuggled up to Max from the sheer excitement of it all. He, however, was in a more sanguine mood.

"Imagine — in a year or two these hansoms will be things of the past. And I don't mean surpassed just by motor taxis. As we ride now, fifty metres below us, they are finishing the deep electric underground railway, the Piccadilly Railway. How the world is changing, Trixie."

We were turning from Berkeley Street into Piccadilly, that great thoroughfare of the nation. I noticed that it was now lit by electric lamps, as had been the case in Prague for years; the old gaslamps had gone. The atmosphere of the city that had made such a romantic setting to the stories of Sherlock Holmes was disappearing. At least the fog could never disappear.

The cabby leaned down and spoke to Max, who turned to me: "He says that Swallow Street is closed due to the rebuilding of Regent Street. It's of no consequence."

Oh, but it was! It meant going about Piccadilly Circus, that hub of London — of the World. I had been a silly young girl the last time in London, a virgin, and now I was here again as a grown woman, perhaps with a little of the responsibility that rank brings, on a task that had become something much more than an adventure. In fact it threatened my life.

The Café Royal seemed to have retained all the gaiety of its reputation, but somehow the crowd seemed thinner than I had expected. They hadn't all been exiled like one of its more infamous customers, Oscar Wilde, had they? We sat in the Grill Room, watching the faces of the diners reflected a hundred times in the French mirrors. At least reflections were plentiful.

"It's the smallpox, Trixie," Max explained. "Many people are staying away from the West End. The theatres are having a hard time of it, as well as restaurants. I take a strictly fatalist line: if you are going to get it, then you are — and that's it."

"So you don't bother to look left and right as you cross the street?"

"No, I don't mean that."

"But it's not just the quantity of the crowd here, Max — but the quality. The last time I was here, young and impressionable as I was, there was a more…well, a crowd with more —"

"'Class' is the word I suppose you're searching for. And you're probably right. Things are changing. The old rich are no longer the richest. Thanks to the diamond mines of South Africa, for example, there are now millionaires richer than the King. The Astors are now so well-established here it's impossible to believe that they're just successful Jewish speculators from New York and not the real blue-blooded thing — let alone Protestants!"

"So where will it all end, do you think?"

"I've had a few knocks here in London — not been an easy time, and I'm probably the first von Morštejn to try to earn a living in more than two centuries. So I've had time to dwell on it all. At the moment it's a simple redistribution of wealth to new people who are sufficiently near to the grabbing process to remember it."

"What do you mean? The old families were grabbers, surely?"

"That's precisely it. They've forgotten they were. Ours — it was pretty sharp changing sides in 1620 and suddenly becoming loyal to the winning Hapsburgs, wasn't it? Look at all the estates it gained that way. But ever since it has gradually lost the need to take and thus lost the urge to grab."

"So my father-in-law's escapades at the gaming tables were a substitute, do you think?"

"Yes, he preferred his risks with a glass of whisky in his hand and his bottom on a comfortable chair. He should have been digging in Kimberley or staking a claim on the Klondike if he wanted to combine risk with reinvigorating the family fortunes, I suppose."

I let this die out, then: "Oh, Max. I'm tired of dwelling on this. It makes me depressed. If they have money and pots of it, why do they insist on dressing like that?"

I pointed out a man with large whiskers like a walrus and a silk waistcoat that was dazzlingly distasteful. Max laughed.

"You're incurable, Trixie," he said, before going back to concentrate on his plate of smoked salmon and quails' eggs.

A minute or two later, as the entrée was being served, Max grabbed my arm: "Show me the photograph again."

I obliged.

"Yes. Yes, that's who he reminds me of. Emile Brodsky. Sir Emile Brodsky."

"And who's he?"

"A famous scientist — French by birth…lived here for over twenty years, knighted a couple of years back for 'Services to the British Empire.' Leading member of the Royal Institution, pillar of the scientific establishment — all that kind of thing."

"And what kind of science makes him so distinguished?"

"Explosives. He's one of the world's foremost experts on death and destruction."

It was evidently time for me to tell Max the entire extraordinary story, beginning with the bludgeoned body of poor old Alois pulled out of the Vltava just two weeks before.

The Majestic Music Hall and Variety Theatre was closed. It was, in theatrical parlance, "dark." The once-yellow bricks from which it was built were also dark, but with soot, and its ornate cast-iron canopy bearing a large hoarding advertising *All The King's Mistresses* was unilluminated. In London's East End, as Max had pointed out, the smallpox was a more serious concern. Like all diseases, it preferred to lurk amongst the poor and dispossessed, the homeless or those whose homes are hardly worthy of the description. The East End of London seemed to have witnessed every kind of human tragedy, as was written on the gaunt, hollow-cheeked faces of its inhabitants. For the moment it also seemed they had been steering clear of the Majestic, even with seats at only two pence. Mr. George Buckle must have found it cheaper simply to close the theatre, as the sign on the doors read, "until circumstances permit."

Max rattled the doors at the main entrance. *All The King's Mistresses — A Short Drama Followed By a Variety Revue* had closed two weeks ago. It looked as if, in the parlance of detective fiction novelettes, we had drawn a blank. Luckily, Max had some of the persistence of our Bohemian forebears and refused to give up so easily. "There must be a stage door," he said.

I had visions of the Fenix in Prague. The stage door of the Majestic was even less salubrious — down a rubbish-strewn alleyway between the theatre and The Leg of Mutton public house. There was an electric doorbell with a plate "The Majestic Theatre Company & Henry Buckle and Sons Limited." Max pressed, keeping his finger on the bell-push longer than was normally socially acceptable. At length the door opened just a crack, secured on a door-chain. Revealed was a thin slice of a man's face with deep-sunk eyes and a sallow complexion. As Max spoke to him I scrutinised the man's features by the light of the one gaslamp in the alleyway. His far from healthy skin showed none of the telltale red spots of the pox.

That we were the second enquirers about the two Edwards was obviously of some concern to the man, whom Max quickly found out was our Mr. Buckle, son of Henry Buckle, the theatre's founder. In fact he really didn't want to speak on the subject at all except that Max had managed to jam his cane in the door, so it had to stay open — even just this little bit — as long as Max desired it to be so.

"All right, all right I'll tell you what you want to know. The actor whom I eventually engaged for the second run was Mr. Preston Cavendish. The one who didn't get the role this time was the Reverend Gerald Swinnerton."

"The Reverend?" asked Max.

"Yes, he's a vicar. Acting is a pastime of his, but he's very good. You see, the play was due to run over Easter — too many days off. Yet he was by far the better."

"And where can we find them?"

"Cavendish, after I closed down, went off—I don't know where. Maybe some of the local pubs might know. The Reverend, well, I'm sure you'll be able to find him. That's all I'm telling."

Since it was clear our interview was at an end, Max withdrew his cane and we got back into the hansom which we'd had waiting. Max ordered the cabby to take us to Bow Library. In the reference section, a copy of Crockford's Clerical Directory told us that the Reverend Swinnerton was the rector of a parish in Poplar, a neighbouring district in the East End.

Finding nowhere suitable to take luncheon, we decided to go on to Poplar immediately. I was imagining one of those cold, dark, pitch-pine panelled Protestant rectories that I must have read about in a novel. The kind where there are ghastly secrets hidden from the world, a place reeking not of incense but of incest. I couldn't have been more wrong.

The rectory turned out to have been built thirty or forty years ago in that cottage style so beloved of designers then — of warm red brick, full of nooks with fireplaces and hand-hewn oak beams in the ceilings. Throughout it was wallpapered with intricate floral designs, of the kind I dearly wanted to point out to Max for his apartment in Mayfair.

Gerald Swinnerton, of course, needs no describing. He was the perfect double of His Majesty King Edward VII, even down to the twinkle in his eyes and an obvious love of life and its manifold pleasures, although as a man of the cloth I presumed that did not include philandering. Like His Majesty he was in his early sixties, or at least appeared to be no older.

"We've come to ask you to help solve a mystery, but we cannot tell you what the mystery is — partly because we don't know ourselves, and partly because if we did know what it was, I feel sure we would not be permitted to speak about it," I said, after we had introduced ourselves.

The Reverend Swinnerton lay back in his generously padded armchair, his big hands gripping the floral printed covers of its arms, pondering what I had just said and looking at our cards.

"Countess, Mr. von Morštejn — some tea, perhaps? I hope you like a China blend. I get it straight from the importers. There are some advantages in a parish near the docks. Martha will get it for us," and he rang a bell.

I didn't know quite where to begin. Luckily he helped me, answering my not yet uttered question:

"About my acting, I suppose. Firstly, I assume you must want to know how I combine being a priest with being an actor. It's quite simple really: theatres are closed on Sundays — and I have ample time during the weekdays, except when there are matinées, to attend to my parish work. It's more than a mere pastime, however. Both occupations are callings, and I learn much about the human condition from both."

"But *All The King's Mistresses?*" interjected Max.

"I don't take myself too seriously. I daresay my royal duplicate doesn't either. A little gentle lampooning never did any harm. And as I am sure you know, in the end I couldn't be in the second run of the play."

The man was disarmingly frank.

"And has anyone else asked you to play the King recently?" I asked.

"And now you come to the point! Yes, there was a curious offer only three weeks or so ago. A man called without warning, just as you have. There was a very special play to be performed abroad — the engagement would be for two days only, but with two weeks' rehearsal, and the salary would be more than the Majestic would pay for a whole year's run. Apart from the fact that I couldn't be spared from my parish for the three weeks or more that this would entail, there was something in the man's manner I didn't trust. And when someone offers something so ridiculous, then I simply smell a rat. The theatrical business is full of rogues — as well as rats. I believe in God's providence, but not to that extent."

"Can you tell us the date when this play was expected to be performed?" I asked.

"I believe he said early in May."

"And where exactly?"

"That he didn't say. Just that it was 'on the Continent.'"

Max was now as fired-up as I was. "And do you know where we can find Mr. Preston Cavendish? I presume he must have been asked also."

"Dear old Preston. After a few drinks he would always get very belligerent — that wild Irish temper of his. I knew him well. We were always standing-in for each other since we looked so similar. But then this means you don't know."

Max and I stared at him. I could feel some kind of bombshell being loaded and detonated.

"It was two days ago. I was with him till the end. The doctors said it was because of his drinking. The funeral is tomorrow."

∽

"Well, what do you think, Trixie?" asked Max in the hansom back to civilisation. A visit to the East End was like crossing to another continent. Soon there were familiar landmarks — the Bank of England, the Mansion House, St. Paul's Cathedral.

"Well, you know what Mamma always says," I replied. And we both joined in a chorus: "Never trust a man with brown shoes!"

"But why is Mamma such a snob, Max?"

"When you have real money and real rank, you don't need snobbery as a prop. All this talk of class that's constantly on her lips — and on yours too, I've noticed — is for those whose hold onto class, and all that goes with it, when it is tenuous or threatened. And God knows, Mamma must have felt threatened with all those de Clyfforde relations with their great houses and vast estates in Yorkshire, while she, the daughter of a youngest son of a youngest son of an Earl — and one who had died in action in the Indian Mutiny, to boot — before he could inherit what little he had to inherit, while she was being raised nearly as a pauper, on a charity for the 'distressed families of gentlefolk.' It was a real *coup* to have landed our father, don't you think?"

"Well, I suppose so. We got a 'von' for a 'de'. A one letter increase."

"And you live in a palace in Prague —"

"Rent. And Prague isn't London."

"No, it's far prettier. And Bohemians are far more inventive. Small countries have this capacity. Look at Britain, with her huge empire — in some ways she is far more old-fashioned. I read recently that she has the biggest navy in the world, but also the most inefficient. For modernity, it must be Paris or Prague. If I could earn the kind of money there that's possible here, I would return home at once."

"Well, my dear Max, maybe it's also possible not to lose as much there!"

Max ignored my jibe. "Money is becoming the new class," he said. "And all you have to do to get money is to be smart, to use your brains."

I was thinking of everything I didn't know: how, I supposed, my brain was singularly underused. I was far from smart. I could see in my memory those terrible private tutors of mine, and that school in Switzerland with all the distractions of growing up to compete with learning anything more than becoming an attractive clothes-horse with a pea-brain and a penchant for putting down anyone who was cleverer as having no class. And in that bracket had gone all the rich girls whose fathers were in the jute trade or making fabulous fortunes building railways in some jungle.

It was late in the afternoon by the time Max and I arrived back at Mount Street. Sabine had done a wonderful job. The apartment felt airy and entirely habitable. Windows had been thrown open and sunlight seemed to have appeared for the first time in the sitting room, where also a bright fire was burning in the grate. There was even an aroma of cooking lurking in the kitchen. Max and I sat down to talk.

"Your instincts have been entirely right so far, Trixie. But I still can't put the puzzle together, however many pieces of the jigsaw you seem to find."

"Let's put it on little slips, shall we?" and I carefully put down all the characters on separate pieces of paper which I cut out with scissors. I cut a lot more slips than the few I had started out with in Jindřišská Street.

"We begin with an actor impersonating old Alois — or, rather, before that, there's the death of old Alois. Then there's the Tontine — that gets a slip of its own. So far Mr. Pinkerstein, the other one left in the Tontine — or indeed the board of directors of the Tontine Financial Association — haven't actually figured in this mystery."

"So what will happen to the theatre when the Tontine is all wrapped up?"

"Max, I don't know. I presume it simply goes to the winner. And once you take in the Fenix Theatre, then the cast of characters increases: there's a whole ballroom of what would appear to be Austrian nobility. There's an Edward VII double, two doubles for Sir Emile Brodsky, and who else?"

"You said that the actor in Prague could do an impersonation of the Kaiser."

"Yes, of course — so there's a Kaiser double as well. And lastly, we have the masterminds — or are they working for someone else? So here's a slip for Jenks, and one for the late Duvalier. Oh, and a slip for the Tobacco Factory in Marienbad."

"The fact you've missed is the date in early May," Max reminded me. That was no doubt of key importance.

It was tempting to think one had the puzzle complete — but still the purpose of it all eluded us. "We've forgotten the explosives," I said. "Brodsky's the expert."

"Do you think this is a big kidnap plot? That all these people — the real ones, that is — are going to be kidnapped? No, it's too far-fetched." Max had immediately doubted his own perfectly reasonable theory.

"Nothing's too far-fetched, Max. I believe this is something extremely serious and could threaten the lives of important individuals, don't you?"

"Absolutely right. This is far bigger than you or I can possibly cope with. I have a friend of mine, Rupert Talbot-Fane. He works directly under the Home Secretary. I shall contact him straight away."

Obviously the brief description of our puzzle which Max had given to his friend Rupert was enough to open doors right at the top. The next morning we were to attend on the Home Secretary himself, at his office in Whitehall, across from the Houses of Parliament. That electricity, that energy I had felt in Piccadilly was increased by a million volts to be at the very seat of power of the British Empire.

I had decided it was to be Sabine's last day before her holiday in Paris. She had worked hard to create a very respectable, but also very seductive (I hoped) Bohemian Countess. Such creatures were rare in London. Since there was a weak sun — bright although still cold — I carried a parasol. It gave me something with which to twiddle, for there were bound to be awkward moments. I begged Max that under no circumstances was he to mention the Tontine.

Brother and sister looked each other over for minor flaws in our *accoutrement* as we waited outside the tall double doors of the Home Secretary's outer office. I flicked imaginary dandruff from the velvet of his collar, as one does. It strengthens the woman's position. Precisely at nine-thirty the doors were opened by a smart young man who came up and shook Max's hand. I was introduced to Rupert Talbot-Fane.

"The drill's quite simple," Talbot-Fane said reassuringly. "I will lead the way and introduce you to the Right Honourable Mr. Akers-Douglas, His Majesty's Secretary of State for Home Affairs. He will show you where to sit."

Akers-Douglas was a dapper man, in his prime. He was courteous to a fault. His office was huge, with clusters of columns and a gilded ceiling. An enormous desk was placed at an angle across the corner by one of the windows. Several other officials were in the room too, but whether they were deputy ministers or simply high-ranking clerks, I didn't know.

"Some coffee is being brought. I know you both have a story to tell — a fantastic one, if I am informed correctly. However, be that as it may, I am afraid I have an unpleasant duty to perform first."

So saying, the Home Secretary opened another door, a smaller, single door nearer to his desk. As it opened, it revealed — sitting rather uncomfortably, hunched forward, holding his hat in his hand which he had evidently been turning like a Rosary — none other than Inspector Schneider.

Chapter Seven

St. John's Wood

As Schneider stood up and entered, the Home Secretary continued, "He comes from Prague with a warrant from the Austrian
police. It is for your arrest, Your Ladyship, on being involved
in the murder of a gentleman on a train at Karlsbad last week.
I am sure these details come as no surprise to you."

Schneider advanced, brandishing a document. I really didn't need
to read it and I waved it aside. "I think, gentlemen, that you owe
it to my brother and me to give us a fair hearing, do you not?
We came here to give you information concerning some sort of
conspiracy which is afoot, the aim of which is undoubtedly to
do harm to one or more extremely important persons."

Brave as I sounded, I felt the blood draining from my cheeks.

"We have sent a message to Count Mensdorf, your ambassador. Count Dubski, the First Secretary, has sent back only an
acknowledgement as His Excellency is in the country. However, I
am prepared to listen to whatever you have to tell us," the Home
Secretary replied. He motioned for Max and me to be seated.

Schneider also sat down and I began the tale. I brought out my slips of paper, and when I placed the fake Austrian nobles on the Tobacco Factory in Marienbad with the early May date — just to test their reaction — I could see that this Right Honourable was more than a little shaken. But I concluded with a suggestion that could be followed up almost immediately: "It would seem that possibly the life or the work of Sir Emile Brodsky is threatened. Surely — since he lives in London — it would be easy enough to warn him, and in so doing to find out if he knows anything?"

Akers-Douglas nodded. "That makes sense. But there are other aspects of this affair which I think need to be reported at once to the Foreign Secretary. In the meantime we have to deal with this warrant. What is your view now, Inspector, having heard the bigger picture?"

One of the other men in the room turned out to be an interpreter and after a delay during which the rest of the story was translated I could see that Schneider was slightly taken aback by the layers of complexity which I had uncovered, or — rather — which he had missed. He was silent for a second.

"Her Ladyship is, of course, half British," the Home Secretary continued, without waiting for Schneider's answer. "That adds considerable complication to the warrant, don't you think?"

Schneider agreed that the very first step would be to contact Sir Emile Brodsky. The Home Secretary fired off a message for Talbot-Fane to send round to the Foreign Secretary and asked to see if there was anything in the files on Jenks. "Get me Sir Charles on the telephone," he asked another assistant. In a moment he was engaged in a conversation with him.

"Sir Charles is the Metropolitan Police Commissioner," Max whispered to me.

The Home Secretary put down the instrument and came over to us. "I think we can sort this out in a gentlemanly fashion. It seems that we all are interested in only one thing — the solution to this complex riddle. What if I were to suggest that for the time being Inspector Schneider and the Countess of Falklenburg were to work together? He could keep an eye on the subject of his warrant and perhaps they might come up with a much more interesting answer so that Her Ladyship doesn't have to be dragged back to Prague in handcuffs. The Metropolitan Police will be sending over a good man to assist."

Schneider nodded his assent. It was hard for the young Police Inspector from Prague to disagree. I agreed on the basis that it was better than being in prison. The Home Secretary dismissed us, but assured me that my presence would be necessary again — once the Foreign Office was involved.

As we were leaving, Big Ben was chiming ten-thirty from across Parliament Square. It had all been accomplished in one business-like hour. Closer to Schneider now, I noticed his collar was quite soiled. Poor man, I thought — he hadn't prepared for such a lengthy journey and God knows what lodgings he could afford in London on the expenses of the Prague Police Department. But as for his warrant, that was an outrage. Even so, it did not look at all good for me: I had fled from the carriage. It had been Karel's gun. It could seem I was as guilty as hell. And the nice Inspector would simply tell me that he was only doing his job if I were to be taken back as a prisoner under arrest!

The villa of Sir Emile Brodsky was in the district of St. John's Wood on a tree-lined avenue behind Lord's Cricket Ground. It was smaller than I had expected for such an eminent man, with one room on each side of a columned porch and three windows of the first floor above it. Our party was in two hansoms — myself and Schneider, for we were now to be inseparable, in the first, and Max with a London Police Inspector following.

Once we were all assembled on the porch, Inspector Grey — for that was our London man's name — pulled the door-bell. We could hear it lazily swinging on its spring from somewhere deep inside the house. Presently the door opened and we were confronted by a couple — a rather surly man and a shrew-like woman, perhaps in their forties. They stood in that unmistakable attitude of "They shall not pass."

Grey explained that we wanted to meet with Sir Emile on a very important matter. The woman said that her employer was not at home for the moment and looked to the man, who said he would go and telephone Sir Emile. In the meantime this woman held her ground like all three Horatii, for which she had the stature. In a short while the man returned and said that Sir Emile would be pleased to receive us in an hour's time at the rooms he kept in Albany, the name of the distinguished gentlemen's chambers just off Piccadilly.

It was March, there was still the smell of coal-smoke in the air and the possibility of one of the dense London fogs that so beset the capital. But I detected another scent in the air. Whilst we were being watched by the servant couple as we made our way back to the hansoms, I pretended to drop my handkerchief and in stooping to pick it up I was able to get a better view of another building beside the house — erected in the garden. It was quite a substantial, rectangular structure of one storey. It could have been, for example, a laboratory. It had a single chimney and the smoke and flying ash from what can only have been burning papers were pouring forth from it.

There was nothing particularly strange in this. People often have to burn papers, but somehow it was one of those facts that one should retain "to lie on file." I was beginning to learn that detective work is ninety percent slogging around obtaining one seemingly meaningless fact after another — or so it probably seems at the time. But these facts eventually form part of a much larger and fuller picture…pieces in some giant jigsaw puzzle. Up to now I didn't think that Trixie had it in her to be patient and, indeed, to have any real skills at all apart from putting the right people next to one another at dinner parties and choosing suitable menus. Oh, and picking out the most expensive dresses!

So next on our round was Albany, that exclusive male preserve (no women may rent its rooms) in a private courtyard between Savile Row and Piccadilly. Sir Emile's set of rooms was in the wing which backed onto Burlington House. We were welcomed in by the man who so much resembled our French actor. I saw Max giving me a glance and a smile — it was, after all, his recalling of Sir Emile's face that had brought us here. There was the high-domed forehead, the bushy eyebrows, and that same intensity of expression. His black hair was shot with grey and I guessed him to be in his mid-sixties or thereabouts.

Soon, after introductions, we were all seated in his sitting room while we waited for the man he had sent off to return with coffee for us.

Inspector Grey decided to open the conversation. "We are here, Sir, merely to establish that you are in good health. We have received reports that quite possibly you might be the target of some criminal gang."

"Well, you can see that I am here, quite well," he said with a relaxed air and in a thick French accent. "So am I to know the source for your reports?"

"I'm afraid we cannot divulge that," replied Grey. "I am sure you can understand the reason."

I sat there looking at him intently. He was either the intended victim of this scheme or, if not, then perhaps its originator. He certainly had the brains, but for the life of me I could not fathom out any coherent reason. I looked at him again — did he look like someone who has just been told his life is perhaps threatened? He seemed to have read my thoughts, for he said, "I must admit, it is rather disturbing to think that there are those out there who would 'do me harm,' as you say..." he left the sentence dangling, perhaps deliberately encouraging one of us to say more than we should in reply.

When no-one spoke, he started again. "And Countess, how are you involved in all this? No harm to you, I hope."

"Let us just say," I said, "that it's a case of feminine intuition."

"I didn't know there were any old wives' tales about taking dastardly revenge on scientists!" he said, smugly.

"I think that's because in those days they were called ogres," I found myself countering. I regretted I had said it at once, of course. "But then in those days they were ignorant of the possible benefits of wizardry — what we call science today." I was trying, somewhat desperately, to make-up for my earlier *faux-pas*.

He was viewing me intently as his hand stroked his chin. I didn't think we could get any further with him. We had already agreed between us not to ask him anything about Jenks. If Brodsky turned out to be more involved in this than we first thought, then we wanted Jenks to lead us to the evidence, and to be unsuspected in the eyes of his possible master.

As we stood up together Grey asked: "And are you expecting to be travelling anywhere in the next few months? Abroad perhaps?"

I could clearly see Brodsky's thought processes, or so I fancied. He seemed about to say 'Oh, no — not at all' — then he calculated for a moment, the smallest moment, but it was a change and I recognised it.

"Why, yes," he said, "I am going to the Bohemian spas for a rest cure at the end of next month." He cast his gaze about us, his eyes ending on mine. "Do you think I shall be safe there?"

"Of course we shall all endeavour to ensure your personal safety, Sir Emile," replied Schneider with some good old-fashioned Austrian courtesy.

Soon we said our good-byes and were let out.

We needed to discuss the situation. Inspector Grey suggested we go to the Tea Room of Swan & Edgar's, the unfashionable department store on Piccadilly Circus. I was about to say that Fortnum & Mason's was hardly any further when I received a sharp tap on my leg from Max. All right, I had to give in. I couldn't imagine that Swan & Edgar's would be in any way a worse place than Fortnum's for such a discussion — but, simply, who would be seen dead there? Just because I lived in Prague didn't mean I didn't know the right places! Max was becoming perfectly tiresome in his drive against snobbery.

"So, Mr. Grey, perhaps you could tell a novice such as I what the secret is of detective work?" I asked.

"Research. And when you've done the research — then do more research. You cannot know too much about your subjects. So what have you discovered about Sir Emile Brodsky, for instance?" He was certainly to the point.

"Well…" I began, not knowing which waffle to start off with. Max rescued me, somewhat.

"We know that he is a very eminent scientist, and his speciality is in explosives."

"That's what everyone knows," Grey retorted. "People's weaknesses lie in information not everyone knows. Information that perhaps they don't want everyone to know. Why don't you begin by going to a library and looking up all his patents, for instance? That might be a very good start."

Suddenly, I felt about one centimetre in height. He was perfectly right. I realised how little I knew about the Tontine Financial Association, for example, or who actually held the lease for the Fenix Theatre.

"We can go down to the London Library. It's only in St. James' Square and I keep a subscription." (Max was ever helpful.)

The two Inspectors began talking about how they would coordinate the meetings with the Foreign Office and my concentration wandered. We were sitting by the window on an upper floor. The room was decorated in an English version of Paris-Prague *Art Nouveau*, with chairs from the Thonet factory in Moravia. Actually, although I dared not admit it, I was happy we were here. The window overlooked the famous Shaftesbury Monument, crowned with its winged statue of Eros. My eyes were drawn to a four-wheeler cab crossing towards the Haymarket. It was unmistakable: with three other passengers sat the recognisable figure of Jenks. I could see his red hair. So he was in London, after all. This was what could only be called a stroke of luck. I thought of asking Grey how much luck figured in the detective's work.

I stared hard again, with only the shortest glimpse of the cab now possible — maybe my optimism was getting the better of me…but no, it really was Jenks…I recognised the ungainly set of his shoulders.

I should have called the alarm, but to what purpose? We would all have run out of the building, only to find the cab had already disappeared down towards Trafalgar Square and The Mall. It was enough for me to know that the man was indeed in London. The picture I was constructing seemed to make sense again. Then for a moment I again doubted I had seen him — surely there are lots of rough-looking men with red hair in this city? Yet all my senses told me that it must have been him. I had to learn to trust my informed instinct.

By the time we were at the London Library we were down to three of us. Grey had said there was nothing more he could usefully do until we would meet him at the Foreign Office tomorrow morning. Schneider, of course, had to stay with me.

Max returned to the desk where we were seated with a thick directory in his hand.

"This will be good for patents applied for up to the end of 1902. It's the latest edition; came out in July 1903."

Soon we were looking at a very long list. Between 1899 and 1902 were these entries:

An Automatic Disinfection Spray for Hospitals and
    Workhouses.
A Rotating Barrel Gun capable of firing 300 rounds
    per minute.

Device for the Alleviation of Drought in Hot
Countries.
A Colourless and Odourless Explosive Material
(Application Withdrawn).
A Gas VM12Y10.
A Gas VM12Y11.
A Gas VM12Y12.
A Gas VM12Y13.
A Gas VM12Y14.
A Gas VM12Y15.
A Gas VM12Y16.
A Gas VM12Y17.

"So what does this 'Application Withdrawn' mean?" Schneider
asked.

"I haven't the foggiest," Max answered, "but supposing someone
bought the invention but didn't want it published — that could
be a reason. Or perhaps the invention was found not to work.
I'm afraid I'm not familiar with the Patent Office's rules."

"And the gasses?" Schneider queried.

"Inspector, as I said, I'm not expert in any of this," Max answered.
"A gas is a gas. They could be used for anything from filling air
balloons to fertilising the soil. Although I have my suspicions
they are probably for a more warlike purpose."

I was looking through *Who's Who*. "Can't see that he's married.
No children obviously. Usual list of clubs — one in Paris as
well. Usual sports — shooting, tennis, chess. Nothing about an
army career or universities or antecedents. I suppose because he
is French. Not a lot to go on."

"So what do you think, Trixie? Are you as impatient as I am?"

"To see inside that laboratory of his? Certainly. It only remains for us to convince our Inspector here that a little common burglary is strictly necessary in the circumstances."

Darkness descended by seven o'clock, the time we set out. We took a four-wheeler to Lisson Grove in St. John's Wood from where we would walk, so as not to attract too much attention. I was wearing one of the plain dresses that Sabine had had made for me — quite nondescript and allowing for more freedom of movement than the styles one would normally wear in Society. I did not wear my far more practical urchin outfit, as I thought I might yet need to fool Schneider in the course of the unfolding of these events. After all, the Home Secretary had never said I wasn't under arrest. Max's reaction to my becoming a boy would also be something I did not want to hazard. He had nearly caught me when I had been dressing in the morning without my wig.

We had no particular plan ready in advance, although Max had visited an ironmonger's in Paddington on the way and procured a variety of things he thought would be useful.

The only lights visible in the residence of Sir Emile Brodsky were at two windows in the basement, to the right of the steps that led up to the porch. The laboratory — if that's what it was — was to the rear, left of the house. The lights were evidently from those rooms occupied by the couple we had encountered earlier. It would seem that the house's owner preferred to stay at his rooms in Albany.

Fortunately there was a narrow path skirting the side of the garden we wanted to enter. It ran by the fence until that became the wall of this building that we hoped would answer at least some of our questions. After the wall the fence resumed. There was a wooden gate.

"We can scramble over and then open it for my sister," Max whispered to Schneider.

"I think not," he answered. "I'm just here to keep watch on the Countess. You open the gate and then we can both walk through."

"I see," said Max — obviously disappointed that some rules Schneider had suggested earlier were actually to be kept to.

In a couple of seconds Max was over the gate, and had drawn the bolt on the other side. Our next obstacle was the entrance to the laboratory itself. Luckily a glazed door which led out into the garden, was only a few metres from where we were standing. The far end of the building appeared to be joined by a short corridor to the house.

Max tried the door, but indeed it was locked. He looked at the keyhole and shook his head. From the bag he had brought — a small Gladstone, suited more for a doctor than a house-breaker — he took out some sticking plaster and a pair of scissors. He was intending to prepare one of the glass panels of the door for smashing. Schneider shrugged his shoulders, sighed, and dug into one of his trouser pockets, bringing out a large bunch of keys which he handed to Max — skeleton keys for a hundred different locks.

So far, so good. We had managed to get into the building without waking anyone or even making any visible signs of our entry. During the day the large room we had entered would have been full of light as it had tall windows overlooking the lawns. The blinds were still up and Max thought it would not be good to switch on the electric light, making our presence very visible indeed if either of the couple were to go to the back of the house. Max had brought a little paraffin-oil cycle lamp which he proceeded to light and this was our only illumination.

Yes, it was a laboratory — or had been a laboratory. There were the numerous gas-taps necessary and one cardboard box full of test-tubes but otherwise it was completely bare. There was not even a chair or a desk. At one end were various cupboards built into the wall. Schneider watched me as I opened one; it was empty.

Max had walked through the long, barren laboratory to a smaller room beyond. This had evidently been some kind of office. It had a fireplace with a grate. A door led from this room into the short corridor connecting it with the house. Again, as I caught up with Max, I could see that this room too was completely empty. Max was kneeling by the grate, pointing his lamp into the cinders. He fished out the charred remains of an envelope, the torn flap embossed with a headless eagle. He put the two torn edges together — an eagle with one head.

"Not ours, you see. A Prussian eagle."

Turning it over he put the lamp closer still, trying to make out a postmark as the area of the stamp had been burnt. "Yes, Berlin."

"Well, there's nothing wrong with corresponding with the German government at the moment, is there?" But I knew as I uttered the words, it probably wasn't quite the thing for a man knighted "for services to the British Empire."

"There's nothing else that means anything here," Max said after sifting through all the ashes, "but there was an iron stove in the laboratory. Let's try that."

We returned to the first room, where there was a large cast-iron stove. Its sides were still warm to the touch. Max opened its round plate and shone the lamp down into a chamber that we were soon to see was filled with the half-burnt remains of leather-bound notebooks.

"I'll take a couple, shall I?" I asked. The contents, being examined by Max, seemed to be all the same — pages and pages filled with an intense mass of formulas, scientific symbols, calculations. Max found two which were less charred than the rest and handed them to me.

In the meantime, Schneider — despite his attempt not to be active in this crime — was casually opening the doors of the row of cupboards, the first of which I had looked into a minute or two before and which had been quite empty. The others were no different, it seemed. Then he found them.

He opened the last cupboard, and its contents spilled out onto the floor — so full it had been. With a soft leathery patter out fell a huge pile of dog collars. They seemed to be for dogs of all sizes, but larger ones predominated — and they were all comfortably used. Some even had brass tags with such English canine names as "Rover" or "Rex."

"That's another slip of paper for you," said Max. Schneider didn't understand Max's little joke. But the collars weren't funny. They were sad, poignant. They reminded me of a photograph I had once seen of a great pile of boots taken from the bodies of Italian soldiers killed in battle — for each pair represented the son of a grieving mother.

I sorted through these strange relics, picked out a collar identified as "Biffer" and put it with the other souvenirs of our visit. Again, the more one seemed to find out, the deeper the mystery became.

The beam from Max's lamp was off me and I couldn't see where Max was for the moment. Then he came running back.

"Quick. We've got to go. Schneider — are you ready?"

Schneider was more than ready, he was out of the door in a flash. We hurried out into the garden at Max's urging. Through the gate, into the lane — then further down the lane, not back up to the street. There was a mews — some stables with coachmen's rooms above — serving several houses. This emptied out into another street. There was some commotion coming from behind us, but it quickly subsided. No-one had come out into the lane.

"What, Max?"

"Look, I went into the passage from the laboratory and thought I'd take a look into the house. I must have been a bit more heavy-footed than I thought, for soon I heard voices and doors opening."

"Did you find anything?"

"Yes. It's strange. The whole place — apart from, I presume, the rooms for that couple of his — is totally empty."

No wonder this pair was anxious for us not to set foot inside.

The Foreign Office was even grander than the Home Office. Max, Schneider, and I were shown into an anteroom at the head of a sweeping marble staircase surrounded by graceful columns with gilded capitals and under painted ceilings all undertaken quite recently, so I was told, in the Italian Renaissance style. Here was a palace fit for the Medicis, or perhaps more appropriately the Borgias, but such petty princes of the Italy of those times could never have envisaged that any single nation would rule over a quarter of the Earth. The style suited, nonetheless.

I noticed Inspector Schneider wiping his hatband as we left the four-wheeler in Whitehall; now he was turning it in his hands, a nervous habit of his I had observed before. Max seemed relaxed; we were amongst those he liked to think of as his peers. My own nervousness sprung from the doubt I was having that I would retain my liberty and not be sent away in chains, the prisoner of this lower-grade Inspector.

The clock-winders must have gained immense satisfaction from the fact that as Big Ben began to boom out the hour, so a small French mantel clock over the marble fireplace began, synchronised to each bong, its own more sweet but humble repetition. Waiting encourages the mind to wander into such frivolous speculations. Then the tall double doors of the Foreign Secretary's office opened and we were ushered into a room which contained six or seven men.

A tall, grey-haired gentleman of dignified appearance at once approached Max and myself, extending a hand.

"Henry de Clyfforde, Lord Chudborough. We have never had occasion to meet — although I am sure you will know I am your mother's second cousin. Looking at you now I can see some de Clyfforde in you both. I only heard yesterday that you, Max, have been living in the capital for some while, although the reason for my information was concerning you, Beatrice — and I hope we may settle this uncomfortable business to your satisfaction, my dear."

"Thank you, My Lord," I replied.

"Henry — please. And may I introduce Lord Lansdowne?" And here a distinguished, but younger man, only in his forties stepped forward. Despite the pomp of his office, he had a rascally twinkle in his eyes. "The Marquess of Lansdowne is, as I am sure you know, His Majesty's Secretary of State for Foreign

Affairs. I think you have met the Home Secretary, and this is Sir Frederick Ponsonby, His Majesty's Assistant Private Secretary."

So they had procured one of our relatives for this matter — this was obviously to soften me up for something: to make something terribly bad seem right and proper, that, or they needed something. Perhaps they had finally grasped the possible importance of what I had begun to uncover. However, I had already made the decision not to tell that I had stumbled on a horde of dog collars. I felt it somewhat devalued the international significance of this affair.

After the usual formalities, the offering of refreshments, the seating and so on, Akers-Douglas, the Home Secretary, approached a slightly bewildered Schneider and asked him if he might wait in an adjoining room as secret matters of State were possibly to be discussed. He looked relieved rather than offended as, still with hat in hand, he was led away.

Again, it was our mother's second cousin who began and addressed himself to me: "The matters which you laid before the Home Secretary yesterday have been extensively considered. I was called from the country when it was known we were related, and naturally I vouched for you both as honourable — and only half Austrian! You were right in thinking this affair is important. How much, may I ask, do you know of His Majesty's visits to Marienbad?"

"I know that His Majesty has been several times and that the visits are usually in August," I replied.

Ponsonby — which, I should add, is pronounced 'Punsunby' — broke in: "His Majesty has always believed in the value of informal diplomacy, of talking face-to-face, often in a social setting. That is His Majesty's way."

I nodded, as if I knew that already.

"I am sure you are aware that there are some extremely grave international tensions at the present time," our second cousin continued.

I nodded sagely again. This time I did know; Max had told me.

"This Russo-Japanese situation, do you mean?" but Max's question was not at once answered.

"But it may not be known to you, since it is known to hardly more than the people in this room — and I was only told of the possibility a few minutes ago — that an earlier, and additional, visit to the spa is planned this year. This will be in order to be able to meet and discuss the crisis that your brother has so correctly identified with — shall we say? — another player of great significance. We are gambling on averting a war which would draw-in all the nations of the civilised world. A World War, in fact, if such a thing could be envisaged."

It was time I said something intelligent, and yet I found myself questioning all this: "Is this war between Russia and Japan that significant?"

The Marquess, as Foreign Secretary, felt obliged to answer. "All the countries of Europe have webs of treaties with each other. The French have been making overtures to the Russians, for example, and we are allied to the French. We have a treaty with Japan. You can see how awkward things will get, especially if Germany picks sides."

I had never really given much thought to the labyrinthine machinations of international politics — but even I could see that trouble could indeed ensue, and Austria, whether we liked it or not, was firmly allied to Germany. The Prussians had seen to that.

"And this revolution in Russia everyone keeps talking about — is it likely to happen?" asked Max, ever the brains.

The Secretaries of State exchanged glances. "Quite probably, if the situation in Japan goes against them," the Marquess stated, "and the effect of a weak Russia would be that the Germans could attack France again with impunity. They could easily win a war on only one front."

Our second cousin brought the conversation back on course: "We think there could be a threat to His Majesty by these people you have uncovered. Like you, we have no idea how the threat is to be carried out specifically — and, most importantly, why. But your help is required in further discovery. The authorities represented here would like you to continue your investigation of this mystery."

"But why me?" I asked. Now that the offer was being made, I felt a horror of it. "Surely Inspector Schneider is entirely capable?"

"Quite apart from the fact that His Majesty travels to Bohemia as a private citizen, incognito hardly — but not in the status of King Emperor, and so your suggestion would present complications. Apart from that, we feel your tact and skill at handling this would be far preferable," the Marquess replied. "Naturally, all assistance will be given you. That, I am sure, the Inspector will understand."

"Well, of course. I am deeply honoured. And Max..." I began. Max completed what I had not set out to say:

"...but I am afraid I cannot really assist personally. I have helped here in London, and naturally wish my sister every success. Anyway, too many cooks spoil the broth."

"There is another aspect to this too." Sir Frederick Ponsonby spoke this time. "His Majesty is adamant that Sir Emile Brodsky is quite to be trusted. In fact they are old friends. It would seem from what you have managed to find out that he is possibly one of the intended victims."

"Albert Jenks is a different matter, however. He has a long record of criminal activity — the usual burglary, selling stolen goods, some extortion. Several lengthy stretches in Dartmoor." The Home Secretary was consulting a file. "But I must say there is to date no evidence of him associating with anarchists or revolutionaries. The police in various countries will be alerted, of course, but our opinion is that it is better to allow him to travel freely for the moment, until the purpose of his travels can be better understood."

So I was to be left alone following or being followed by a known criminal and certain murderer. This was all more than I had bargained for. I hoped at least I could travel with Schneider, of whom suddenly I was almost fond, for the resolution of this mystery must lie in Marienbad.

The Marquess of Lansdowne wrapped up the proceedings: "The British Ambassador in Vienna and the Consul in Prague will be notified and they will, I assure you, give you any assistance within their power. Inspector Schneider will also take with him a message for the Commissioner of Police in Prague."

Old de Clyfforde took my arm, "It goes without saying that we all wish you well. A lot might depend on it."

— such as whether I would ever get invited to see my grand relatives, although the necessity of this, I was beginning to feel, was something that didn't bother me. It had concerned our poor mother all her life; she would kill me for not caring a jot.

The big question was now whether to try to find Jenks in London, or to return to Prague and Marienbad, knowing that sooner or later he would come back there. Max thought that we had probably reached the end of what could usefully be discovered in London. He would keep me posted on any news concerning Sir Emile Brodsky, although as yet we had no certain evidence to suggest he was linked with Jenks. Schneider, quite naturally, wanted to return home. He had originally followed Sabine to Marienbad for her to lead him to me, expecting to be back in Prague the following day, the next at the most.

On returning to Mount Street, a telegram awaited us. It was from Karel:

YOUR UNCLE BERTY DEAD STOP FUNERAL ON
FRIDAY STOP FELICITATIONS KAREL

"What does this mean?" I asked Max, but knowing already it had some connection with the ghastly business in hand — the mystery which had turned into a nightmare.

"It means we have to buy your ticket home this minute. We can walk round to Thomas Cook's in Berkeley Street. There should be a *de Luxe* leaving first thing in the morning.

Chapter Eight

Crossing the Border

The wind was teasing what passed for my hair. It was cold, but I was warmly wrapped. By the ship's rail, the flag of the railway company steamer billowing in the breeze, I could see England receding, the famous cliffs becoming just a thin line of white chalk on the horizon. Max — unless he was a dark horse — had never pulled a woman into the shape of her corsets before, but with Sabine gone for the time being, it had been a necessity. Thank Heavens he didn't have to sew me into my dress. In my new regime Sabine had managed to have two of my favourite dresses converted to buttons. However, Max had still cursed. Sixty of the things, he had said, was an inordinate number. And he had used an expletive.

It was proof, so he had said, that I hadn't entirely lost the art of being feminine — that I wasn't one of these ghastly women Socialists. I had read about them of course: those Pankhurst sisters with their Women's Union. They would not rest until women had the vote. I suppose that up until very recently I had been content for men to run men's affairs on the mutual understanding that they did not interfere with what I ordered from the dressmaker or looked too closely at the flirtatious notes

I passed to certain admirers, harmless as they turned out to be. Then it had seemed the world, and by that I mean the harmony of the sexes, was in perfect balance. In the space of less than a month I was beginning to see cracks in the impervious male facade. Why should men be the only ones to have adventures?

Schneider was lounging against one of the large trumpet-like ventilators that gave air to the deck below on which the *de Luxe's* carriages had been manoeuvred aboard en route for Paris, Strasbourg, and Prague. He lit a cigarette. I didn't know he smoked. I noticed he had a clean collar — a little too big for his neck. He must have had some difficulty buying a new collar or two in English feet and inches.

"Aren't you supposed to be watching me, Inspector Schneider?"

He threw me a questioning look.

"I mean," I ploughed on, "you are smoking on duty, are you not?"

"I don't think travel of this kind counts," he replied somewhat testily.

"So do you mean I am not under your supervision?"

"Didn't the Home Secretary tell you we had agreed to suspend the warrant in the light of all you told us?"

"In short, no. However, I rather relished the prospect of travelling across Europe as a bad woman!"

Schneider blushed. "I don't think I could ever see you as that, Countess."

I chose to ignore the improper use of the term Countess at this juncture. I was flattered by his compliment. Perhaps it was the delayed reward for my revealing my stockinged ankle.

"Steamers make one romantic, do they not, Inspector?" I said, not waiting for a reply. "Thank goodness that there isn't time for a shipboard romance."

On a crossing of barely two hours there would hardly be time for the culmination of such a romance, let alone all the courting which women demand to justify the effort for that short act of consummation. I cursed again my English blood and suddenly was envious of Sabine's doubtless honest, down-to-earth way of satisfying…well, her lust. I was aware, by reading a certain volume that Karel kept turned pages-out in his library, that in Paris there were certain hotels that hired out rooms by the half-hour.

Soon there were only three hours left before the train would arrive in Paris. For those three long hours after we had set off from Calais I sat in my sleeping compartment, which served as a day carriage — the door locked. Memories of the journey to Karlsbad overtook me, the realisation that if I had been in my compartment when Jenks and Duvalier had come — of what might have become of me. Then I dwelt on the terrible news of Uncle Berty's death.

Karel's telegram had said virtually nothing. How had he died? Was this yet another mysterious death? At least my anxiety might be reduced by news at Paris. I had telegraphed my husband to respond to the train at the Gare du Nord. No sooner had we pulled into the station there when the conductor was rapping on my door and soon handing me a telegram from Prague.

UNCLES DEATH SUICIDE STOP HIS LETTER
AWAITS YOU AND AM CURIOUS ABOUT
CONTENTS STOP WILL MEET AT STATION STOP
FELICITATIONS KAREL

Suicide? If there seemed to me a man least likely to commit suicide it was Uncle Berty. I believed there was another mystery in this. Perhaps none of this would have happened if I hadn't agreed to start investigating for Uncle — but, no, the mystery of old Alois and the Tontine had already begun by then.

After the train set out from Paris for Strasbourg and Prague I felt so incredibly nervous, alone in my compartment, that I had the conductor go and find Inspector Schneider. I would treat him to refreshments in the Dining Car. He was, of course, travelling in the rear coach reserved for the servants of the First Class passengers. The Prague Police Department was evidently careful of its budget.

Schneider was adequate company. At least he kept my mind off my apprehensions about Uncle Berty, or what might be lurking in my compartment.

"I shouldn't worry," he said, "the Metropolitan Police were sure there was no-one suspicious on the train and the Railway Police made sure no-one boarded at Dover. Of course, in France we're in the hands of the French."

"How reassuring," I observed. Irony was something that came naturally to me, unfortunately.

"You are not married, Inspector?" I asked, after a pause as more of the flat French countryside crawled by the windows.

"It's not a job which encourages it. Late nights, travel like this on occasions — no regular hours. I don't know as a wife would put up with it."

He could see I didn't believe a word of that. He went on, however: "Well, perhaps it's a case of not finding the right girl."

"Yet," I added.

"At my age, I am beginning to discover that all the best ones are married."

"Then that leaves you plenty of scope, surely?" Although I doubted whether he was at all adept at playing in bedroom farces. Yet. He might do well if I introduced him to some friends, the sort who had such stuffy husbands — a banker or two, the Commissioner of the Prague Drainage and Sewerage Enterprise, those on the boards of companies whose unappetising brass plates one hurries by when going to dressmakers or milliners. If only Karel would take a mistress, then I would feel entirely justified. I often surprised myself that I did have a moral code, although it assumed flirtatious conversations were permitted, of course. They really didn't count. I could dream of being unfaithful; that was quite enough. I could not countenance all that tiresome undressing.

"Do you mind if I smoke?"

It is impolite to refuse any such request, but I gave him my best "if you must" look, a weapon that Mamma had taught me so eloquently.

Smoking occupied him. The flat fields, the lanes lined with poplar trees, the red-brick villages, and domeless spired churches sped by the partially opened window. I would stay here, I decided, until the next station, by which time my nerves would surely have calmed. Schneider had at least succeeded in banishing the bogeymen from my mind.

As the *de Luxe* steamed in towards Strasbourg I decided at last to return to my compartment. During the stop I would take a stroll on the platform and visit the Powder Room there. Entering from the corridor, as I felt the train gradually reducing speed and the click of the wheels on the track becoming less frantic, I had the distinct feeling that someone had been inside. My bag…

it didn't seem quite so neatly put on the rack as I had placed it. And beside my bag, where was the parcel which contained the charred remains of the two books of formulas taken from Emile Brodsky's laboratory? It was gone. The window was open slightly. I had left it closed. I had a sudden horror that perhaps the intruder was still here — although plainly he wasn't, was he? My mind was spinning. I screamed.

My scream merged with the whistle of the train as it entered the tunnel before Strasbourg main station. I think I would have fainted, but I managed to contain myself. I mustn't succumb to these fits of fright. Mustn't. In the sudden darkness, the rattling of the wheels accentuated by the partly open window and the walls of the tunnel, I saw a dim shape emerge from under a blanket on my berth. The form rose up in front on me — it would overwhelm me; I was helpless with terror. It pushed past me, however — hurrying past me and out into the corridor.

I could feel the brakes gripping the wheels as the train slowed. Suddenly the compartment was flooded with light again. I noticed the dust on the windows. Everything was normal except a cast-aside blanket, my disturbed bag, and the missing parcel. As the train pulled to a halt with people on the platform blurring past me, I was thankful I was alive.

I didn't think I would ever be so glad to see someone I knew as I was now happy to see Schneider. He was hurrying along the corridor to my door. To hell with decorum! — I sobbed into his arms.

We had forty-five minutes. In the Refreshment Room of the station he calmly analysed the situation. Whoever it had been had had ample chance to slip away in the crowd. He had timed it well. But it meant we had been watched in London. I told Schneider that I had seen Jenks in Piccadilly Circus. He couldn't understand why I hadn't said anything at the time. I couldn't either, when I reflected on my silence. People's motives and actions are not only often incomprehensible to others, they are sometimes incomprehensible to themselves. I did remember, though. It was immediately after that Inspector Grey had made Max and me seem about a centimetre tall, castigating us for not doing our research. I had been in a mood, sulking because someone else had been right.

For the rest of the journey, again to hell with decorum, Schneider would have to share my compartment. It had the spare berth that all sleepers do if you book singly.

As it got dark on the way through Germany, Schneider offered — naturally — to stand in the corridor whilst I got changed and performed my *toilette*. While he was standing there, the carriage bucking over some uneven junction, he found the door opening a crack and that crack filled with the back of an alpaca dress in a pretty shade of blue.

"Inspector — if you please. You will find in front of you a vertical line of sixty rather irritating buttons. I would be grateful if you could undo the first forty from the top. The rest I can manage. I would call you an angel, but I don't think that is appropriate nomenclature for the occasion."

At Nuremberg I had a telegram dispatched from the station:

```
DEAREST HUSBAND PLEASE COME TO CAR 8
COMPARTMENT 5 ON ARRIVAL AT STATION TO
PULL ME IN STOP TRIXIE
```

I could hardly expect this Inspector to do my corset laces. That would be going too far.

In the dark of the speeding compartment, the throbbing of the wheels as our constant companion, I could just make out Schneider's shape on the opposite berth by the faint glimmer of the gaslamp's pilot.

"I don't think your life was at stake," he was saying. "I am sure he was just after the notebooks and that was all. In fact I don't even think Duvalier's death was murder either."

"Oh?"

"Seems to me they were reaching up for your bag. You said the revolver was wrapped up in some clothes in the bag. Am I correct?"

"Yes — that's what I said."

"Now tell me, was the revolver's safety on?"

Oh dear. I remembered all too clearly. "Well, I can't say precisely."

"And you said that your butler had been sent to get it from your husband's drawer. In my experience there's plenty of men who keep guns in their desks with the safety off. 'What's the use of needing the thing in an emergency if you've got to fiddle with the damned safety catch?' — that's what they think."

"Oh."

"Indeed, madam, Countess, Your Ladyship —"

He'll never understand the correct protocol, so to hell with that too: "Countess will do."

"Well, indeed, Countess…have you ever properly handled a gun? I mean, do you actually know where the safety catch is?"

So saying he reached up and took a gun from a leather harness that was hanging with his jacket. Its dark steel glinted in the dim light. He turned it over in his hand as one experienced, explaining to me the various parts of the device. He broke it open at one point, spilling out bright bullets onto his palm. There was a thrill of excitement about this at night, under the blankets so to speak. I was looking at his strong fingers stroking the barrel, which he did with a certain sense of intimate familiarity.

"So you don't think Jenks meant to murder Duvalier?"

"No," he replied, "it was an accident. Albert Henry Jenks is a violent man, no doubt about it, but so far in his career he's stopped short of murder. He can handle prison, it seems, but fears the gallows."

The *de Luxe* arrived in Prague FJ1 Station at five-thirty in the morning, but it was the custom for the blinds to stay down and the train to rest at the platform until six-thirty, when the passengers were roused and coffee and breakfast rolls served to the compartments. The passengers would then leave between seven and seven-thirty. However, a panic seized me as soon as the train arrived. Of course there were good reasons — for my personal safety, for one — but I did not particularly want Karel to find me sharing a sleeper, especially as now I knew that he was perhaps one of those men who probably kept the safety catch off. That notion had given him a new dimension.

"Quick, quick, Inspector, time to leave."

He turned over in his semi-conscious state.

"My husband —" I began.

He shot up out of his cot and I turned away as he dressed at the speed of light. I wondered if he hadn't done this kind of thing before. Perhaps my little Inspector was a dark horse, after all.

"If I may, Countess, I shall call you by telephone later."

And with that he was gone. I lifted the blind a little. Dawn was just streaking the azure sky beyond one of the great iron arches of the station's roof. Pigeons that defied the netting were busily identifying their morning's pickings, looking down with relish at the bakers' delivery boys with their baskets of fresh rolls heading for the kitchen car of the *de Luxe*.

Just after six I was ready for him. Sometimes, after a long journey or some enforced separation, a wife should try to please her husband. In the book kept without its spine showing on his favourite bookshelf I had long since discovered what my husband's tastes were. Similar, I shouldn't wonder, to those of a million other men. I put on the body linen that covered my bosom; my corsets were loose about me; I smoothed the stockings over my legs — a new pair. It wouldn't do for him to have seen even the neatly darned toes of so many of them. But I did not put on my drawers or pantaloons. That sight, bare below the midriff, would be my gift for his patience — and for sending me more money than was strictly necessary in my hour of need.

A short while after there was a soft tap at the door. I would have expected a harder knock from the Count, but maybe this was his notion of romance: the velvet touch. I flung open the door.

"Madame!" Sabine cried, for it was she.

As soon as she had recovered from the surprise of seeing her mistress in such a state of wanton undress, I could see her looking about the compartment — at the unmade bed so recently occupied by a tough man whom I had allowed only to soothe his pistol. I knew I would make a useless adulteress, or even as an amateur detective I should have pulled the covers over. But, I pleaded with myself, beds are things which just…which just get made somehow, don't they? How was I to know?

"But I thought you were in Paris?" (Ignoring her obvious observation of the bed was the most prudent course of action.)

"Madame, two days — and nights — were enough. 'Ee was very — as you say — very vigorous."

"Well, I'm glad to hear it." That's just what I could be doing with at this moment, I thought, some good vigorous attention by a member of the male gender. I was feeling very crestfallen after being in such an adventure, often in a state of inner commotion. I needed strong relief, on a par with dangers I had faced, and not this.

"Your husband gave me the telegram."

"Then you'd better pull me in, Sabine. I don't suppose you brought any more drawers, did you?" How disappointing that Karel had sent Sabine — thoughtful but thoughtless at the same time. How absolutely typical of him.

"Of course, Madame. Now that we are home in Prague, I thought silk."

"Cotton for travelling, silk for the city" — one of Mamma's mantras. Sabine got to work.

"And has Madame been eating properly? I can pull you in by almost another centimetre," she said, straining hard.

She pulled with strength, that I give her, but I was hoping for Karel's more forceful method which involved placing his booted right foot in the small of my back. When he did this I felt I was being saddled like one of his old cavalry mounts. If only he'd wear spurs.

Sabine had also thought to bring black. The black taffeta suited the occasion perfectly. Black silk drawers, that accompanied the dress, were a novelty from Paris. I had noticed in London that the press was full of articles denouncing black silk as something that would corrupt morals! Our palace on Jindřišská Street was in mourning. Müller was very deferential and he had the urchins lined up on the staircase like members of the household, their heads bowed in respect. No-one said more than was necessary to get me to my boudoir, where I encountered two envelopes and a card on the silver salver on the side table. I opened the one from Karel. The other was addressed to me in Uncle Berty's hand. The card, edged in black, was the invitation to his funeral.

My Dearest Trixie,

(began Karel's missive)

> *Since Sabine returned and recounted some of your adventures, and I understand you are safe and well, I thought it best she should attend to your requirements. I have had to go to South Bohemia for a few days and I regret that I shall miss Uncle Berty's funeral. Please*

convey my regrets and condolences. I will try to tele
phone you soon.

Ever your loving husband with sincerest felicitations,

Karel.

"South Bohemia" was his euphemism for going to stay with old
Count Paar. He would be hunting down in those huge forests
of his around Bechyně Castle. There were worse vices.

Next I opened Uncle Berty's letter.

Dear Trixie,

*I can tell you things I would tell none other, and I tell
you these so that you may understand your old Uncle a
bit better and perhaps forgive his errors, so that what is
laid to rest is not such a damned enigma.*

*For most of my life I have hidden my true self behind
the whiskers, bluster and falseness of Austrian Society.
In the Army one is never called to account as a person
so long as one continues to obey orders from above,
and when one is oneself in that superior position then
the orders one gives must simply excite no passions and
break no regulations.*

*However, I have lived a lie. I have lived a secret life
and you must do your best not to judge but to understand. You will be the only person who could even begin
to. I have been guilty of those crimes — that is, crimes
according to the rules of Society — that finished Oscar
Wilde. It is difficult to think of a military man having
anything in common with an aesthete, a namby-pamby
— but it is God in his wisdom who selects those who*

will follow one path and those who are destined to follow another.

A great scandal is brewing and many of us will be unmasked. I hope by my death my name will either not surface or be brushed over inconspicuously as dead and gone; that way I can minimise scandal for our families and for poor Ludmila. The tentacles of these scandals travel far and go deep into corners least suspected. There will be the usual telegraph lads, guardsmen and chorus-boys but when I tell you that there will be in this an internationally famous Russian ballet dancer, a Grand Duke of the highest esteem, an eminent scientist — also of world renown, at least one member of a criminal gang as well as a theatrical impresario whose recent death will allow him, at least, to escape the worst attentions of the press and quite possibly the courts.

I could not have borne the scorn, the hypocrisy, the rejection of what we call Society and could not have stood up to the rigours of prison life at my age. So I leave you and wish you farewell.

Ever your loving and devoted Uncle,

Berty.

P.S. With my will there is an envelope to be handed to you which also contains a letter to be given to the Tontine Financial Association. I am giving you all my proceeds from the Tontine, although you alone understand what these may or may not consist of. Your Aunt Ludmila is taken care of by my General's widow's pension and from her own family money. I hope, if played carefully, the Tontine might yet provide for you both. B.

I stood there, still holding the letter but staring vacantly before me, unable to comprehend all that it meant. Uncle Berty — who could have thought? But at his club — there had been something. I had felt it. I had even seen the signs — but I hadn't been able properly to interpret their full implications. These, these peculiar individuals, were totally outside my knowledge. After nearly a minute, I suppose, I went into the library and took down the appropriate volume of the encyclopaedia and looked up "Sodomite."

There, on its pages, was a graphic and unemotional account of the condition. As I was shutting the book, I heard Müller's distinctive tap on the door, followed by his appearance holding out a selection of newspapers on a tray.

"Forgive my intruding, Milady, but His Lordship was desirous of giving you these. They are yesterday's Vienna and Prague papers, and they each contain an obituary of your late uncle."

"Thank you Müller," I said, taking them. He glided out without my noticing as I opened Uncle Berty's own favourite, the *Wiener Zeitung*:

> General Albrecht Schönburg-Hartenstein acquitted himself bravely at the Battle of Königgrätz in 1866, holding his sector of the line with the regiments under his command despite the murderous slaughter inflicted by the Prussians. He witnessed the death of 10,000 fine Austrian men in under an hour on that day. He had always been an advocate of Army Reform and for re-armament with breech-loading rifles which had been rejected at the highest levels and had given the Prussians the advantage of being able to fire five times as quickly and from concealed positions. He never spoke out publicly but he is known to have been deeply affected to see his troops mown down whilst standing reloading their rifles. Since retirement he had been a patron of the popular theatre and had a wide circle of friends beyond his old regiment and his clubs. He leaves behind a wife, who was born Ludmila von Morštejn, and has no issue.

I wondered if the "wide circle of friends" was already a veiled reference to what I already knew. However, the usually out-spoken *Neue Frei Presse* of Vienna made no mention of what I now knew — veiled or otherwise.

This matter, this problem, of Uncle's deeply shocked me. It was a subject that was never mentioned during my childhood — or even now, for that matter — but it was, unsung and deeply covered over, the darkest sin imaginable. Yet I would honour his obligation on me not to judge but indeed to try to understand.

The funeral was to be the following day. I had time to accomplish something I felt I needed to do before the ceremony. I would seek advice from a priest. Maybe that would settle my spirit, which was by now far from at ease.

Father Svoboda was taking confession at three in the afternoon. St. Jakub's was only a few minutes' walk away and not worth the trouble of having the carriage taken out. The exuberant facade of the church depicted the life of St. James in a writhing mass of baroque sculpture stuck onto this ancient basilica, built as a Franciscan monastery. Inside, the same seething, restless orgy of baroque statuary continued. I rather enjoyed it, although the style was now very much out of fashion.

When my turn came I crossed the old paving stones to the pol-ished wooden confessional booth. I had the extra cushion for my knees that Sabine had procured for me and which was by now well used. At first I hesitated. After all, I wasn't here to confess anything really, other than the prejudice which the Church itself endorsed. That was my problem.

"What is it, my child?"

I could see part of his face vaguely through the grille.

"I do not understand," was all I could find to say.

"And what is it you do not understand?" — his calling was certainly one of infinite patience.

"Well —" and here I was going to launch into the whole argument of why Society rejects these people, and am I prejudiced or right? "Well, I don't understand..." I found myself saying, and then it just popped out: "What is a sodomite?"

That appeared to have shocked the Reverend Father as much as it surprised me. I hadn't meant to be quite so blunt, but at least it was out now. That's what I wanted to know — not the description of the act, the encyclopaedia had told me that, but the rest: the spiritual dimension, if you will.

"One who comes from the city of Sodom. Just as Moabites are those from the City of Moab."

"And nothing more...?"

"The Bible says nothing more. And why is this troubling you, my child?"

"I had a relative. He is now deceased. I didn't know...I am told now he was being persecuted."

"Persecuted?"

"Persecuted because he was a sodomite. He was about to be exposed to the world. The hostile world."

"He alone — or were there others?"

"He mentioned those who are pillars of Society, or those in the spotlight of attention: an eminent scientist, a Grand Duke, a famous ballet dancer."

"Russian? A Russian dancer?"

"Yes, but...?"

"And bishops — did he mention bishops, or priests of the Church?"

"No, Father. I don't believe so."

I thought I detected a sigh of relief. It wasn't just the very faint sound but I could sense his whole posture seeming to relax somewhat and through the grille I could see a single bead of sweat glistening in the grizzled hairs of his temple. After a moment, as if collecting his thoughts again, he spoke:

"Persecuting groups that don't conform in some way — Jews, gypsies, homosexuals, even the deformed — this is all just an excuse for the majority to hide their own insecurity. The men of Sodom didn't conform."

"And what my conscience tells me is wrong then?"

"Conscience is sometimes just the wish of the majority. Would you have helped your relative if you had known he was being persecuted?"

"Of course." I had not thought of it before, but indeed I would have.

"And you would help me?"

"*You*, Father?"

"These are what you must stop, Countess."

And through a crack below the grille slowly appeared a postcard. He began the Absolution and I mumbled along with him as I pulled it from my side of the division — in sepia a pair of powerful legs in the hose and shoes of the ballet, a jewelled bodice with exaggerated sleeves — a young man with piercing black eyes and a shock of black hair like a horse's mane.

I pulled the card free. The other side showed that it was addressed to Father Svoboda at St. Jakub's. It seemed written in an ill-educated woman's hand. The stamp bore the profile of the Tsar, postmarked from St. Petersburg only a few days before. The space for correspondence contained a single word in capital letters, made by a pen heavily pressed into the card: SODDOMITE!

For a moment I didn't know what to say or think. Then I realised he had called me Countess. I really didn't think I was known here — that was why I never made my confessions in St. Jindřich's. Did he mean me to investigate this? Was this yet another mystery I was being asked to solve? Was it something like this that Uncle Berty had received? If cards like these were being circulated in the open post, then no wonder Uncle Berty had been alarmed.

"Father, if I delve into this then I shall have to uncover some unsavoury truths. You realise that?"

"But then you will be preserving the memory of your great uncle from scandal."

I knew deep down that this was somehow related to old Alois, to the Tontine, to the Fenix Theatre.

He wondered by my momentary silence if that reasoning had been strong enough so he added: "— and your family from disgrace."

"I shall be discreet," I replied. "But I really do not know if I am able to do this."

"Your great uncle had real faith in your abilities — that I know."

I curtsied and left the confessional and sat down for a moment in one of the pews at the back of the church. All this added another burden to a head which was already spinning with wild theories. I didn't know that I could cope. I was only a person of the weaker sex. If there had been some nice man to catch me, I would have swooned into his arms.

Walking back to Jindřišská Street, under the great gate of the Powder Tower that had been part of Prague's medieval fortifications, I felt my confidence returning. Prague's ancient solidity, surviving many vicissitudes of fortune, would always have a restorative effect on me, as it did now — helped by stopping at the confectioner's on the corner of Na Příkopě, where I had a cream *Dort* (or was it two?) and a cup of strong Viennese coffee.

As I sat at one of the spindly tables which were just big enough to place a cup and saucer and a small tea-plate, I imagined my slips of paper. In my mind's eye I laid them out before me, like cards in playing Patience. There were the new slips now — Grand Duke, Russian dancer (and this one had a photograph), eminent scientist. And if I dropped "eminent scientist" onto the same slip as "Sir Emile Brodsky" then the whole web was connected. The Tontine, the Union of Servants, the mysterious goings-on in Marienbad, Paris, and London — all were linked. To solve a puzzle, first one must be aware of its existence. Thus was the puzzle, in my head at least, all spread out before me.

Old Alois had doubtless died of natural causes and perhaps Duvalier's death had been, in the end, an accident — but there was certainly one death in this saga that was as near murder as could be: Uncle Berty's. I turned the postcard over in my hand.

The spidery handwriting of the address, as well as the blunt one word message, had been written by the murderess. I looked again at the ballet dancer's photograph. Despite the fact that his lips appeared rouged and his eyes rimmed in mascara — which could of course be taken for standard theatrical makeup — he did not appear effete. He was the kind who could perhaps be wildly attractive to women, I felt sure.

Oh, I'll admit it, I knew so.

There were things to attend to at home before the arrival of Mamma in the evening. I did not get on with my mother and had made an excuse about having to redecorate the one bedroom she really liked, for she was extremely critical of my skills in choosing curtains, bed linen, the right colours — in fact, almost every-thing. As a consequence I had booked her a suite at the brand new Hotel Paris, a few steps from the Powder Tower. This would at least give her a chance to praise to high heaven the qualities of the principal *chef de cuisine* — knowing that Monsieur Yves had been so recently poached from under my nose.

The silver tray in the hall had several cards on it. I shuffled a too-well-fitting glove from off my right hand and looked at the cards hurriedly — yes, friends who had called with condolences. And there was a telegram. It was from Max:

HOW DO WE KNOW THAT THE BRODSKY WE SAW
WAS THE GENUINE ARTICLE QUESTION LOVE MAX

I couldn't believe that the suave, though slightly guarded, per-formance of Sir Emile in Albany was that of an impostor. But it was another possibility to be added to the slips. No idea could be ignored.

I was glad Max had made contact. He had apologised the night before I left for not coming with me. He said, by way of explanation, that I would never be aware of just how precarious was his situation. "This Russo-Japanese War could easily wipe me out," he had said, "me and many others I've advised."

Having been back for almost half a day, it was finally time for me to review the garrison. I had the boys summoned to my office on the ground floor — which, I noticed, had been entirely changed back again into the arrangement of furniture as my husband's Business Room. This annoyed me, but I kept the emotion to myself.

Müller knocked and entered. We exchanged glances over the resurrected arrangement of things — but he wore the kind of helpless look he adopted when my husband had had strong words to say to him. However, it was time for the young men, as I preferred to think of them, who were already entering the room and standing before me. They seemed in awe of me as someone who had, since our last meeting, travelled across Europe and even gone overseas (a one-hour, forty-five minutes' passage over the seas).

"So what is there to report?" I began.

They explained that they had kept constant watch at The Invalides. The impostor had only returned once, his visit evidently timed to coincide with an inspection by the Army Department. Having been duly noted down as still residing there, he was soon off. They had successfully followed him this time. The catalogue of his dreary comings and goings was of no interest — to his seedy lodgings and back, sometimes to the office at the Fenix Theatre, to pubs and cheap restaurants — except for one thing: he had made three visits to a tailor's, Kohn & Kohn, in Josefov. I knew of this establishment. It had supplied my father.

"Müller, would you find out if this Kohn & Kohn has a telephone, and if so, would you call and ask the following — exactly as I say it: 'Is the Kaiser's uniform for the Fenix Theatre ready yet?' You might also commiserate on the fact that, at the price, it will obviously be far too good for the theatre."

While Müller disappeared on this errand I asked the young men about The Union of Servants. I was told that it had held its next Saturday evening ball and that it was well-attended. Yesterday a notice had been pasted up outside the theatre. It was fully described and remembered verbatim by Jirka Minor:

WANTED
For Employment

Singer with voice and looks of
Ema Destinnová
(The rising star of the Prague Opera)
Short Term Engagement
Good wage for correct artiste
Apply side-door office
Mondays & Wednesdays, 8am - 11am

'Emmy' Destinnova was the country's favourite singer. Hadn't I heard somewhere that she was also a favourite of King Edward VII — or rather, as the Prince of Wales, when he had visited first in 1899? Another slip of paper.

Müller returned, a surprised look on his face: "Yes, Milady, they said it will be ready next Wednesday. And I mentioned the price, as you said. They promised me that there could be no better quality — for the money — than theirs. Except they said it wasn't the uniform of the Kaiser they were making, but that of a British Field-Marshal. On this Mr. Kohn was adamant. Were these the answers you were wanting, Milady?"

I nodded, but like everything else in this mystery, every answer contained a dozen more questions. I would simply have to make out a slip of paper and hope that in time it fitted with some other clue. Next I addressed the young men, praising their careful work and asking them to continue looking out. Now that I was back, there would be other tasks for them as well. I noticed how much better they were looking, nourished by regular soup, dumplings, and a half-decent place to lodge. It looked too as if the Na Struze Street Baths were having their effect.

I wondered what might become of them when this affair had drawn to a close. Perhaps I could get them taken in by the Church. I could just see them as altar boys. On second thoughts, perhaps better not.

As they dispersed, I spent a few minutes with Müller. There were engagements for the theatre and opera to cancel, as I was in mourning. There was tonight's small supper party to oversee. I was shown the menu, which seemed perfectly satisfactory and not worthy of any particular discussion with Cook. I had invited an extremely dull couple, which only made four of us. No doubt my mother would take pains to remind me that six is the absolute minimum for a dinner party, and I will argue "*Supper*, Mamma, *supper* party. Four is nicely intimate in which case." Besides, this was my first day back. The couple: the British military attaché to the Embassy in Vienna with his even duller wife. He had business in Prague and had left his card. With any luck their scintillating conversation should make my mother wish to go back to her hotel by nine, half-past at the very latest.

As we were coming out of the church, Mamma drew my attention to it: the particularly smart horseless carriage waiting by the gate to the cemetery, its occupants still within. The rain had been falling steadily all morning. The mourners were shuffling from the church to the gravesite in black, under black umbrellas and under a thunderous black sky. The church of St. Peter and St. Paul in the Vyšehrad fortress, although sitting on the site of one of the most ancient shrines in Prague, was so new that the pews and fittings still smelt of fresh varnish. Outside, the twin towers with hollow spires seemed meagre and had none of the power of the medieval that it doubtless replaced. It was not one of architect Josef Mocker's best creations — far from it. It seemed an odd choice of burial place. Vyšehrad was for artists and men of letters. The Schönburg-Hartensteins, military people, were from near Linz; perhaps that was too far. At least all this was being done without a whiff of scandal. Even suicide had been hushed-up.

"Look!" Mamma said, almost pointing to the motor, which was one of the new Pragas. I knew she would embarrass me. Nevertheless my eyes were drawn to it. A portly well-dressed man — almost floridly dressed, considering the occasion — descended with a diminutive wife and joined with the rest of the mourners. "They didn't come into church," she continued in a very audible whisper. "They're Jewish."

"Sush, Mamma — please." I tried to carry on respectfully, remembering that my dear mother had once suggested to me that we should take our opera glasses to a funeral. I agree they would have come in useful, but how ghastly!

We were catching up with Aunt Ludmila. Mamma should have been right behind her. "Anyway, who are they?" I asked almost casually.

"The Pinkersteins, didn't you know?"

The Tontine came flooding back into my brain. There, in his coffin, was one of the last two contestants in the game. Following him, at a respectful distance, was the other. How long the charade of old Alois could be kept up, I had no idea. The fact that such a swindle was entirely morally reprehensible also crossed my mind. However, it wouldn't all go away without some action on my part now. I decided then and there to see if a compromise might be possible — and this was the ideal opportunity to make Mr. Pinkerstein's acquaintance.

Mamma was digging me in the ribs. "The Pinkersteins — as rich as creases!"

"Croesus, Mamma. As rich as Croesus."

It had been Mamma, who in a fit of rage and threatening all hell and damnation to me once — over something as overwhelmingly important as the folding of napkins the "correct" way — had made mention of the "Four Horsemen of the Acropolis." She had also been sent to that same school in Switzerland for "finishing."

"Croesus—mentioned by Herodotus…" I started to explain.

"Oh, some Greek, you mean—how simply ghastly! I'll stick to creases."

After the prayers and the tearful lowering of the coffin I found myself looking at poor Great Aunt Ludmila. She was bearing all this so nobly. Didn't she have any odd feelings about…about, well…sodomy? Perhaps she still didn't know.

The mourners were filing past now, each putting a handful of earth down onto the coffin. Opera glasses would have been quite useless, I was thinking: how well umbrellas cover the face, especially on a dark day. At the rear of the column — partly hidden amongst the clusters of grey marble obelisks and other funerary monuments of the great, the good and the gone of Czech Society — were a few odd types who weren't family or dignitaries. Their breasts did not glint with medals. Some, to my horror, looked quite young and — shall we say? — theatrical. There was one in particular, and as he turned to throw his moist clay, I saw clearly those dark eyes I had first seen yesterday in a photograph, that shock of black hair. Not effete, but what else? — something else, I could not put my finger on it. It was he. The Russian ballet dancer.

Mamma leant across excitedly. "You know who that is?" she said in her irritatingly loud whisper.

"You mean the dancer?"

"Yes, that's the famous Vasily Pilipenko."

"From St. Petersburg?"

"Yes, he's the star of the Imperial Court Ballet. I read about him in one of the journals. Handsome man, don't you think?"

For a split second our eyes engaged. Mine and the dancer's. Apart from the distant rumble of thunder there was birdless, bell-less silence. The new towers of the church were empty, waiting for the foundrymen to deliver. I felt sure he must have known who I was — there was that suppressed flicker of recognition. I could see the wild romanticism that doubtless made him exciting, but those eyes were also mean, heartless orbs of black ice.

On one of his fingers, hardly visible as he shook the sticky clay off his perfectly white hand, was a ring. If the custom in Russia was the same as Bohemia or Britain, then it was a marriage band. I looked at Aunt Ludmila again and it all seemed to become clear. Now, at least for a certain part of this puzzle, there was a motive.

Chapter Nine

Another Message from London

"Mr. Pinkerstein," I said, "I don't think we've ever had the pleasure."

He was just helping his wife into the saloon compartment of the motor, juggling with the door handle and an umbrella as well as handing her up. The correctly uniformed chauffeur sat stiffly at his controls in the open front section, ignoring the rain that was trickling down the collar of his tunic. This was obviously the new etiquette, the expert mechanic concentrating on things mechanical while the passengers have to fend for themselves.

"And this is my mother, the Countess von Morštejn."

"Madam," he replied, "we haven't had the pleasure. My wife, Lili. And —"

"Countess von Falklenburg."

He reached into his waistcoat pocket. There was a gold watch chain the solidity of which could have lifted anchors from the deep. Even the fatness of his fingers didn't demand quite such heavy rings, surely? He fished out the silver case for his visit cards and handed me one.

"I presume it is business you wish to see me about?"

How quickly he had made the point. "Yes, could I call upon your office at three in the afternoon on Monday?"

"Certainly. I shall look forward to it. The directors of the Tontine Financial Association have informed me of the situation. I am so sorry about your great uncle."

He tipped his top hat and climbed into the motor which — with the smoothness and ease that only well-oiled riches can buy — glided away towards the gates of the old fortress, its warning klaxon echoing in the vaults of the archways under the old ramparts.

I looked at the card:

Isidor Pinkerstein
Mikulášská 22
Prague Old Town – Josefov

Mamma was looking eagerly over my shoulder. She was impressed by class, but even more impressed by a surfeit of money. However, she would never admit this.

"That's on the new avenue they're building from the river to the Old Town Square, isn't it?" she described rather than asked.

Indeed it was. But I just thought of it as a new street driven right through the heart of the old ghetto — just like the boulevards had been cut through the soul of Paris half a century or so ago. The ghetto may have been overcrowded, ramshackle, even insanitary, but it was a place of wonder and enchantment which somehow captured the mysteries of the teeming Orient on our own soil. I wondered if Pinkerstein cared about any of that.

"Beatrice, shall we eat at my hotel tonight? The Paris is so *à la mode* and the interiors are all in this *Art Nouveau* style — you must see it."

I looked doubtful. I was beginning to reach saturation point.

"I mean, I thought you could enjoy, let's say, a little home cooking?" — thus spaketh my mother with forked-tongue.

As we were walking towards the traditional carriages with living horses which were parked lower down for more turning room, Mamma's curiosity, which I could feel itching me, was getting the better of her. For her disguised reference to my loss of Monsieur Yves I was determined to let her stew.

Finally it broke the surface.

"And who or what is the Tontine Financial Association?" she asked.

"Oh nothing, Mamma. Just something I'd said I'd look into for someone."

And which could send me to prison or to be murdered or even make me rich, I could have added. But didn't. It is the lot of parents to find out about the activities of their offspring by first reading about them in the newspapers.

That night, having succumbed to a disagreeable dinner at the Hotel Paris — disagreeable, that is, in its aftereffects — I couldn't sleep. My poor stomach was trying valiantly to digest the truffles, the meats roasted in liqueur sauces, the rich chocolate and sugar confections of the desserts that Monsieur Yves had presented to our table. He seemed overjoyed at making me thoroughly ill, and as I had booked Mamma into the hotel in lieu of providing her a bed at home — and as the dinner was so graciously added to the room account — I even had to pay for the torture.

I had found the nerve — over braised asparagus — to simply ask her straight out: "Mamma, what do you honestly think of homosexuals?"

"Unspeakable, Beatrice. Perfectly unspeakable — at least that's what I hope I drummed into you as a child. But you asked for my honest opinion? Well, for one thing they are the backbone of the British Empire. Think of all those far-flung outposts. They look absolutely tip-top in uniform and don't fraternise with the natives, that is, marry the devils. They are quite content to fraternise amongst themselves. That's why the French or the Italians will never have an Empire like ours — and I'm talking about our British blood now, of course. Can you imagine those Latin Lotharios colonising anywhere without impregnating the natives and causing heaven-knows-what imbalance in the natural order of things? I think not."

I had looked surprised at this outburst.

"Yes, Beatrice," she had gone on, "and it is all due to the British Public Schools System. It has devised a good method to nurture these people for the Empire, and yet, when duty calls, to be able to grin and bear it and sire children with their proper race and class."

"But I mean, Mamma, doesn't it disturb you — what they actually do — between themselves? I mean, with their 'thingies'?"

"Thingies, my dear?"

"You know, their *thingies*, Mamma."

"Oh, their thingies! My dear, men are simply beasts. They find they have to put their 'thingies' somewhere. If deprived of proper opportunity, they will put them anywhere. Nothing would surprise me, or even shock me. But it's the kissing I can't imagine."

Her answer was far more forthright than I imagined it would be. I changed tack slightly, aiming more directly at home this time:

"Uncle Berty never had any children, did he?"

"What on Earth do you mean, my dear?"

I had let it go at that. I don't think she could have possibly believed it in her own family. It was certainly strange that she had been in favour — in her own way — of homosexuals (I was beginning not to call them sodomites), but I could hardly have called her attitude liberal.

I would have slept very soundly as that day I had managed to catch the elusive solution to part of the mystery. None of the puzzle made sense without a motive. The "why" had been bugging me ever since old Alois had been found not to have been old Alois.

Looking at Aunt Ludmila had done it. If I had been her, I would have been furiously jealous to have my husband having affairs, even if they were with men. Either she didn't know or she had got used to it over the years. Perhaps she was thankful that old Uncle Berty hadn't strayed with other women. Or perhaps the terrible nature of his unfaithfulness had killed something inside her — for jealousy only comes from strong passion.

The postcard with its simple, frank message — daring anyone to see it: that was the kind of reckless, devilish behaviour born of a great passion — a terrifying jealousy. I could imagine the poor wife of this Vasily Pilipenko scratching out these desperate messages. One of his lovers, if love was the correct word, had been Uncle Berry, another Sir Emile Brodsky — perhaps this Duvalier had been one. Somewhere there was also a Grand Duke — and maybe a bishop or a priest as well. Certainly it began to draw the threads together. But it just seemed doubtful. Without the moderating influence of women, I was sure male love would be more predatory, but with such a string of lovers? There must be another explanation. These questions, churning about in my mind, did not in fact permit me to sleep.

I was counting the hours by the bell of St. Jindřich's. At least I was sure I was until…until I awoke to find Müller opening the curtains and drawing the blinds and my breakfast tray being set down on the counterpane.

"And would Milady like my little egg and schnapps concoction to settle her stomach?" he was saying, very gently. What he was really saying, of course, was would I like something for my hangover?

The headache I had had the previous evening had been entirely caused by my mother. In any event, as every grown-up woman knows, the very best cure for a hangover is a glass of champagne on the breakfast tray the following morning.

The romance with which this architect Mocker had put exciting, turreted, gothic top hats onto Prague's towers — despite his other failures — was continued by other romantic architects into Mikulašska Avenue as each of the new apartment blocks vied with the next for the fussiest, fairy-tale silhouette. Number 22 was a very new block standing amidst the partly demolished remains of the old ghetto. Opposite was the Jewish Town Hall which would be preserved, along with the principal synagogues and the old cemetery, as the sole remnants of a Prague that had virtually disappeared.

Prague was, of course, almost three distinct cities — the Czech, the German, and the Jewish. After their unanimous defeat in 1620 by the Hapsburgs it was prudent of those Czech aristocrats who had survived to pretend to be Austrian — which meant adopting German culture. But with the recent growing feeling of Czech nationalism, we von Morsteins had taken to spelling our name 'Morštejn'. A tiny, but quite significant change. It was a signal and a plea not to burn down our property if there were to be a Czech nationalist revolution. We were one of "them."

On Monday at the appointed hour I was waiting in the very elaborate ante-room of Mr. Pinkerstein's offices. To create that temporal vacuum of waiting is the best trick that exists to unnerve the steeliest, and I was very far from steely. What courage I had possessed as I had picked my way over the little cubes of cobbles being hammered into the new pavements outside, or in the new lift with its gold trellised gates, was fast evaporating. I had been thinking of what my proposal to Mr. Pinkerstein would be all the weekend. It was important now that this matter seemed to me as nothing — a mere trifle, something so terribly inconsequential which I was only bothering with now simply to brush it away for the sake of a clean writing bureau.

I had ordered Sabine to polish my nails, adding a little rouge to the lacquer. Mamma — now thankfully returned to the decrepit splendour of Morštejn Castle — would have called this vulgar. If she had seen this room then she would have repeated the adjective more forcefully. There was what might be described as a wholesale quantity of green marble and gilded metalwork. If it had been possible to fashion as well the curtains and cushions from these materials, then I am sure they would have been thus executed.

Mr. Pinkerstein had a fearsome reputation, now that I had checked with my husband's solicitor, fabricating, as I had to, some reason to pass the time of day with him on the telephone. He had told me an eye-opening story:

One of the Sternbergs — sorry, the Sternberks (they too had seen the value of a tiny concession to their Czech roots) — had been wanting to invest in a cattle ranch in Nebraska, in the United States. He was a younger son and his brother, only a year or two older, was fit and well — so he perceived his chance of inheritance at very little. It was said that Pinkerstein purchased the younger brother's reversionary interest in an estate estimated at four million krone for a mere one percent of its value — the appropriate gambler's odds at one hundred-to-one, so Pinkerstein had said, of the young man gaining the fortune. Within two years, however, the older brother had died in a hunting accident without having sired any children, and the one percent invested in Nebraska had dissolved into a lost dream. "The only winner was Mr. P.," the solicitor had said.

"Come on in, Madam," Pinkerstein said expansively on opening the double doors to his office. On closer inspection his flabbiness had that clean, soft, dumpling-like texture that comes from the Turkish baths in the Old Town Mills — or the mud treatments at Lázně Toušeň.

He offered coffee, mineral water, and little wafers made as in the spas. These things had been brought in on trays fashioned from yet more green marble with gilded sides and handles.

"And what can I do for you this bright, sunny afternoon?"

"Mr. Pinkerstein, we are the last two in the Tontine and I have come to make a proposal to you."

"Which is?" (No small talk. I had been warned to expect none.)

"Neither of us knows when our nominee might pass from this Earth — it could be tomorrow, it could be much longer."

"It might have been yesterday," he said with a grin.

My heart nearly failed me. Did he know something of my real situation? He looked at my drained countenance, and felt sorry for his little joke. But he was also being serious:

"I mean…have you checked? Do you check every day? I certainly don't, Madam."

"So my proposal is this: we end the Tontine now and divide the capital equally. I am sure that this is within the rules or could be made so."

He thought for a second. He had not expected this.

"Well the answer, I'm afraid, is no. It doesn't really mean that much to me and I may as well wait until it is resolved by itself. I gambled a thousand guilders twenty years ago and I've got this far. I'll keep my stake in. I hope that doesn't disappoint you too much."

But I couldn't help but look disappointed. Apart from the immediate money it would bring it would save me from having to keep up the dishonest charade any longer — and it wasn't even I who was keeping it up. I would have given anything to have settled it now. However, I had information to get as well. I cleared my throat and tried to sound as nonchalant as an impoverished countess could.

"Tell me, Mr. Pinkerstein, what does happen at the end of the Tontine?"

"The capital asset — that's the theatre — gets given to the winner. It's as simple as that."

"And what would you do with it, if I may ask?"

"Kick those bloody actors out fast. When I put my money down twenty years ago, the Vinohrady area was then in need of a synagogue. It was my idea — if I had won much earlier — to have pulled the theatre down and given the site to our community here. For only a thousand guilders out of my pocket it would have made a very handsome gift. But I was younger in those days and couldn't see that this would last twenty years or more. I had visions of daily reports of train crashes, more battles with the Prussians, epidemics. In fact, most people actually live out their allotted span, more or less."

"And now?"

"The site is worth far more than the theatre's rent for rebuilding as an apartment house — fine, good apartments with a fine view in a quiet and prosperous neighbourhood. But that wasn't the plan of your great uncle. He was mad keen on the theatre and wanted to keep it going. No, if he had survived and his nominee had outlived mine, then he would have granted them a new lease, even with the unfortunate death of this Duvalier. But tell me, what will be your plans if you are the lucky winner?"

I replied honestly. "I simply haven't thought. It seems a shame to close a theatre, but then all things are transient, are they not? People had a good time there — but now time itself has moved on."

"That's very wise, Madam. However, I am sorry to disappoint you on a compromise. We rich people like a bit of a gamble, don't we? Who knows what the future will bring. I like that uncertainty, don't you? It adds a little spice to the otherwise boring routine of accumulating wealth, don't you think?"

The solution to the Tontine part of the mystery had been handed to me, so in that, I was happy at least. It was those managing the Fenix Theatre who were anxious to keep old Alois going — for while he lived the lease on the theatre was theirs. And if he could be kept alive long enough to outlive any other claimant, then the future of the theatre would be secure. That was all well and good insofar as the solution to the mystery went, but it did not assist at all in delivering me my strange inheritance. Who was master of the theatre now? When would they stop sending this impostor to take old Alois' place?

I reasoned that the Fenix Theatre was certainly needed for a few weeks more, for the plot being hatched at Marienbad seemed to need the assistance of the Union of Servants — or, to stand this reasoning on its head, the Union of Servants, using the theatre, had probably been created especially for the execution of their scheme. I was safe for the time being. But I doubted that a character like Mr. Pinkerstein would take being cheated very kindly if it were to be discovered. I could envisage my own corpse being dragged out of the Vltava before the spring was out.

My carriage had crossed the Old Town Square and was heading down Celetná Street towards the Powder Tower. I would have to think of a way to find out more about this dancer Pilipenko. I would tell Müller to get our young men to watch the theatre day and night. He would come there at some time or other, without a shadow of a doubt. Through him I could find his wife. One or other of them must know the solution to much more of the puzzle, of that I felt sure.

It was my mother on the telephone. She rarely used the instrument. Müller held mine out straight for me as if we had to keep the wire taught between Morštejn and Prague like playing with tins on strings as a child.

"Ludmila is in a state. I have just spoken with her. She won't ring you directly — you know what she's like — but she would dearly like you to come round and help her sort out Uncle Berty's study. Apparently there are drawers full of all sorts of things and she just doesn't know where to start and you know how difficult it must be for her…Beatrice dear, are you there?"

"Yes, Mamma. I will send a note round by pneumatic so as not to disturb her. Of course I'll go and help." I was sounding simply dutiful but in fact I was dying to get a look at Uncle Berty's papers.

"Now, Beatrice…" she continued. I knew that ominous note in her voice. "Now that I am a safe distance away, can you tell me? Whatever have you done to your hair?"

"It was a wig, Mamma." I knew this would shock her.

"A wig! Whatever for?"

"Because I've cut off all my hair."

There was a pause, all I could hear was the electrical crackling on the wire.

"And are you becoming one of those Suffragettes — a Pankhurst girl, then?"

She didn't allow me to answer, just ploughed on; typical Mamma: "Well good, very good, Beatrice. We should have had the vote centuries ago." And at that she hung up her instrument.

Yes, but it will take another few centuries for this to happen in Austria, I thought. Even in London it would be difficult.

I wrote immediately to Aunt Ludmila and by mid-afternoon she had replied. My suggestion for the following morning was accepted.

The residence that now was occupied solely by my great aunt was in a large block of apartments on Sokolská, one of the two broad avenues that stretch out from the top of Wenceslas Square to end in the Karlov Gardens with its great open vista to the south, ironically including the old fortress of Vyšehrad, where Uncle Berty now was lying, and the great Vltava River flowed down its path between towering cliffs and forested hills. Down in the valley directly below the gardens and the town ramparts, speculators had built the bustling suburb of Nusle with its terraces of houses rising on a hill opposite — the last outpost of the City of Prague and straddling the winding road to Brunn and Vienna.

All the family had wondered what had persuaded Uncle Berty to remain in Prague after his retirement. He would have been much more at home in Vienna, or in one of the houses on the family estates in Upper Austria, they had said. That Aunt Ludmila would have wanted to be nearer to my mother or the other Morštejns would have probably been of no consequence to the old autocrat. He had always had his own way. Or had he? This whole business now was exposing a weakness that none of his family could have known about, perhaps not even Aunt Ludmila.

"You understand that I don't want to go into that room, not for the present." Aunt Ludmila was standing on the threshold of Uncle Berty's study. "Don't move the small rug near his writing table, will you? It hides a stain. I will have the whole carpet taken up and burnt as soon as I can," she warned. I knew what the stain must be. So it was in here that Uncle Berty could finally stand the pressure no longer.

The top of the table which served as his desk was completely bare. This must have been due to the cleaning up. However, a

desktop would usually be a good place — I would have thought
— for an appointment diary, odd keepsakes, recent correspondence (perhaps as yet unanswered), plus postage stamps, even
an address book. All these things, if they had been there at all,
were now gone. So I began with the table's two drawers.

They were full to overflowing with silver and gold pocket-
watches, card cases, cigar cutters, spoons, forks, tie-pins,
spectacles and eyeglasses, napkin rings, ashtrays, small silver
dishes…in short, anything which could be pocketed. Here were
the results of a lifetime's kleptomania or at least the items over
which dear Uncle Berty had never been challenged. I paused at
one curious-looking device. It was like a small pair of scissors,
but with blades that formed a circle and which were armed with
cruel teeth. I imagined it had some barbaric or even some —
shall I say — medical purpose. Then I remembered. As a child,
our governess had one to cut the tops off our boiled eggs every
morning. This was a curious collection. I ventured over to the
bookcase, which had drawers below the glazed book presses.
They too were filled with the same assorted bric-a-brac.

So I turned my attention to the bookshelves. The key to the
doors I found hanging on a string behind. I went through the
entire contents of those shelves, book by book. There were no
false books with hidden compartments, no hidden caches of
letters — just one album of personal photographs: regimental, wedding, Ludmila in a studio setting — her hand poised
somewhat unnaturally on the back of an ugly chair — hunting
in Austria, a castle somewhere with a house party on the front
steps, a holiday in the South of France, Egypt in front of the
pyramids, this apartment building with the trees on the avenue
noticeably younger: nothing for the last twenty years or so.

There was another album of photographic copies of many of
the posters advertising past productions at The Tontine Theatre,
but again nothing too recent. It was just so strange that none

of us — his family, that is — knew anything of his secret life connected with the theatre. An investment in a building was one thing, but this was something different. Otherwise, apart from the volumes of military history (Julius Caesar to Prince Eugene and Napoleon, nothing afterwards) and the usual classics, some as school prizes — plus some surprising volumes of poetry — there was really nothing deeply personal. It appeared the old man had done a good job of wiping out his past, or at least all its intimate associations.

I decided to re-examine the writing table. I rummaged in the right-hand drawer first, putting my hands under the trinkets, trying to see if there were any hidden papers. Nothing but the lining paper in that one. The second drawer yielded the same result, other than some pens and pencils in a leather case, two small tins of snuff, a magnifying glass, a bunch of door keys and a clutch of old tickets — opera, theatre, concerts. So I crossed the room again and took a chance with one of the bottom drawers of the bookcase. Guarded by its gold and silver hoard, or so it seemed, I felt a flat envelope which I managed to withdraw without emptying the other contents.

It was a plain envelope, larger than for normal social correspondence. Inside was folded a second envelope, which had been torn open and was empty. Its postmark was Prague Central Office, and dated less than two weeks ago. The handwriting of Uncle's address was a scrawl — the writer had clearly tried to disguise his or her hand, but I recognised it as having certain Russian characteristics and it was written with that same spidery thin nib and dated almost at the same time as the postcard to Father Svoboda. On the back of this envelope was written an address in pencil, in Uncle Berty's hand. It was for a house in Jeseniova Street — 166 Jeseniova Street. But what had become of the letter?

It was very hot in the room. The window was shut tight and the curtain drawn to allow only a thin column of light. I touched the ceramic stove, which was cold – the heat was coming from hot water radiators and pipes. But maybe the old stove was still usable. I opened its door and, indeed, in the grate, were the ashes of papers, recently burnt by the look of them. Their contents, as innocent or incriminating smoke — for it made no difference by then — had been dispersed to the four winds.

I had a very light repast with Aunt Ludmila, mainly so as not to leave her lunching on her own — but that, she would have to get used to. I could summon up no appetite. It didn't feel right, that room, the stain on the floor, the near presence of Uncle Berty — and then the contradiction: that apart from a scribbled address in pencil, I had learned nothing more about him whatsoever.

Father Svoboda was again taking confession at three. I could feel him tense when he saw me. I had waited until last, and it was by now nearly a quarter to four. I pushed the envelope from Uncle Berty's study through the crack beneath the grille. The very sight of it made Father Svoboda draw breath.

"Did you receive a letter in a similar envelope, Father?"

"I did."

"Can you tell me what kind of letter it was?"

"Yes. It was an extortion. A blackmail demand. I don't know how they thought I could ever afford such a sum."

"Did the blackmail involve this dancer, or perhaps the Jeseniova address?"

"It was a *maison de passe*, or slightly more — a kind of club. It had been set up some years ago by a man called Hammond, who had done something of the kind in London. He couldn't go back there and wasn't allowed in France either. I didn't really like him."

"But you did like what he offered?"

"To my shame…to my shame, I did."

I could sense him shuffling uneasily on his seat. He went on:

"Then nearly two years ago this Pilipenko appeared and Hammond went off. But six months ago he closed Number One-Six-Six. First it was the postcards from his wretched wife, and now these letters."

Jeseniova turned out to be a street continuing out into the fields beyond the suburb of Žižkov. It was a road that wasn't made-up and resembled more the country track of its origins. There were a few villas, some vegetable gardens, the bare trees of orchards and land lying in wait for speculators who would be "improving" this street as soon as the bustling populations of Vinohrady and Žižkov expanded outwards.

It had to be number 166, which we were now approaching. It was a small, drab villa standing on its own amidst vacant land. It appeared to be boarded-up. There was a "To Let" sign, with an agent's address, on the rough planks which covered one of the front windows. Strange that this sordid building could have been any kind of place for pleasure. But men are strange in the way they must degrade themselves, as if making love wasn't already an animal enough act even between husband and wife.

I can't deny that I have noticed — and perhaps been fascinated by — the night butterflies who solicit for their trade quite brazenly at the top end of Wenceslas Square after dark and I can't help noticing how old, addled, and ugly many of them are — yet many a good husband will take them, when at home he has an adoring wife who is still pretty enough. Perhaps the whole attraction is this sordid degradation which men seek — and women certainly do not.

I was about to call to the coachman to stop so that I could take the agent's address when I noticed a figure — it was a woman — stepping out of a side door, very plainly dressed and carrying a large enamel jug for water. She was walking to a pump.

"Drive on," I said to my coachman. He was new, I noticed. It was another wearisome sign of the times that the turnover of staff was so frequent. "Just drive on, then turn left or right then head back for home."

But there weren't any side turnings, and the poor coachman simply looked round at me from the box, wondering what to do.

"Just turn right round, then, and back the way we came."

He wheeled the brougham round by a field entrance and we came trotting back past the house again. I was intent on looking forward, not appearing to be taking any notice of the house. However, the woman was now standing by the gate and she had been joined by a man. All I could observe, by not staring, was that she had rather thick black eyebrows. The man quickly turned away so that I was not able to see his face, but he had a head of wild black hair.

As we finally turned into Jindřišská Street I broke the habit of the last twelve months: "Drive on past home and drop me outside the Post Office." This meant also passing the vulgar Palace

Hotel, which I still refused to acknowledge as even existing. But I was in a hurry to get a telegram wired.

I couldn't remember ever having been in the building before. The sending of mail or cables or the collection or dispatch of parcels was something Müller would send the hall-boy to do. I sat myself down at a writing desk and waited there. In due course an official came and took my instructions. I certainly had not intended to wait amongst the throng. The official soon returned with the form and I began to write my telegram to Vienna.

In my bag I had put the note that Violet Northcott had sent me, thanking me for the supper last week. Colonel and Mrs. James Northcott were the couple I had invited to soften my dislike of spending too much time alone with my mother. At least her thank you — what is called a "bread and butter" note in England — gave their address in Vienna, which I did not have. But violet ink! How tasteless, even for one called Violet.

Had it been a posted letter, I should have written:

Dear Mrs. Northcott,

It was so pleasant to make your acquaintance and to meet your husband again. During supper your husband mentioned that he had good connections with the Ambassador in St. Petersburg. I was wondering if he might be so good as to pass on a request for information concerning a certain dancer, a principal of the Imperial Court Ballet — one Vasily Pilipenko. Anything your friend might be able to tell me would be most helpful. I would appreciate this information at your earliest convenience.

In addition, in a parlour quiz recently the question arose: 'What would the Kaiser want with the uniform of a British Field-Marshal?' Do you think your husband might know the answer to this brain-teaser?

I am, yours most sincerely,

Beatrice von Falklenburg.

But since it was a telegram, paid by the word, after much scratching out and eventually after having acquired a fresh form, I sent the following:

```
THANKS LETTER STOP REQUEST INFORMATION
FROM HUSBANDS PETERSBURG CONTACT
CONCERNING IMPERIAL BALLET DANCER
VASILY PILIPENKO SOONEST REGARDING
URGENT MATTER STOP ALSO WHAT DOES
KAISER WANT WITH OUR FIELDMARSHAL
UNIFORM QUESTION VON FALKENBURG
```

Quite succinct in thirty-two words — who really needs the social niceties?

I walked back the two hundred or so metres to the Harrach Palace and got Müller to summon the young men for a meeting as soon as they could be found.

The watch on the theatre was still being maintained. The news was that the actor impersonating old Alois had now started coming in to run the theatre office on Monday and Wednesday mornings, but who was in overall charge there after the death of Duvalier remained a mystery.

"Then there's the man with the red hair," said little Honza Minor, "He's back. And he has bought a small dog — a little terrier."

The reappearance of Jenks was significant. I wondered if the dog needed a little paper slip, but a detective, I was discovering, couldn't afford to ignore anything. I explained to the young men I also wanted the house at 166 Jeseniova watched, and to report to me any unusual comings and goings. At six-thirty, as the light was beginning to fade, they set off again to keep their vigils — happy, I supposed, for having a proper diet and gainful employment. I wondered if I should report the sighting of Jenks to Inspector Schneider. My decision on this could wait until tomorrow.

I was exhausted by the day. Uncle Berty's study had thoroughly depressed me, as had thinking about the empty future of Aunt Ludmila, as if the past hadn't probably been empty enough for her, as now I realised. I had undressed and was just preparing to go to sleep at almost ten o'clock when there was a knock on the door of my boudoir and I heard Sabine's voice:

"They want you to come, Madame. They say something's up at Number One-Six-Six — and that you'll understand."

I thanked Sabine and asked her to get my urchin's outfit ready for me. In a minute it had been carefully laid-out for me as if it had been a precious evening gown from Worth. I had to stop Sabine from brushing it down! Putting it on was somewhat easier than anything from Worth, however. Oh how quickly a man can dress! In the space of three minutes I was running down the stairs to the front entrance. Müller was standing there, trying to do up his collar.

"I've already summoned the carriage, Milady," he said, and then slightly under his breath he added, cocking a characteristic eyebrow: "Sabine has told me all about the outfit. You could have fooled me, if I hadn't known it was you."

'There was a clattering of hooves and jingling of harness in the courtyard. Against the silence of the night it seemed all the more noisier.

"Why don't you come, Müller? You'll only be waiting for me otherwise. Can you bring a lantern?"

"Indeed, I would rather accompany Your Ladyship, yes. You may need rescuing again, Milady."

Müller put a dark topcoat over his suit and thus looked only a little less like a butler on some lordly errand. The night was clear and crisp, frosty but dry. Jeseniova, when we got there, was already a part of the countryside: shadowy and still. Behind us the hill of Vitkov was alive with human activity, dotted with gas and electric lamps and the illuminated cars of the electric tramways which were still plying the route back and forth to the Old Town.

We stopped the brougham a good way off, concealed by the darkness, and descended. The coachman blew out the lamps and stilled the horses. Jirka Minor had run the errand, while Jirka Major kept watch nearer the house. The two Honzas were engaged at the theatre. Jirka Minor wouldn't tell us anything, as he wanted the bigger boy to tell us. Shortly before we got to the fence around the plot on which the infamous Number One-Six-Six stood, Jirka Major suddenly appeared out of the darkness.

"What is it?" Müller asked.

We could see the side door of the house was open. The gaslights were still burning and a great pool of yellowish light spilled out onto the rough ground — otherwise all was dark and silent.

"It's like this, Mr. Müller," Jirka Major began, "about an hour ago — the door being closed then — there was a great commotion inside. There was only a dim glimmer upstairs, coming from the light downstairs."

Indeed, that much fainter light was still visible now. Both a downstairs and an upstairs room at the back had not been boarded up. Jirka Major continued his story:

"There was a woman's scream — two, three screams. Then suddenly, out rushes a gentleman. Just a dark figure. He rushes past us, and up towards Žižkov. I didn't think to follow him. It happened so quick. Then there was silence — just like it is now. And I thought we should send for you, as you had asked us."

I thanked Jirkas Major and Minor and turned to Müller.

"Are you prepared to go in with me and find out what has happened, Müller?" I thought that sounded very brave and positive. In truth I was terrified. If Müller had declined, then we would have all gone home to our beds. But he said yes. He knelt down and lit the wick of the oil lantern, and when he stood up with it alight, I beckoned him forward. The two Jirkas were right behind us.

"Do you think they should see whatever's inside?" I asked Müller.

"They probably won't be stopped by us. Anyway, four of us will give us all a bit of Polish courage."

The room we entered by the open door was plainly furnished — a simple table and a couple of nondescript wooden chairs, a cupboard and some shelves with kitchen things. Through an open doorway beyond, in darkness, lay the kitchen itself. There were sheets of blank paper both on the table and scattered on the floor, and an ink bottle had been toppled over, spilling its dark liquid on the table, over the papers, and then onto the tiled floor. This was the first sign of a disturbance. The gas mantles hissed steadily.

If we were to find the staircase, it was going to be found more to the front of the house. The door out of the back room was open but no lights were lit. Müller held up the lantern as we moved towards the front hall. Now the decor was different. An attempt at *faux* gentility or tasteless romance or both had been made. The walls were decorated with a velvet-flocked paper. Curtains and drapes were swagged and tasseled. All was of an insidious red colour. There were some tawdry divans in the main room we came to, but no other furniture.

Then there was the staircase. As we climbed I noticed the shapes on the wall of pictures that had been taken away; just their ghostly outlines in the dust remained. Some vulgar plasterwork of poorly sculpted cherubs heralded the entrances to four bed-rooms. A short, narrow corridor ahead led to the room over the one at the back by which we had entered.

None of us said a word. We hardly breathed. Müller was ahead with the lantern, which threw grotesque shadows of those who followed him onto the constricted enclosure of this corridor. I felt Müller recoil back for a moment as his light fell on the scene in front of him, then he turned.

"I think Milady should go no further."

"I must, Müller." I had to steel myself to anything. Adventures were not for the faint-hearted. I must not show weakness.

He stood back, holding the light aloft. Half on the bed in the room, half propped against the wall, was the body of a woman. It had been as artlessly arranged as a glove tossed onto a chair. I recognised her eyebrows — but how people are different without life, without any ability to respond or to answer or to look. What had been a woman was now just an object for our horror and curiosity.

Her face was spattered with deep blue ink as well as blood, and the most gruesome feature of this scene was that she had been stabbed violently across her chest and neck. I wanted to be sick.

Jirka Minor seemed to be far more robust than I. He had spotted something in one of the woman's hands and gently prised open two fingers of her closed fist. The fact that this was the corpse of a brutally murdered woman seemed not to concern him. Stuck to the palm of her right hand, by the bulb of the base of the thumb was a postage stamp. The young boy loosened it and held it up. It was a Russian stamp bearing the familiar head of the Tsar.

"I think I have to leave, Müller," I said.

I was back in the carriage again. I can hardly remember how I was brought there. Müller was pouring something into a glass from a silver flask with the nonchalant air of a summer picnic.

"A little schnapps, Milady?"

Jirka Minor held out for me a cheap notebook with cloth covers. "This was under a chair in the downstairs room — beneath some papers," he said. "Is it important?"

"I am sure it must be," I replied. Actually my one thought was getting back home. I felt weak. "Your work is finished here. Come back the both of you and get warm by the kitchen stove. Are you too young for some medicinal brandy?"

Before I retired, I had just enough energy for Müller to get a connection to Inspector Schneider's home telephone. The Inspector had insisted on giving me his card with this number and the other information prominently printed on it in shiny thermographic ink — the poor man's form of engraving.

"Inspector," I said as brightly as I was able considering the terrible things I had witnessed, "I think you had better send men around immediately to 166 Jeseniova Street. I am led to believe there has been a murder there. I would be obliged if you would call on me for what very little I know about the affair at eleven tomorrow."

"Eleven…morning?" he said, sounding a little confused. Perhaps he had already gone to bed and I was awakening him. A man his age should be up all hours, for Heavens' sake.

"Inspector," I remonstrated, "now, would I mean eleven in the evening?"

"You already have — and more," was his very apt response.

Sleep was again elusive. I was haunted by the staring eyes of the dead woman. The more I saw them in my mind the more I was impressed by the idea that they also had looked surprised. Could such an expression linger after death — in the way a watch can be stopped permanently, recording the exact moment of some catastrophe? If the deed had been done by her mad, unstable, wayward lover or husband — then she could hardly have been surprised.

But for certain she was the sender of the postcards. They had been written in Prague and sent to St. Petersburg for posting back. I guessed that she lacked credit or friends there because she had to have the stamps already stuck onto them. It had been an elaborately staged plan to spread panic amongst Number One-Six-Six's clients. She had also been the writer of the blackmail letters. I was suddenly reminded of the notebook which Jirka Minor had handed me. Where was it?

I got out of bed and opened the door to my boudoir. I switched on the electric light. Yes, the notebook was there — along with my hastily discarded boy's clothes. There was a blood spatter on the cover. All the papers scattered about that lower room had been blank sheets, that someone must have been thorough enough to try to remove anything which gave any clues to the woman's activities. The notebook had apparently got hidden from view and thus overlooked.

It was the register of callers to One-Six-Six, with — wherever possible — their real names and addresses or scraps of addresses for them. It was in two distinct hands. The first was in a recognisably English hand — that of this man Hammond, perhaps, who had started the establishment. The second was the Russian woman's.

There were perhaps two or three hundred names here, maybe more. I knew several personally from just taking a quick shuffle through the pages. I knew of many more: some were names at the very top of Society. Each one was the possible target for blackmail. This book with its greasy covers and cheap lined paper could ruin the reputations of so many men who were otherwise going about by day as the most respectable of citizens. In the eyes of the world their abnormal propensities would make outcasts of them. My Uncle Berty, had he been, as the writer of our encyclopaedia had put it, "a female soul trapped in a male body"? I just didn't understand. Female souls weren't generals, surely? And would female souls wish to risk all they had in dirty little villas like the one on Jeseniova Street?

I did understand that this book could do no one any good. I threw the shawl over me that had been draped over a small settee and went out into the corridor. The palace didn't have the luxury of central heating and the big ceramic stoves in each room were charged by small furnace doors in the corridors so that servants could do this work unseen. I opened the door to the stokehole behind the boudoir and threw the book in. I waited a moment to ensure it was fully consumed by the flames which licked up and around it, shrivelling it quickly to black wisps of carbon. It was gone. For good. And for this, at least, I felt an enormous sense of relief.

"I can't work out, Countess, if trouble simply follows you around or you manage to cause it," said the Inspector. I took this as some kind of humorous aphorism. "But how came you to be there in the first place? That house — we had words with the owners a few months ago: 'Either you close or we close you down.'"

"Oh, so you knew about it?"

"Look, of course the police know these things. Our job is not actually to persecute *Widernatürliche Unzucht.*"

"You mean sodomy?"

"Well, in law it's defined as 'unnatural lewdness' — that's good for five years. But the authorities don't want the prisons full of men just following their urges."

"Especially if those men are generals, judges, bishops, financiers?"

"So we allowed the Café Carl to go on, and the Café Scheidl. They are harmless enough. Safer than men meeting anonymously in the Karlov Gardens after dark. But when it comes to an out-and-out male brothel, then there are the dangers of pimps, procurement, blackmail. That Russian dancer who took it over — we didn't like him a bit."

"What about Hammond — the man who started it?"

"You are well informed. Yes, Charles Hammond. The Metropolitan Police in London sent us a file on him. He ran the notorious male brothel in Cleveland Street, which they closed down in 1889. Since then he has been in various places in Europe. He tried to do something in Turkey for a while, perhaps it was procurement. But he found out just in time that British subjects there, are in fact under British jurisdiction, and got out just in time. We had a report of him in Budapest — advertising his *Poses Plastiques*, then he turned up in Prague. He was a friend of this Duvalier. In the last six months we haven't seen him, which means he's either dead or he's up to something bigger."

"And in London, did he have any connection, do you think, with Sir Emile Brodsky?"

"I've not thought to connect them. You see, all relevant records in the Cleveland Street files have been — shall we say — lost. That affair was reported in our papers, but never in the London ones, that someone of the very highest rank was involved besides the two lords who were named. Someone much higher. It was all hushed-up. I don't want to burn my fingers by delving too deep. But you still haven't answered my first question."

"The address was written on an envelope in my late Uncle Berty's study. General Schönburg-Hartenstein was the subject, I believe, of an attempt at blackmail."

"He and others. If only we had all the names."

"Then you would have, no doubt, a comprehensive directory of the sodomites of Prague. That could be used to protect them — or to destroy them."

I realised I should have spent more time at that wretched house on Jeseniova Street. I had only entered one of the upstairs rooms, but I didn't have the stomach for more. Perhaps I didn't really have the stomach for this work at all.

I told Schneider a slightly edited account of last night's activities, and that I believed the woman to have been one of the black-mailers. But now there was another link, this man Hammond with Duvalier. But the Russian?

I could see the telegraph boy in the street outside as I was watch-ing Schneider cross the road and make his way back to his office. In a minute, Müller was handing me an overseas cable. It was from Max in London:

INSPECTOR GREY INFORMS BRODSKY LEFT
COUNTRY YESTERDAY TRAVELLING BIARRITZ
STOP BEING FOLLOWED STOP THATS IF ITS
BRODSKY QUESTION STOP SOMETHING NOW
BEGINNING AM SURE STOP MAX

Biarritz, I was thinking. The seaside, at this time of year?

Chapter Ten
The Scheme Begins

Nothing much happened for the next five days. Hans Grübbe, the actor, continued to attend the office of the Felix Theatre which was now receiving callers resembling Emmy Destinnova. The Russian dancer was not seen and neither did Jenks visit the theatre. I had cancelled invitations, as I was in mourning, and yet, I was in no mood to see Aunt Ludmila again. With all that I was beginning to discover about Uncle Berty, what could I possibly say to her?

Only one small incident occurred. Müller informed me that he had been passing by the back of the empty Royal Court building, next to the Powder Tower, where he had seen our old chef, Monsieur Yves, handing over a sack to a gentleman. Yves had seemed rather embarrassed to have been spotted, especially by Müller. As Yves came away, Müller caught him and engaged him in conversation.

It transpired that the gentleman was in the habit of buying empty champagne bottles which Yves had procured from the Head Waiter of his hotel in the street opposite. "And just as when they are full," Yves had said, "he pays more for the best vintages. Best prices for 1880 to 1887."

"The gentleman had red hair, I suppose?" I asked Müller.

"Yes, Milady," he said gravely, "our friend Jenks."

"And tell me, Müller, I suppose too that these gatherings at The Union of Servants are strictly teetotal?"

"Oh yes, Milady. Strictly — but how could you possibly know that? Anyway, for our gala outing next month they are to make an exception."

"So you are still going?"

"Only if I can be of use to you, Milady."

"Good. That's settled then."

I dismissed Müller. Yes, it was all beginning to add up. For example: His Majesty King Edward VII had a small, long-haired terrier.

I toyed with the idea of informing Schneider about this sighting of Jenks, for it would be easy to set a trap for the man. I toyed, yes — but I would keep this to myself for the moment, to use this avenue when I needed it. In the end, Jenks would lead us somewhere, I felt sure.

On the Monday of the following week I received a letter, a cable, and a telephone call — all in the space of half an hour. It was exciting! The letter was from Max:

> *My Dear Trixie,*
>
> *I have been in regular contact with Inspector Grey. Contrary to the opinion you probably have of them, the Metropolitan Police have been intensely interested in Sir Emile Brodsky and his visit to Marienbad — despite the fact that there are instructions from the highest in*

*the land that there can be no suspicion attached to his
activities. This does, of course, pose the question as I
stated in my telegram that is 'If it is the real Sir Emile
in London?'*

*No more has been seen of this man Jenks here, and
despite a watch on the ports it is believed he has slipped
away. On Tuesday Inspector Grey told me that Brodsky had left London that morning on the boat train,
destination Biarritz. He was alone without even a valet.
Grey said that they had managed to place an officer on
the train and his whereabouts would thus be monitored.*

*Henry Chudborough has been round to see me twice
now. The Foreign Secretary has apparently been asking a
lot of questions about you, and Henry thinks they either
mean to solicit your help or to arrest you! I think whatever is planned by these villains in Marienbad must be
important.*

*I will write more when there is anything new to
report. I admire your courage in following all this
through and trust Uncle Berty's funeral passed well.
How was Mamma?*

*Before I finish, I do have one thing more to report. I
did as you said and telephoned Mr. Elderbridge at The
Times. Yesterday I received from him by post a cutting
from about 4 months ago. It simply reports that in the
area of St. John's Wood and Marylebone over the previous few months there have been no less than twenty-two
missing dogs reported. I suppose they are the owners of
the collars!*

*By the way, I popped into The Times today, just to
thank Mr. Elderbridge for his trouble. Did you know*

*he's the All-London Graeco-Roman Wrestling Champion
in his weight?*

Ever your loving brother,

Max.

P.S. Trans-Siberian Railway shares continue to fall.

I could never have believed that of the diminutive Mr. Elderbridge. It evidently pays never to believe only what one sees.
The overseas telegram was also from Max:

BRODSKY HAS GIVEN THEM THE SLIP STOP
WASNT ON TRAIN AT BIARRITZ STOP MAX

The telephone call was from Colonel Northcott:

"Beatrice, if I may?"

"Of course, Colonel…James, isn't it?"

"I am responding to your telegram. I hope you don't mind me
telephoning, but there's quite a bit to tell you. I contacted my
chum in St. Petersburg. This Vasily Pilipenko was indeed a dancer
at the Imperial Court Ballet, but hardly a big star. He danced at
the Mariinsky Theatre. In fact he got into rather a lot of trouble
— missing money or something — and he was forced to leave
the company. Then there were rumours of an even greater scandal
involving a Grand Duke. I think the police were told to keep a
lid on it, and Pilipenko was offered the chance to get out of the
country or face charges for theft. He and his sister — Olga, her
name was — left forthwith. Not a nice piece of work, I'd say."

"Sister? What about his wife?"

"Nothing known about any wife — just this sister Olga, a nasty piece of work, so I am told."

"When was this?"

"This would have been about two years ago. Now, in answer to your other question — that's simple. When Heads of State meet, it is customary on occasions when one of them particularly wants to honour the other, for them to exchange uniforms. It's no secret if I say that later this year His Majesty is coming to Bohemia and Emperor Francis Joseph will visit him in Marienbad. One of my tasks here has been to get all the details correct for an Austrian Field-Marshal's uniform for His Majesty."

I was learning secrets by the second. I wanted yet more: "Oh, do go on," I said.

"Well, actually, Archduke Frederick has already been to London to deliver the thing, but since His Majesty did not permit his correct measurements to be sent to Austria, it was — of course — far too small. My job has been to discreetly pass on the correct ones, especially those relating to girth."

I thanked him very much for calling and our conversation ended.

Well! Pilipenko's *sister*. All the postcards from St. Petersburg were part of their cold-blooded scheme to make it seem like a jealous woman on the rampage. Perhaps Pilipenko had said as much to his victims. Now, for all her scheming, Olga Pilipenko was in the morgue.

More slips of paper were beginning to fall into place. So the Kaiser would be meeting the British Head of State. Except that King Edward would not be meeting the Kaiser at all, but a poor actor named Hans Grübbe. Was that what was being planned? And for what purpose? At least it didn't look any more like a plan for an assassination. For that, you could turn up in any clothes, hide behind a tree, and simply lob a bomb at the appropriate moment. No, this was much more subtle. If only I could understand Brodsky's role in all this.

The day after Max's letter came I heard the doorbell ringing very insistently at nine in the morning and callers being admitted by Müller. He showed me two cards: one was that of the British Consul in Prague, a Mr. Wentworth-Forbes, and the other of my friend Colonel Northcott. I understood that the police, if going to make an arrest, never make an appointment. Maybe what Max had said in jest was true, and I could imagine Northcott being polite but rigidly firm.

"Show them into the drawing room, Müller. I shall be there in a minute."

He stood there a second, a look of confused bewilderment on his face — an expression he had perfected when, without uttering a word, he objected to something.

"Yes?" I snapped back. I was getting nervous.

"The drawing room is unheated, Milady. The stove has not been lit, as you instructed."

Yes. My damned economies. My fault. "Then they shall be permitted to keep their coats," was my only concession.

He bowed in that hurt way of his and silently padded out.

I looked at myself in the mirror. I presumed that prisons did not have mirrors. The curve of my bottom, I noticed (as if for the first time) seemed entirely satisfactory, but my wig — I was thinking it was a little too blonde. But again, in prisons I supposed prisoners had to sport their own hair, not the poor, boughten, once-treasured and severed locks of some peasant girl from Romania or the South of Italy. It occurred to me to ask Sabine to pack a little case, but she was out for half an hour on an errand.

"Gentlemen, do sit down, won't you?"

They did. That was a good sign. Arrests, I assumed, began with the words "Now this won't take long," with no time for settled conversation.

"Some coffee?"

Yes. That was another good sign — although it could have been merely for the warmth to be gained by holding the cup.

This Mr. Wentworth-Forbes — he of a stout neck and optimistic eyes — began:

"Lord Chudborough was asked by the Foreign Secretary to form an opinion as to whether or not you can assist us. You are not a British subject and I am sure your loyalties are to the Empire of Austria-Hungary. But in matters which do not affect that country, Lord Chudborough ventured to suggest that your loyalties in the next tier, so to speak, would be firmly to the United Kingdom. So we would like you to confirm that this is so before we go further."

Loyalty? What a nightmare it would be if I did have to choose. I felt entirely comfortable being both Czech and English combined, to be at home in shops in Vienna or London, as I wished.

"Certainly. As you know I am related to Lord Chudborough through my mother and all I can say is that my sentiments are very much English, perhaps sometimes to the detriment of my feelings towards this country. Were the Czechs free of the Austrian yoke, of course, then my father's blood which courses through my veins might alter things. But I shall always drink Jackson's tea, eat cucumber sandwiches with the crusts removed, get my brother to put a small stake on a favourite horse in the Derby every year for me, and look down upon anyone who calls a lavatory a 'toilet.' So do I pass muster?"

"Delightfully put, if I may say so," said Northcott, relaxing back into the sofa and drawing his topcoat around him.

The sofa was covered with a floral chintz. I had wanted the room to become a flower-bedecked bower and two years ago, when there had been a little money in the coffers to undertake the redecoration, mauve had been the very last word in modern colours. But I wondered now if I liked it all....

Wentworth-Forbes went on: "You brought to the attention of His Majesty's Government last month clear evidence that a criminal scheme is being prepared which we believe directly relates to an important, private, and to all intents and purposes, secret visit of His Majesty to Marienbad. He is already due to come to the spa in August, as he usually does, and this year part of that visit will consist of a formal State Visit to meet His Imperial Majesty Francis Joseph. As you are aware, the Russo-Japanese War is threatening to destabilise the whole of Europe, and His Majesty feels that a private, social meeting with his nephew, Kaiser Wilhelm, is necessary and urgent. His Majesty will therefore be travelling to Marienbad, where the meeting will take place, on May 4th."

"Well, I'd guessed that."

"I think we realised that you have been able to collect enough evidence to make that assumption," Wentworth-Forbes ploughed on. So much hot air. If it hadn't already been April, his breath would have been visible in the decidedly chill air here. It was undoubtedly warmer outside.

"The thing is," Northcott cut in, "I am actually coordinating Secret Service activities in the region and we are very concerned that there has been a leak. Only a very select few knew of the plan to visit Marienbad, and yet this criminal band has been targeting May 4th for some weeks. If only we knew their intentions, then we could act. I knew you'd come across something with that question of yours about uniforms."

"I couldn't agree more about trying to establish their intentions. It's the motive, or the end result which they are trying to achieve, which has me completely foxed," I admitted.

"We want you to officially assist us," Wentworth-Forbes announced, splitting an infinitive.

"And in what way?"

"Firstly, to identify the intended crime. Secondly, to accompany His Majesty's party in Marienbad. You will be the one most familiar with all the people involved, so your presence, in my opinion," said Northcott, "is vital."

I needed a moment to think — just a moment. Wentworth-Forbes took this as a bad sign:

"Rest assured that your services to the British Crown will in no way compromise your loyalty to Austria. And if any doubt did arise, then it would be resolved diplomatically between the powers, and your position would be maintained."

"You mean I wouldn't have to emigrate to South America and live out the rest of my life rearing ponies on the pampas?"

"Exactly." Wentworth-Forbes was certain, although I did notice a bead of sweat now running down his temple, making part of his face glisten like his oiled hair.

By chance rather than design I happened not to have asked for any reward. Threadbare aristocracy is always too proud or stupid to demand a fair wage for its services. Everything from clothes brushes to bottled pickles are sold under coats-of-arms as "By Appointment to the Duke of this or the Prince of that" without any percentage of the profits going for this noble sales-boosting assistance. In this new century *Noblesse oblige* means "noblesse obliges us to pay the rent as anyone else." This reverse of the mercenary spirit in terms of my lack of demand of any kind was taken as a sign of devout loyalty. It was, of course, merely naiveté.

"I am sure His Majesty will be very thankful," Wentworth-Forbes added. I could guess what "thankful" meant, or rather exactly what it didn't mean. However, I was charmed, flattered, honoured to be asked.

"So let's begin with what must end up as the key to the mystery, shall we? It's this man Sir Emile Brodsky." I was getting in form now.

"But it's quite simple," Northcott replied. "His Majesty is going to Marienbad ostensibly as a private person and will attend a party at Sir Emile's invitation. Sir Emile is going there for the cure and is giving a small, but significant, dinner party on May 4th."

Well, that stood everything on its head.

"So where is Sir Emile at this moment?" I asked.

Wentworth-Forbes and Northcott looked at each other. Each saw a man blue with cold, hunched in his overcoat, and trying to avoid answering this particular question.

"I can tell you," I went on. "I believe you've lost him. He's given you the slip. He did not go to Biarritz, despite having set off for the place with a ticket. Why should he behave like that?"

"I'm afraid we just don't know," said Northcott. "It's odd, I grant you, but he has been known for his eccentricity in the past."

I didn't know if this was the time to tell them about Hammond, Number One-Six-Six, and other unsavoury links in the chain. Perhaps not. Maybe there was an explanation, but I had certainly come away from London with the clear impression that Brodsky was behind the whole plot. Max still thought that Brodsky had been replaced by an impostor — but that, I felt, was just too fanciful. The actors who had been engaged to play him would have had no chance to study the man at close quarters, to get into the role. And for Heavens' sake, why were there two actors?

"I want you to stay in touch with Colonel Northcott. There will be a full briefing nearer the date which the Colonel will arrange. If there is any assistance you need, please make contact. In the meantime you will receive a formal invitation to the party on May 4th, but let's hope by then we all have a clearer idea of what to expect."

I turned to Northcott: "I presume I can ask Violet for information on what I should wear? Is it a ball or just a supper? Tiaras or not?"

"I am sure she can find those answers for you — certainly better than I can, at any rate." He allowed himself a little smile, sharing it with Wentworth-Forbes, before going on: "Most of the agents I run don't have tiaras, unless they've just purloined one and it's

under their arm in a sack as they shimmy down a drainpipe."
James Northcott was eventually showing a grain of humour. I
could warm to that.

My darling Husband,

*In reply to yrs. of yesterday. Of course I understand
that you must spend more time with Count Paar. Keeping up what social connections we have is extremely
important, and I know he was kind enough to lend you
that money last year when you were in a fix. But don't
expect the same this year, the Paars are quite canny with
their wealth. By the way, Max says on no account to buy
Trans-Siberian Railway shares if anyone tries to tempt
you. Sell them if you have any.*

*The great British Empire in its wisdom has now
finally decided to believe what I had found out in
Marienbad and the possible danger to His Majesty. They
could have saved themselves several weeks if they had
acted earlier on what Max and I had to tell them in
London — but there, the wheels of government grind
slowly.*

*I have been asked to perform a special service for His
Majesty. I am not at liberty to disclose the date or other
details. However, it will require a new dress and trust
you will not mind if I go ahead and order. Don't worry,
it will be from Prague. Fortunately I cannot afford the
time to get to Paris and to Worth's!*

I feel I haven't seen you in such ages. Now I am even beginning to miss you a bit,

Your loving,

Trixie.

And in reply to that:

My dearest Trixie,

I am overjoyed that the British Empire finally appreciates you. However, I have to say that I have heard of the 'special services' that that old rascal Edward demands of his female acquaintances from time to time, especially in Marienbad. I hope what you intend to render him does not fall into this category. However, the place is full of divorcées and adventuresses of all kinds so I doubt whether he will lack for excitement.

Of course you must have a new dress, but only if you wear it. I would feel foolish lavishing money on it if (a) it were to used to cuckold me (b) and in so doing it was not to be worn at all! Just get the dressmaker, milliner etc etc to send the accounts as normal.

I am thinking of you while shooting in these woods and trust to see you soon,

Ever your loving husband with sincerest felicitations,

Karel.

P.S. I think I shall go on to the Hatzfeldts' at Sommerberg. Charlie Kinsky will come with me. We've been invited to stay a night or two at a snug little shooting

box of theirs a kilometre from the castle — good view of
the Rhine, I'm told — bachelor party — every comfort.
Couldn't resist. K.

Now that I was being taken a little more seriously as a solver of mysteries — although in this case I felt I had only managed to ever deepen what had started out as a simple matter — I decided to set out the complete theory of just what I thought the rogues' scheme to be.

In my office — once more rearranged to my liking (if not to Karel's) — I cut up a pile of unsent "The Count and Countess von Falklenburg are pleased to announce that they have moved house" cards (printers always assume one has far more friends than one does) into new shapes roughly the size of playing cards. On the blank backs of these I transcribed all the slips of paper. Armed with this deck of pertinent information I then set about trying to put together an intelligent sequence of people, places, and events.

It wasn't a card game that I would have recommended to anyone. It wasn't as self-contained as Patience, although that is precisely the quality it required. In the end there were plenty of loose ends — including the white-haired terrier. However, I concluded that the scheme, which must be some kind of elaborate swindle, involved a Kaiser. It involved a ballroom of Austrian guests — unless they were to be used to create some kind of diversion, which was entirely possible. I decided that there must be only one fake Emile Brodsky in play, perhaps I had misread the situation at the Gare du Nord: I mean, why on Earth two? In any event, Brodsky's cards included "Dog Collars" and "Dogs Missing in St. John's Wood."

As for the possibility of a fake King Edward, I concluded that this was part of an alternative plan which had been abandoned for the sensible reason that their first choice of actor had died and their second was not interested. There was obviously to be some amazing sleight of hand which could have been performed either by a King or a Kaiser. In fact if it weren't for the three corpses and the unsavoury characters involved, I might have reckoned it all to be some form of harmless prank, a hoax, the climax of which would be some astonishing feat of prestidigitation. But sadly it was clear that that's what it was not. This was a project for a reward for which it was worth committing murder.

As for old Alois, the theatre and the Tontine, at first this had just seemed a coincidental occurrence. The late Gerard Duvalier had wanted his theatre lease and had done what was needed to keep it alive. I presumed that Uncle Berty was more than an investor: his enthusiasm for the theatre had been fuelled by the smooth posteriors of young actors, which predilection had later — after Duvalier's death — been turned into the seeds of blackmail. But there was a link to the main fraud, I felt sure: it must be this — how was all this pantomime being financed?

If Brodsky was not involved, then all the others were a fairly threadbare lot — Jenks, Duvalier, the Pilipenkos. They needed the theatre for its offices, for the training of the guests. And for additional cash — to pay the principal actors of their charade, to buy spent champagne bottles, to rent the empty tobacco factory, to order plates of chops in Paris — yes, for this cash requirement they had the chance of a few of their blackmail victims in Prague paying up. It must have been some row between the Pilipenkos over the conduct of this milking of their hapless victims that resulted in Olga Pilipenko's terrible murder. One thing was certain — there was no big international finance behind this; an ingenious fraud was being enacted on the cheap.

I felt that this theory should be officially communicated to Colonel Northcott. In this Business Room of my husband's there was an object that I had seen adorn many business premises, and I was pleased to see that he had acquired one. It sat under a cover on a table all its own at the end of the room I had not yet disturbed. I removed the cover with a flourish: a shiny black Consul typewriter.

It took several hours, but I was quite determined. For a machine which was supposed to facilitate writing, it was surprising it had so many ways to hamper the eager author. It appeared to wage a war against my imprinting anything in an orderly fashion, but it had not reckoned on the warrior-spirited woman pitted against it. From the de Clyffordes who had come to Britain with William the Conqueror in 1066 (or at least that was what was inscribed on the Battle Abbey Roll after a discreet bribe to the monk in charge of the document early in the sixteenth century) and the von Morštejns of Bohemia whose ancestors a thousand years ago had accompanied the wandering Slavic Chieftan Čech — King would be too fine a word for him — up to the top of Říp mountain (and who on looking down at the inviting broad landscape spread out below had uttered the immortal words 'This will do' and had stayed), no daughter of these antecedents would be defeated by a mere lifeless automaton.

The next morning I asked Müller to send the footman round to the British Consulate with the completed document. All I had to do now was to make sure that anything else I found out would have to conform to my theory. This is the way, surely, that theories survive and have respectable lives of their own? What would happen to any contrary discoveries, I had not as yet decided.

℘

The formal invitation arrived, surprisingly from — or at least in the name of — Sir Emile Brodsky. It was his party, after all. The address for replies was, however, that of the British Consulate. I attended the detailed briefing with Northcott — learnt all kinds of indescribably dull facts, to which I knew I should be paying more attention: that His Majesty would be travelling with only two equerries — Oliver Montague and Sir Francis Knollys — and his private secretary, Sir Frederick Ponsonby; that the King's normal Mercedes motor would not be driven over for this visit for the King did not want his nephew the Kaiser to see his reliance on German mechanical skill; that Mrs. Keppel, his official mistress, would not be in attendance (although his young Czech milliner, "our little Mizzi," a resident of Marienbad, would not be ignored); the royal terrier would not be accompanying His Majesty on this particular visit; the famous Ema Destinnova would be singing; as usual, the Royal party would be lodged at the Hotel Weimar. Monsieur Ménager, the royal chef, would not be coming and reliance would be made on the hotel restaurant. Staff at the hotel were being called in early to prepare, as the Marienbad season only starts on May 1st — cutting it rather fine for putting on an impressive show.

As Colonel Northcott was relating all these details I remembered that I hadn't made up one of my cards for Ema Destinnova. But I decided I wouldn't make her a card: she didn't fit my theory. If I had bothered to look in any of Uncle Berty's books on famous military disasters (I imagined that all generals kept such books to hand) — although my morning in his study was hardly conducive to this task — no doubt I would have encountered numerous instances of theories made to fit, regardless of the facts staring the ever optimistic Field-Marshal, General, or plain despot in the face. But there was an explanation. Destinnova had been part of the King Edward imposture, and that I felt certain had now been cancelled in favour of a fake Kaiser.

Sabine brought the dressmakers to see me. If it was to be a ball,
then I favoured a white tulle skirt with a white silk body adorned
with jet — "jet" in Bohemia being very cleverly fashioned black
glass; one could never tell the difference. If the occasion was
supper only — and the wretched invitation had been criminally
vague on this point — then I favoured the white tulle with
pâquerettes, a very striking creation from a Paris pattern book
which would be made here in a workroom in Josefov. Of course,
by "a dress" in my note to Karel I took that to include a new hat,
evening bag, shoes — and as my long white gloves looked a little
tired, new ones there too. I declined a new parasol, however.
Early May did not warrant such an extravagance.

So the days passed. Müller had taken it upon himself to find
out when Monsieur Yves intended delivering his next cargo of
vintage champagne empties and organised the young men to
have Jenks followed. Pilipenko — too dangerous for our little
poor chaps to follow — had anyway disappeared.

At the beginning of the third week in April the two Honzas
reported back to Müller. Initially they had followed Jenks to a
warehouse on one of the narrow streets that go down to the river
between the vodka distillery in Zlíchov and the big brewery in
Smíchov — a district therefore of drifting aromas. He appeared
to spend his nights there, camping out on the job. There were
various comings and goings: plenty of deliveries, carters, and
general labourers helping during the day with whatever work
was going on there. This work appeared to include packing a
large quantity of china and glassware into crates, taking in a con-
signment of chandeliers, even dealing with several large potted
palms which had arrived one morning. Then on April 22nd
three carts left the warehouse laden with crates and boxes and
made the short journey to the West Bohemia Railway Company's
goodsyard — the big sheds and sidings opposite the brewery.
The potted palms were on the last cart.

The following day a four-wheeler fiacre took Jenks, the small white terrier, and a large amount of luggage to the FJ1 Station. He left on the Eger train which would be stopping at Pilsen and Marienbad.

I thanked Müller for his very thorough report, and gave him money for the young men. I called Sabine and asked her to pack as soon as possible. Our journey to the great spa for the resolution of this intriguing and doubtless tragic affair had begun.

Chapter Eleven

A Royal Visit

As Sabine and I were driven from the station, it was clear that spring was in the air. The surrounding forests gave the streets of Marienbad the distinctive aroma of pine needles. Cane chairs were being unloaded from carts to be set outside numerous cafés; men were at work repairing awnings and hanging up flower baskets; the large hotels were busily recruiting the last members of their staff who were lining up for interview outside the larger establishments; and at the few restaurants which were already open, waiters hovered for their expected guests. Over the season some of the richest men in Europe would make their way here for the cure. How different the whole place seemed from the empty, shuttered place of just a few weeks before.

The British Consulate had arranged for myself and Sabine to stay at the Weimar, where the King — under his pseudonym of The Duke of Lancaster — would also be lodging. It was the grandest hotel in the spa, whose façade resembled…well, to put it truthfully, an overblown opera house in some provincial French city. Although it was a few days before the season started officially and finishing touches were still being put to the great hotel, the restaurant was one which had already re-opened. Our suite was fine and airy.

King Edward was not only a favoured regular customer, but under his patronage Marienbad had blossomed into one of the most famous spas in Europe. It had in part achieved its fame for the two types of individuals it attracted: fat men with money and dubious women without. The spa was a Mecca for beautiful adventuresses of every nationality. There were American divor-cées, Russian *demi-mondaines,* and fascinating Austrian widows of doubtful origin. An ambitious young writer who last year had attended several of my Drawing Room soirées once said to me of his then-recent visit here: "To mingle with monarchs whilst losing superfluous weight was to glimpse the sublime."

The forest-scented air, the bubbling trickle of streams, the splash-ing of the fountains — all this would aid my concentration, I felt sure. I sat in my corner room on the third floor with my cards laid out on a small writing desk. Now here was a card whose significance I had overlooked: "BRODSKY TO BIARRITZ: Alone by train. Gives police the slip *en route.* Does not get there."

In the context of this Brodsky being an impostor, then naturally he would need to lead the London police on a false trail and actually head for Bohemia. But what if he had been the real Brodsky? What then would have been the reason? The Biarritz ruse could put off anyone else following him — such as Jenks — but it also could be used to give the man a few days in a state of limbo. He would re-surface in Marienbad for his party in early May, or perhaps some while before to complete arrangements, but he would have had a few days off the official record. Now the clue this offered would have to wait until I could possibly imagine what he would need this time for. It might have some-thing do with this man Hammond, whose whereabouts were also unknown at the moment. The homosexual half-world might just hold the answer.

There was also the fact that this meeting — this party — must be very important for the King to come to Marienbad in May, when usually he only came in August.

The afternoon light was turning into the warmer hues of evening and I remembered I had agreed to take a walk with Sabine. Our route would take us down the Haupt-Strasse then a right turn into the lane that led past the old tobacco factory.

As we walked along together we not only looked like the first of the season's promenaders but also its first pair of adventuresses. Sabine, being French, managed to look extremely *chíque* even on the modest wage I paid her. I probably looked a trifle overdressed, for there was no one else of my class taking the air tonight or probably in the entire spa. I wished I had purchased the parasol to go with my tulle dress even though the sun was now in fast retreat and the shadows lengthening with every step we took. It would have given a jaunty spirit to the outfit.

As we turned to the right off the Haupt-Strasse, Sabine gripped my arm: "We're not going *there* again, are we?"

"It's all right, Sabine. We're not going to climb in through any window. I just want to go past — to see what's happening."

There was the mysterious old convent once more. Its main entrance was now shrouded in a wooden framework draped with a tarpaulin. The windows appeared to be boarded-up from the inside with very new wood. Certainly there was no way we could see anything within.

Everywhere in Marienbad was the sound of hammering — for those last minute repairs which were still being completed in time for May 1st. Everywhere too was the sound of the beating of carpets. It was a mania. Large carpets dragged from hotel dining rooms, druggets from corridors, rugs from bedrooms

— all were taken into the unfamiliar outdoors and punished severely: bruised into docile, dustless submission for the start of the Season. The rich, famous, and fat could then walk all over them for another summer.

"Listen," I said to Sabine.

"It's not coming from over there, is it?" observed Sabine, pointing in the direction of the Haupt-Strasse, where all the hotels, restaurants, and pensions were busy repairing or improving.

No, it wasn't. Coming from inside the old tobacco factory was the distinct sound of hammering and sawing, but outwardly there were no visible signs of life. I wondered just what the secret activity inside could be. However, I couldn't see how we were to discover more by just standing here.

We turned away. As we were walking back down the lane, not one but two very large motorcars began making their way up the thoroughfare towards us — or, rather, towards the old tobacco factory. At the sight of us they appeared to change their course, quickly turning down into the shorter route that led to the railway station. Other than their drivers, the motors were empty.

It was clear that they had not wanted to be observed.

"It seems everything is in pairs in this mystery," I muttered.

The following morning, after the kind of hearty breakfast that one only eats in hotels, I gave some errands to Sabine to run while I visited the estate agent's office where Jenks had procured the rental of the tobacco factory. I was curious to see if other premises had been let to this team for the purposes of their scheme. It was only while Sabine had been running my bath for me that an idea to get this information came to me.

I stood by the counter in the estate agent's and adroitly rang the bell. The same clerk who had dealt with Jenks came out of an inner office. I could see his breakfast had been more modest, consumed this time at his office, for there were still remains about his mouth and clinging to the ends of his moustache which he was trying to remove with a handkerchief. If I was to get anywhere in this interview I would have to forget I had seen this disgusting exhibition. I proceeded to do so.

My dress was one of the plain, workaday items that I'd had Sabine get made for me. With any luck I didn't look a Countess. I just hoped that my face did not betray my loathing for bad manners. If I had had a napkin with me I would have given him it, together with a lecture.

"Can I be of service, Madam?"

"I am writing an article for the *Rodina Illustrated Weekly* on the subject of family holidays at the great spas," I began. "The cost of hotels is rising so steeply that it is far better for a family — especially a large one — to take a house. I was wondering if you would be so good as to give me some information on the rental accommodation available — or even that which you have let successfully recently?"

"Of course, Madam."

"Naturally, I shall mention the name of this firm. So what about very large houses — country houses, castles, and the like? Our readers also like to dream."

I was thinking that this crew of varlets would need a base somewhere. What better than a quiet castle just out of town?

"Well, Madam, I can say that there are a few large country houses let for the Season. These are mainly for later on, for July and August."

"Have there been any let for the entire Season? I mean, from now onwards? I was thinking of larger castles — like Count Nostitz's at Planá or the Trauttmansdorffs' — Schloss Bischofteinitz, I think it is." (I sounded so knowledgeable as I had been dragged to both of these. Karel liked to shoot at one or other of them in the autumn.)

"No, there's almost no demand for that — and most families don't want to let out their homes for longer than a couple of months in the summer at the most. There are some big houses idle, owned by foreigners. One of those we let recently."

"Oh? Which one?" This would be it, I felt sure.

"Madam, I am afraid I am not at liberty to say. Indeed it was an express term of the contract between both the lessor and the lessee that we kept the matter confidential. I am sure you understand."

"But tell me just a little about the transaction, something interesting for my readers?" I tried rolling my eyes seductively in a way which I thought suited to the class of person I was hoping to emulate — like the shop-girls I'd often observed waiting at the tramstop near St. Jindřich's churchyard. The ploy seemed to work a little in that it reminded the man to put his handkerchief away and smooth his hair with his hand. He looked at me with an earnest gaze.

"Well, I suppose it names no names for me to say that the lessee was a gentleman from Belgium, a director of the Brussels Water Works Company."

So, I had drawn a blank. I couldn't imagine Jenks, Pilipenko, or Hammond hiding behind that alias — although, by that very fact, it would have been a good one to use. However, there was no stopping the estate agent now.

"He particularly wanted the house because it has nearly two kilometres of fishing in the stream that borders one side of the estate. We were, in fact, instructed to negotiate with the Grand Duke's agent for the rights to fish on the far bank as well."

"Grand Duke?"

"Yes, Grand Duke Mikhailovich. He is one of several Russians — industrialists as well as the aristocracy — who have estates here in West Bohemia. They enjoy the recreational spirit of the spas and the cure certainly performs its restorative effect on them. I hope you will use these words in the your article..."

But I was gone.

The Ladies Reading Room, the warmth and shelter of which I had so envied when walking by in a very different guise on my last visit, now provided me with the use of reference works. I was able to discover that this Grand Duke Mikhailovich was, in St. Petersburg, head of the Theatrical Society and the Russian Ballet Company. That all made sense. In another directory I found an address in Bohemia — a castle but a dozen kilometres away. That would make an outing for Sabine and me...a change from the normal sights at the spa.

We had already walked through the woods and up the Dianahof path, but found that the Dianahof Café was still closed, and climbed the hundred steps of the Hamelikaberg view tower (although they seemed like two hundred in each direction) by the time the hotel had found a two-horse carriage that we could hire for a day. The spa was beautifully provided for with these invigorating recreational walks. It was finally the first of May, and the carriages had just returned from their winter quarters, ready for the Haupt-Strasse's promenaders to go — on a whim at the sight of them on their stand outside the magnificent Church — for many outings that were about an hour or two's pleasant drive. It made a change for the visitor weary of trudging those endless woodland paths.

The Marienbad Season opened with some ceremony and with a band playing in the Colonnade. The abbot of Tepl blessed the springs as he did every year, for they were indeed the well-spring of the Abbey's fortunes and put sumptuous roasts on the refectory board every day of the week but Fridays. More importantly, the hammering and the frantic beating of carpets were now forbidden until the autumn. The town, after all, thrived on its air of unreal serenity. It was its currency. To me, this was all like some majestic overture to a drama which I was sure would unfold soon in a more exciting way than any grand opera could hope to rival.

The estate of Grand Duke Mikhailovich was a few kilometres onwards from the small town of Tepl, the great Abbey of which owned Marienbad's lucrative warm springs — the Waters of Mary. I instructed the coachman to drive us to Tepl first, then take the road in the direction of Franzensbad, the smallest of the three great West Bohemian Spas, whose development had lacked the aggressive entrepreneurial spirit of the last abbot of Tepl, the venerable priest who had been Marienbad's tireless commercial promoter.

It was raining gently, as one would of course expect on a holiday, and I was finding Sabine agreeable company. Sometimes it falls on a maid to be a *de facto* companion. One should resist the temptation to get over familiar, as the role of maid would be reverted to soon enough — but for the while we could talk about things viewed from the carriage and what we anticipated of our luncheon, to be taken on returning through Tepl at the Abbey's own hostelry, a short distance from the town itself. Since that was also an establishment of the enterprising monks, we had expectations of a fine repast.

The road beyond Tepl ran through gently undulating, pleasant countryside. Eventually, on the left-hand side, began a long estate wall, made of stone. It ran for over a kilometre until there were gates with twin lodges. As we were passing, a horsedrawn cart was stopped as the gates were being opened for it. It appeared to be carrying a large quantity of freshly sawn timber.

I had the driver turn round and we drew up before the lodges. The gatekeeper was by this time just closing the heavy iron gates, upon which were iron plaques of a coat-of-arms I did not recognise.

"Is this the Nostitz Estate?" I called down to the man.

"No, Ma'am. I'm afraid it's not."

Insolent fellow! He should have told me whose it was. All my senses were so roused that I was in a continual tetchy mood...

"Anyway, the place is let for the Season," he went on.

"And may I enquire to whom?"

"I'm afraid not, Ma'am. If I knew, I'm told not to tell."

I shook my hand in a way Sabine knew was for her to take out my purse. The man's face brightened as Sabine handed it to me.

"Then can you at least tell me if they are at home, then?"

"They comes and goes. That's all I can say."

"And the timber waggon — are they doing repairs to the castle?"

"Oh no, Ma'am. That's just for extending the summer house in the park. Nothing up at the castle."

Having tipped the gatekeeper, I ordered the coachman to drive us back to Tepl.

"Inconclusive, I should say," I observed to Sabine. I was thinking that I could somehow bend all this to fit my theory, but the facts as they stood did not warrant it.

"I know what you wanted, Madame. As in those novels when the hump-backed old lodgekeeper says there's been strange goings-on up there, pointing aloft to the dark castle clinging to its crag in the distance?"

"Yes, you're right, Sabine. Nothing in the least romantic." Now I knew the kind of novels she read.

The bells of Tepl Abbey were tolling and clanging at the same time for some festival in that discordant way of Continental Europe as our carriage rattled across the cobbles of the Abbey's forecourt and to lunch.

The night before the King's arrival, on May 2nd, Colonel Northcott telephoned me at the hotel. I had to report that I still did not understand the plot which was obviously in motion. I hadn't been able to gain admittance to the old tobacco factory, or even to peek inside. On two further occasions, as Sabine and I passed, men obviously walking with purpose to the building diverted their course on seeing us. However, I could only say that I didn't think it was life-threatening. Assassinations are carried out by small groups or even single individuals and this didn't have that feeling, not that I had ever witnessed such an event. All I had to go on was my intuition.

"I will give you HRH's programme when we meet tomorrow," Northcott said. "We are keeping it secret until the very last minute. It's the best policy."

"Don't you think your leak is in fact from Sir Emile?" I said. There was just no one else who could have known anything about the King's visit. "I mean, he had to make arrangements for his party…invite other guests?"

"HRH has absolute confidence in Sir Emile, as I have said. But I suppose it is just possible that one of his staff might have let the cat out of the bag."

He could see I still had my doubts, and went back on the defensive: "We are lucky to have a monarch who values genius — inventiveness which can attract capital, technology which advances the Nation. This is a new era, and we must accept that there are new people who hold many of the best cards. HRH is a man of a very different mould than his mother. I suppose Her Late Majesty would have frowned on HRH's present social *milieu*. But it is not my place to make any kind of judgement, and I must respect his complete confidence in Sir Emile."

We left it at that. Tomorrow the fireworks would begin.

Northcott himself arrived at about eleven in the morning from Prague. He had with him three gentlemen in suits that were very slightly too small and who had that bull-necked look of professional prize-fighters, the tortoise shape of their craniums emphasised by their bowler hats. In short, they were an advertisement for their profession: bodyguards! Northcott had come straight to the hotel and I lunched with him in the restaurant.

"Here's the programme," he said, starting off briskly. This was business. "HRH is arriving on the early evening *de Luxe*. It's a very small party: HRH, two equerries, private secretary, two detectives. Usual valet, footmen, and so on. He'll dine here in this restaurant — in the private room — and then he'll have the rest of the evening off."

"Off?"

"Well, no duties. Not to be disturbed. You understand?"

"I think I do," I said. This is where "HRH" visits his pretty Czech milliner, I assumed. "He'll be trying new hats?"

Northcott smiled.

"So that brings us to Saturday. It's been arranged that you will be introduced to HRH just after lunch, at two-thirty. You may tell him what you know, but no suspicions of Sir Emile, as I said. He wouldn't want to hear that. Oh — and no mention of that man Charles Hammond. After the Cleveland Street affair, HRH never wants to hear of him again."

I looked puzzled. Northcott lowered his voice to a confidential whisper: "The late Prince Eddy, HRH the Duke of Clarence. An unhappy business. Only by a miracle was it not in the press. And, quite frankly, only by another miracle is he not with us today. Could you imagine the King's eldest son, the heir presumptive, one of *those*? So you can see why this topic mustn't be mentioned — ever, at all."

"Anything else I shouldn't say?"

"No, not really. Otherwise HRH is very broad-minded and likes talking to attractive women, so you should have no difficulty."

I couldn't work out if this was a sly compliment from Northcott — and with a wife like Violet, as plain as a pikestaff, I could understand his need to spread his wings occasionally — or whether it was just in the line of "business."

"Anyway," he concluded, "the rest of the programme we will give you at the interview with HRH. The dinner party is, as you know by your invitation, on Saturday evening."

Before I left Northcott to go to the smoking room to have his cigar I asked him if I might have the use of one his men to follow Brodsky if he arrived later. We agreed I should go to the station first and try to find out if Brodsky had already arrived and if not, then Northcott would assign a man to watch for him there. All this was on the strict understanding that HRH would not be informed.

I still had the photograph of the actor Jules Lefèvre and I showed it to the ticket inspector at the railway station, asking if this man had been through the station in the last day or so.

"Now that's a funny thing!" he exclaimed, "— in fact the funniest thing I've seen in a long time. It was about this time yesterday. Your man comes, but there's three of him! Three of this gentleman, all dressed the same — same monocles, same ties, same everything…spats an' all."

I had missed them. I kicked myself for not having thought of watching the station earlier. This detective business was damned far from being easy.

"And were these three men on their own?"

"No, there were two other men accompanying them. Two burly fellows."

"One with red hair?"

"Well, no, the man with the red hair was here to meet them. They went off in a motor."

As I was leaving the station, a figure stepped out from behind the newspaper kiosk. It was Inspector Schneider.

"Good afternoon, Countess," he said, taking off his hat in a gentlemanly manner. "I am here with my men. We are keeping in the background, but we want to ensure nothing happens to the 'Duke of Lancaster' on his visit to Bohemia."

"I'm glad to hear of it, Inspector. I'm still no nearer solving this riddle, however — and are you?"

"In a word, no. We have not found Pilipenko. Jenks has disappeared. Your lads watch the theatre, we know that — but nothing new there either."

"All calm before the storm, do you think?"

"Let's hope not."

"And The Union of Servants?" The day of their excursion had almost arrived.

"Their train's still due to arrive tomorrow at one. We'll be watching them, of course, but as they have done nothing wrong — other than purloining the odd tie-pin here and there — we have no other powers. They're all staying at the Continental, by the way. Management gave them a special rate as the Season's hardly started."

As I left the station I recognised the less than inconspicuous forms of other "men in plain clothes" who were there on the lookout. What a nuisance we were all too late to have caught Jenks with, I presumed, at least one real Sir Emile Brodsky!

In one way the time passed slowly until two-thirty the following day. It was the next event in the sequence and there was nothing more to do until then. I had seen the woodland paths, statues, memorials, fountains, grottoes, and springs of Marienbad too many times already. Now I simply wanted to get on with what I was really here to do. In another way, however, there didn't seem enough time for Sabine to make me ready to meet the most powerful monarch on Earth — the man whom a quarter of the world's population either admired or cursed as their King and Emperor.

"So you are our new detective?" were his very first words to me. I had to get used to this "Royal We." He put out his cigar (a good sign, I was told) and bade me sit down opposite him at the small table in the window — one of his favourite spots in the Weimar's restaurant. Northcott sat to one side.

Here he was: that famous beard and those slightly hooded eyes. I curtsied and as I rose he took my hand in his for an instant. He had stood up. I was surprised at how short he was. One imagines

Kings — but then, here he was — no throne, no courtiers other than Ponsonby and one of his equerries whom I noticed sitting discreetly at another table out of earshot, no fanfares — just a rather portly old man with a short beard, cigar ash on his waistcoat, and a knowing twinkle in his eye.

"Wish all of them were as pretty, Colonel. But dear girl, what have we got to do? We are told we are in your hands." As he looked at me I knew he was a man used to taking in a woman in a single glance.

"Well, Your Majesty…"

"We're a Duke here, a common or garden Duke."

"Well, Sir, I believe there may be some form of criminal undertaking connected with your visit. I am extremely sorry to say that it has been impossible to discover a lot more about it than that. I do think, however, that I shall be able to recognise it the moment it commences, so all I am advising is to keep on one's guard."

"Hhmm," he growled, reaching for his cigar case.

"It could be, of course, a hoax or even some pleasant surprise," I added — trying to sound positive and making no mention of the three mysterious deaths in the matter thus far.

"We hate surprises," was all the King of England could find to say.

"Let's go through the schedule, Sir, if I may —?" Northcott managed to change the tone.

The King nodded. Northcott began:

"Train arrives from Berlin at five-thirty-nine."

"So let's see if we can remember. Our nephew Willy goes straight to his hotel — the Klinger — and has an hour in his room. Six-forty he comes here for the reception in the ballroom. Seven-thirty he changes here from his uniform."

"There is a small ante-room, next to the ballroom, which has been prepared," Northcott added.

"And then at seven-forty-five the motors take us up to Glatzen for Sir Emile's little soirée. Bedtime at eleven or half-past. So that's the drill unless some damned anarchists, revolutionaries, or practical jokers disrupt it, eh?"

In a few moments I was out in the bright sunshine — that very bright sunshine that makes its appearance from dark clouds — on the Haupt-Strasse. So I had survived my first conversation with a King. I had curtsied before Queen Victoria and been in the same room as Emperor Franz-Joseph, but had never had the pleasure of being engaged in a conversation. My mother would dine out on this for months when I told her.

Sabine had been waiting for me and we promenaded together. The colonnade looked quite busy with strolling couples. The band was playing under the graceful iron arches as rain was threatening. In fact the street looked quite busy too, especially when compared to yesterday.

Suddenly Sabine tugged at my arm and was just about to wave. I pulled her hand to me to stop her. "But look, it's Müller, Madame!"

Indeed, it was Müller — dressed as normally, that is, dressed as he would normally be for a day off. He was strolling on the opposite side of the street, along by the green swards of the park, arm-in-arm with a woman of similar age. They made a presentable couple for their class. He made no sign of recognition although clearly he could see us. That I had arranged with him.

So the sudden busy look of the spa was due to the arrival of the servants' outing. It all looked innocent enough. Perhaps I had been deluded into believing all kinds of conspiracy theories of my own making. May 4th just happened to be the same day as a surprise visit of King Edward and his nephew Wilhelm II of Germany, although it must be an important visit for the King to come before August. There was nothing really to link the argy-bargy of the Tontine Theatre with Brodsky other than that he knew — fifteen years ago — this man Hammond when he was in London. Nothing.

But I was wrong. There was, of course. Jenks had just collected Brodsky from the station — that is assuming one of the three was the genuine article, but even of that I wasn't one hundred percent certain. This really wasn't the neat way events unfolded in the casebook of Sherlock Holmes!

Sabine looked a little upset. Maybe she was just a little jealous at seeing Müller with another woman. I felt like reminding her of her Parisian love-life, but it really was none of my business. "They're all just play-acting," I said to reassure her. "Don't worry. He'll be back to being our old Müller tomorrow."

I was dressed and ready for the reception in the Weimar's ballroom at six-thirty. I found several old friends from amongst local people in Society who had been invited. It wasn't a good time in Marienbad with the Season hardly started, so there was no-one particularly glittering, other than some Russian and Austrian women who had got themselves up for the occasion like Babylonian princesses and I presumed would be coming on to dinner (and whatever else) afterwards. However, I was absolutely certain that all these persons were the genuine article — not servants in disguise.

"But where is Sir Emile?" I whispered to Northcott.

"Oh, he will be waiting for us at Glatzen."

I did not want to display my ignorance by asking exactly where or what Glatzen was. It was enough to know it was the place where we would be having dinner, a party of fourteen, I was told.

We were served champagne — 1885, I noticed — and chatted until, just a few minutes later, the King made his entrance. He was dressed in the full dress uniform of a German Field-Marshal, helmeted with a spiky *Pickelhaube* which managed to look more humorous than menacing. He nodded across the room to me as he made his way to various Austrian nobles who were very pleased to be so honoured. But I could see he was slightly tense. He didn't meet his nephew very often, they didn't get on particularly well, and obviously he must have had good reason to wish to meet him now and in this informal setting.

At precisely six-thirty-five the doors of the ballroom opened and in stepped the Kaiser, resplendent in the full dress uniform of a British Field-Marshal, also bedecked with gold frogging, ropes with pointed tassels which swung against the scarlet of the tunic and jingling with, naturally, Prussian and German decorations with those British ones he'd been presented with at meetings similar to this. Under his arm he carried the appropriate plumed, cockaded helmet. He was a full five minutes early. The King was looking at his pocket watch, obviously of the same opinion.

"Willy, how good to see you," ventured the King, striding up to him, shaking his hand vigorously and trying to stuff his watch back into the folds of his unfamiliar uniform.

"Uncle, you look in excellent health and no more portly than many of my own Field-Marshals. Gone are the days, sadly, when any leader could be challenged to single combat as a way of settling differences. That kept their waistlines down, I daresay."

"Yes, Willy. You and I should fight it out ourselves and save Europe the trouble!"

"Now Uncle, this is a social occasion, I trust." The poor man really didn't have much of a sense of humour.

"Of course it's entirely social. Business tomorrow. Pleasure tonight. There's a man there waiting to give you champagne. Come." The waiter advanced.

The King took the Kaiser into the crowd and introduced him to several fawning couples. Very informal. Very Marienbad.

Meanwhile the famous singer Ema Destinnova had taken the small stage and begun singing in her enchanting voice, as I edged nearer the Kaiser. There was that slightly wild look in his eyes which I had noticed from photographs — the kind of look I assumed an angry bull would give one before it charged. The points of his moustache were waxed sharp and elevated upwards, giving the impression of a boar's teeth. Indeed he was a fearsome creature.

One little incident occurred which was mildly embarrassing. The Kaiser had been engaged in conversation with a divorcée who, I was told, was new in Marienbad. She had been married to a wealthy American who had built railroads in the west of that sub-continent. As he was turning away, he caught one of his spurs in the hem of her dress, thus causing it to tear quite badly. She was rather distraught — and I sympathised — as it was an expensive Paquin gown. I supposed that these things just happen, but the Kaiser should have been more careful with his spurs in the company of ladies. He offered neither recompense nor even a gesture of pity.

It didn't seem long before the King led the Kaiser away, and both men disappeared for fifteen minutes. The orchestra stopped playing and those who had been invited only to the reception melted away, leaving those who were to go on to dinner. So far I had not detected anything in the least suspicious.

Northcott came over. "Well, my men shadowed him from the station to the hotel, waiting outside for the fifty minutes or so he was due to rest, then shadowed him again from the hotel to here. Nothing untoward so far."

I nodded agreement and crossed my fingers.

The motorcars were waiting outside — three big Pragas like Mr. Pinkerstein's. It was getting a little dark as we climbed out of Marienbad and into the forested hills. I had managed to get a seat next to Northcott in the second motor and I finally admitted my ignorance. He replied with a sympathetic voice:

"First I'd heard of the place as well, but I'm not a regular here. The Glatzen is a popular hill in these parts. Eight hundred and something metres. Good view of the town. Good hunting in the forests at the right time — and there is a shooting box there. It's a place that HRH likes a lot — most informal, extremely private and one can do what one likes there. It's a good choice of Sir Emile, I think. And he seems to have laid on some striking enough women."

"I doubt he has laid *on* them," I commented.

Chapter Twelve
Taken for a Ride

It was quite charming. Amidst pine trees, but near the summit of the hill — the perfect retreat. A wooden construction in the Alpine Style with plenty of ornamental, fretted work to gables, stairs, galleries — that warmth of pine wood, glowing in the light from the open fire and from the hundreds of candles all alight when we arrived. Oak may be the robust timber of the British Navy, but give me pinewood any day for conviviality.

Sir Emile was at the door to greet us. I couldn't say he wasn't the same Sir Emile I had met in London and of course amidst this great company he hardly had a moment to speak to me — in fact, other than a hearty "hello," not a word.

Dinner progressed pleasantly, if a little noisily. The women who were, shall I say, of slightly dubious ancestry, became very merry on the wine which followed several more glasses of the excellent champagne.

The King and the Kaiser sat beside each other, both now in ordinary dinner suits — no decorations. The Kaiser seemed to be drinking even faster than the King.

"Do you know our host?" the King asked Willy during the sorbets after the meat.

"Of course I know Sir Emile," said the Kaiser — a certain sparkle in his eye. "We've done business together over the years, haven't we?"

Sir Emile looked a little surprised this had been mentioned, but not as surprised as the King.

"Business, Brodsky?" he asked.

"Naturally, I serve Your Majesty, but it must not be forgotten that I am...I am — shall I say? — like a chef. I make concoctions for whoever asks me."

"Whoever pays you, you mean?" said the King, a little more aggressively.

"Naturally."

"So what are you up to with my scientist, Willy?" The King turned on his nephew.

"Oh, nothing, nothing really. A little invention."

"Willy..."

"Well, tomorrow it will all be concluded. So convenient, your invitation."

"We hope you will forgive us, Willy — but we would like a few words with our host, if you don't mind."

The Kaiser seemed to turn his attention to the well-upholstered Austrian widow at his other side. The King virtually hauled Sir Emile to his feet and took him to a corner of the room. I felt it very necessary to hear this conversation and stood up to warm myself a little nearer the fire. This was not impolite as our host and the King were both on their feet as well.

"So what are you selling them, Brodsky?" I heard the King shout, although he was trying to keep it to a whisper.

"It's a new weapon. Only like ones I have sold to the War Department — just an improved version."

"What kind of new weapon?"

"Your Majesty, I am really not at liberty to say."

"Not to your Sovereign!?"

"I am actually French, Your Majesty."

"Knighted — by us — for loyalty to Britain, where you live, remember." Then the King changed tactics. "And how much are they paying you?"

"Two million marks. So you can see it is important to me. It represents some years of work," Sir Emile said calmly.

"Then why in God's name was it not offered to us?"

"Oh, but it was. But your generals, they do not understand that modern warfare will no longer be fought with cavalry or even infantry. In fact my weapon is so deadly that it may never be unleashed at all — the mere threat of its use will bring enemies to book." Suddenly he stopped, then added: "But I have already said too much. I am afraid I must conclude the arrangement tomorrow. It is merely a matter of business."

The King left Sir Emile standing near the corner and lurched angrily back to his seat.

"Willy — so what kind of weapon are you poaching from under my nose then?"

"Something quite terrifying if used, but I believe it will bring peace in the end," he replied.

"Yes, but peace on the terms of whoever has this thing, whatever it is."

There was a look of triumph on the Kaiser's face: "A deadly gas — so deadly it can kill tens of thousands of troops almost instantaneously."

The King stood up again and returned to Sir Emile.

"If the British Government matches the offer by tomorrow morning, where will your loyalties be then? Or does the great chef want a custard pie fight too?"

Sir Emile then said quietly: "Say nothing now, but I'll do it. I should have consulted Your Majesty when the War Department first rejected the idea."

The King was slightly soothed by this, and was returning to the table when Sir Emile added, "The German Government is paying half in cash and half by banker's draught. My solicitor is in Marienbad and I have the formula and one of the test phials."

I couldn't see whether the King was actually flabbergasted or just seemed to be so. I resumed my place and — heart in my mouth — at last took matters into my own hands.

This would be the biggest risk I should undertake in my life (or thus it felt), my throat felt suddenly dry.

I managed to catch the Kaiser's eye. I looked straight at him for a moment, then winked.

He was suddenly still. Not shocked — just frozen for a second. I knew I had my man, now I had to find the courage to speak. I found my voice, thank Heavens.

"Nice try, Mr. Grübbe," I said.

"What the?" said Sir Emile. The King looked confused. Already this little incident had raised his blood pressure — he was as red as a beetroot.

The Kaiser was silent, then suddenly that wild-eyed look of his just disappeared, like someone turning off an electric light. Even those pig-sticking upturned points of his moustache seemed less fierce.

"This is not your nephew Willy, Sir," I said to the King — loudly enough for it to still the entire party. "He is an impostor. He is an actor by the name of Hans Grübbe."

"And what is this, Brodsky? Some kind of joke? We really don't take kindly to..."

"If the game's up, then I am not Emile Brodsky either," the man looking and sounding so much like him said. "I am Jules Lefèvre — also an actor. Look, I don't want any trouble. I'm just playing a part here. I think it's time for us to go."

Grübbe and Lefèvre made for the door. Northcott nodded and instantly four plainclothes men were ready to take them. Two other men who accompanied the fake Kaiser, his "equerries," also rose to leave.

For a moment the King was still looking confused; it was as if everybody was not who they should be. "Countess — then who the devil are you?" he called out.

"I am me. Please do not worry. We have the impostors now."

"So you mean," said the King, turning on the poor actor who had played his nephew Willy so perfectly, "that this fellow is not the Kaiser of Germany?"

"Correct. He is not," I said.

King Edward suddenly stepped back and then lunged forward, hurling his fist at the astonished actor. As he fell back, the look of astonishment continued frozen on his bruised face. He was out cold.

"We've been wanting to do that for years and years," the King said proudly. "We just wish we had the courage to do it to the real McCoy."

There was a ripple of laughter amongst the shocked guests, some of whom hadn't yet realised that the Kaiser was not the Kaiser.

"But then where the devil *is* our nephew?" the King asked.

Northcott looked blank. The Honourable Oliver Montague, the one equerry who had been invited to the dinner, also suddenly looked at a loss. It was my turn again. In a flash I had seen the entire fraud paraded before my inner senses for the first time.

"I believe I know exactly where he is, Sir," I said. "I will have to go and rescue him immediately. He may be in danger. Especially now…if Colonel Northcott can accompany me — ?"

"You can count us in," said the King in strong tones — the kind one doesn't disobey too easily.

"But Sir," pleaded Northcott.

"Where's that motor?" shouted the King as he strode from the warm, candlelit glow and into the cold, hilltop air with the lights of Marienbad spread out below, over the tops of the breeze-stirred pines.

"Do you think this is wise, Your Majesty?" pleaded Northcott. "We could leave Your Majesty at the Weimar, which we will be passing." The motor was speeding down the winding hill road.

"We've told you before. We're just a Duke for the duration. And do you think we'd want to miss this? We are enjoying every minute, especially as now we know Willy isn't buying a deadly gas to wipe us all out."

"So tell us, Trixie — I mean, Beatrice — no, Countess, what is this fraud?" Northcott had quite forgotten himself in the heat of the moment.

"Trixie! We like that. We had a filly called Trixie once. Damned good ride," the King called out from his front seat position next to the chauffeur. His Majesty's somewhat bawdy laugh was fortunately stifled by his cough.

"I think it's like this," I began. "There is not one fraud going on this evening, but two. At the very moment this 'Sir Emile' was convincing the Duke of Lancaster to put up two million marks to match some fictitious German offer, so another Sir Emile was convincing the real Kaiser to match a British offer for — shall we say? — half a million pounds. It was a brilliant idea, so nearly came off too. Can you imagine the weeks of careful planning?"

"But don't be too impressed. We have to catch them and rescue poor Willy safely first. Where did you say they were?" said the King.

"There's an old tobacco factory behind the Haupt-Strasse. We might find them there."

"Might?"

"Yes, Sir. Might. This mystery has never been that simple."

The motorcar behind us had two of Northcott's men on board, and as we passed up the lane towards the old convent that had housed the tobacco factory, out of the shadows stepped Schneider with three or four of his own men from the Austrian police.

Our force burst into the place and we followed quickly behind. The entrance way was now without its covering tarpaulin. It had pillars and two hanging flower baskets, which I had seen somewhere else today...and then the interior: it had been transformed. It had become a replica of the ballroom of the Hotel Weimar, perfectly made in every detail, although behind it were probably timber struts and iron stage-weights to hold them in place — just as I had seen at the Fenix Theatre.

The music which had been playing suddenly stopped. The small orchestra was still standing with instruments in their hands. Emmy Destinnova was sitting with her legs crossed, smoking. Even I was fooled for a moment, but it can't have been her real self. The crowd which was in the place — dressed to the nines as the aristocracy who were their masters — suddenly was quiet. Into the centre of the room strode the King, wheezing asthmatically. I didn't think he was used to this kind of exercise, but nevertheless he was impressive when his blood was up. Perhaps that's why so many women had succumbed to being chased around his bedroom.

The King noticed on the floor several empty bottles of 1885 champagne. "Waste of a precious vintage," he scowled.

"Hardly, Your Grace," said a familiar voice. Out of the crowd stepped Müller, my Müller. "We had lemonade from those bottles until His Imperial Majesty the Kaiser left at seven-forty-five. Then they brought out the beer — but no shortage of that, I might add."

A closer look round at the fakes in their grand attire showed that they were a little the worse for wear. The men had loosened their collars. The duchesses and countesses sitting by the wall had their shoes off. Some were smoking cigarettes. These women, God forbid, were also drinking beer! None of them seemed surprised to see someone looking remarkably like King Edward VII of Great Britain. I doubt whether they would have batted an eyelid this evening if Julius Caesar himself in full battle gear had marched in.

"This is my butler, Müller, Your Grace," I said, introducing the King — Müller having reminded me of the correct form of address for an English Duke (trust him to have done so!), but should that have been a Royal Duke? — Oh, hang protocol! "He will tell us what has been happening, Sir."

"We are just interested to know what has become of our nephew, nothing more."

"As I said, they left at seven-forty-five on the dot. They said they were going to a dinner party at the Gratzen," Müller stated.

"But that's impossible," the King stated emphatically.

"No, a replica Gratzen. An exact duplicate, I shouldn't wonder." I said, then turned to Müller: "Was there any mention of a Grand Duke?"

"I did hear a mention of a Grand Duke this evening. Grand Duke Mikhailovich — could that be the name? They were speaking of the Grand Duke's residence."

"Thank you, Müller." I turned back to the King: "Then I believe I do know exactly where they are."

At that moment Northcott and Schneider emerged from a small room made in this theatre set at the far end. Over Northcott's arm was what I took to be the full-dress uniform of a British Field-Marshal, just as our fake Kaiser had been wearing at the Weimar.

"We hope to God we find more of him than that," the King muttered.

Only a moment later we were on the road to Tepl — the colder evening air blowing through our hair as the Praga picked up speed. We now had an extra two passengers, Müller and Schneider. Although they gave us some intriguing new details, there was still no information on the whereabouts of Pilipenko or, for that matter, the real Sir Emile Brodsky — for I was now convinced that at our duplicate dinner party we would find only another hapless actor playing Brodsky.

I couldn't help admiring the delightful simplicity of it all. "You see," I told anyone who was listening, "the next morning neither King nor Kaiser would mention anything to do with having done another deal with Brodsky. It was in their interests to say absolutely nothing. And as for trusting Brodsky on his word about the invention, it wasn't just Brodsky's word that was being relied on — but that of either the King or the Kaiser in person. A brilliant touch, don't you think?"

"But — Trixie, we hope you don't mind us calling you that — it is late. These situations breed familiarity, don't you think?"

said the King, looking back over his shoulder at me. If only he knew that my hair streaming so romantically in the wind was only a wig!

"Trixie, Your Grace, Sir, is fine."

"But Trixie — how did the fake Kaiser and his suite manage to avoid all the police?"

"Again, brilliantly simple. You remember our Kaiser was five minutes early at the Weimar? Well, all the police were waiting for him to emerge from the Hotel Klinger. Our man — and his "suite" — came in through the back door, out by the front, ahead of the real Kaiser, and is then shadowed all the way to the Weimar. If the police had waited another five minutes, they would have caught the real Kaiser stepping into a motor-car which would take him to the old tobacco factory."

"We see what you mean. Simple! Intriguingly simple!"

We had crossed the silent cobbled square at Tepl, the distant baroque onion-domed spires of the Abbey silhouetted against the only slightly paler sky. Soon we were passing the long stone estate wall of Grand Duke Mikhailovich's castle. The gates between the lodges stood open. The drive wound its way up and over a low hill. In the faint light we could see stately trees spreading their moon shadows on this "English" parkland and on a crag rising up ahead was the dark shape of a castle, towered and turreted. A single light was burning in a single window high up in a battlemented wall.

Before we got to the castle, however, the driveway divided into two. The right fork would take us directly to the castle entrance — so it appeared — while the left fork led to a building nestling in some trees. There seemed to be lights over there, and the sounds of music and people laughing and shouting. Of course — the Summer House. I knew immediately what we would find inside.

Outside were two station-wagons — the kind pulled by two horses each and seating up to ten or twelve persons. The horses looked up surprised at hearing the motors. The noise from the interior continued, drowning out the sound of our arrival. As before, we had a second car following with Northcott's men in it.

The door to the Garden House was not locked. The wall on this side of the building had been clad in fretted pine boards to resemble the Gratzen shooting box. Inside, the replica was more complete. We found ourselves disturbing a scene of considerable debauchery.

The King let out a gasp of astonishment and gripped my arm. However, I was certain he had seen all this — and much worse — before and his strong emotion was more to justify gripping my slim, satin-clad arm than to register any genuine alarm.

The women employed by the fraudsters were somewhat looser than those attracted by the bigger fish at the real Glatzen event. Several of them were in a state of undress. One of them, I noticed, was wearing the very latest American stays, in white. I knew the shop in Prague, and I would call there; they were quite fetching, apart from the ungainly metal suspender clips — six of those frightful things which must have very fractionally increased Mr. Pinkerstein's fortune.

Candles were guttering, some nearly burned down to their holders. The male guests at this — well, it had started out as a dinner, quite obviously — were fairly nondescript. Only one was immediately recognizable. Together, as they now came to each other, one couldn't tell the two King Edwards apart.

The King marched straight up to his counterfeit: "You, sir, are a scoundrel."

"Then God made two of them!" the impostor shouted back. Drink does make one reckless!

"Sir," I said to the King, "may I introduce the Reverend Swinnerton?"

The King ignored me for a moment. He was pointing. A small white long-haired terrier was cowering beneath the table. "Glaring error!" he roared. "We left Caesar at Windsor!"

Yes, even I had to admit — they'd made one small mistake. However, I couldn't help but admire the fact that both were wearing gardenias in their button holes.

"But why? I thought you said you wouldn't be doing this." I addressed the not-so-reverend gentleman. His trouser fly was undone. "Why did you change your mind?"

"They offered me so much more money. I was just tempted. And this," he said, sweeping an arm in a gesture to indicate that which he would now only be able to dwell on as pleasures partaken of, or perhaps about to have been — for which activity he would have, surely, a lot of time ahead in an Austrian prison. He caught my eye again: "And it's been fun. Plain fun."

Suddenly it occurred to us all at the same time. Northcott voiced it first: "So where is the Kaiser of Germany?"

Swinnerton, quite as commanding a presence as his twin by appearance but not by birth, spoke reasonably. He had realised the game was up.

"Look, gentlemen," he said, "I had only a small part to play. Nowhere near as large as in *All the King's Mistresses*. The Kaiser and his party, together with Sir Emile Brodsky, went back to his hotel. They did that nearly two hours ago."

"You were in *that* play?" exclaimed the King. I feared this poor reverend would now certainly be beheaded at the Tower of London for High Treason.

"Yes, Your Majesty, I have to admit I was."

"Good show! We enjoyed it immensely with Mrs. Keppel. Very funny indeed. Bit near the bone at times — but a good evening and we never stopped laughing. Bit near the funny bone, we suppose one might say!"

"Your Majesty saw it?"

"We'll teach you a thing or two about disguise one day. And on the way out, having taken off the appalling wig and spectacles, the people leaving the theatre complimented us on our performance! We'll see we don't press charges, especially if you have ended up swindling our nephew Willy out of two million marks."

Northcott was looking at his watch. "They will have had — by the time we get back there — nearly three hours' advance on us. God knows what will have become of them."

As we arrived outside the Hotel Klinger another motor was drawing up. It was a Mercedes with mud on its wheels and windscreen. Its chauffeur hurried round to open the saloon door, leaving the engine running. Two very Jewish gentlemen with briefcases stepped out and walked briskly into the hotel. As we were walking into the reception hall, they were disappearing into the lift ahead of us.

After some dialogue between Northcott and the night porter, the duty manager then appeared, hurriedly completing his dressing. He was soon shaking his head. "It's impossible to disturb H.I.M. the Kaiser of Germany," he was saying, "even if you are H.R.H. the King of England."

After more dialogue, with the said King of England pacing the reception hall and filling it with clouds of thick cigar smoke and even thicker curses, one of the Kaiser's equerries was summoned. He gave forth the same story: the Kaiser had given the strictest instructions that he was tired and needed to get rest. No phone calls, telegrams, or cables.

After a few minutes, while all this argument was still going on, the lift doors opened again and out stepped the two Jews. The King recognised them. "Good evening, gentlemen," he said.

"Good evening, Your Majesty," they replied, tipping their wide-brimmed black hats in unison. But there was no small talk. They left as briskly as they had arrived. Only one carried a briefcase now, I noticed.

"They are the directors of the Continental branch, in Dresden, of Bischoffsheim and Goldschmidt," the King stated. "Theirs is the only financial house that can finance entire wars if needs must. And at short notice. Monarchs do well to remember such people — they may have need of them."

The implications of this were all too obvious. Before we could do anything, the lift had come down again. As the trellis gate opened, out stepped Sir Emile Brodsky. Another man who was in the lift stepped briskly past us as the King pointed at Brodsky. "Arrest that man," he shouted.

But I was already following the younger man with the shock of black hair — and now carrying a briefcase. I called to Müller and Schneider to come quickly. The man we were following was on foot. There were no cabs around and this man — who could only have been Pilipenko — disappeared down into the Colonnade. It was impossible to follow by motor.

We were still in the Colonnade, with its moonlit, silent forest of cast-iron columns and its fountain of mineral waters still softly splashing, not seeing him. Perhaps we had lost him. Then there he was. We could suddenly see him again running the other side of the Colonnade and across the park towards the New Baths. He was a good fifty or sixty metres ahead now.

Again he disappeared briefly, but by the time we had reached the baths we could see him on the Haupt-Strasse. I had to let the men go on first. I was wearing a wretched evening gown, for Heavens' sake. I tried hitching up the skirt.

Past the Continental and he turned up the lane towards the tobacco factory. Müller and Schneider were heading across the street to follow him there. But there was a shortcut from the tobacco factory to the station — he would lead them up to the factory, making them think he was inside. I ran — as best I could, feeling like a constricted turkey — straight towards the station.

I was right. I saw him darting across the square — from down beside that grubby hotel in which I had spent my first night in the spa — and on towards the railway platforms. A locomotive with a single carriage was waiting, a great plume of steam and smoke catching the light of the moon as it shot upwards. I hurried as fast as my ridiculous costume would allow, getting to the gate that led to the platforms and now only a few metres behind him. A man in railway uniform stepped into my path, saying, "Special train, sorry. Last trains have left for the night."

"Get away, you fool," I shouted.

At that moment there was the sound of a gunshot. A bullet struck an enamel sign hanging above us with a fairground *ping*. The railway man ducked out of sight in panic. I kept on. I was determined to board that train. Pilipenko had now jumped onto the running board of the carriage. "Leave, leave will you?" he was shouting to the engineers on the footplate of the locomotive.

There was the sound of the steam pushing pistons, the squeal of wheels on the track and the train was beginning to move. I just couldn't make it in time. Now Pilipenko was inside the carriage and firing back towards me...me! Help! His shot was almost echoed by another: Schneider had reached the platforms and was returning the fire. Pilipenko ducked down and that was the last we saw of him as the train pulled rapidly from the station. But I was sure I had seen another head in the carriage too — an arm pulling Pilipenko down. Could that have been Jenks, I wondered?

The railway employee now dared raise his head.

"Idiot," I shouted at him.

Schneider was more practical: "What line's he on?"

"Karlsbad, sir."

"Direct?"

"No intermediate halts or stations, no."

"Then telegraph ahead to Karlsbad at once. Get them to get the police out. That man must be arrested — you understand? I am Inspector Schneider from Prague. Mention my name."

I was still panting, heaving great breaths from my unexpected run and feeling the effect of tight corsetry on an otherwise reasonably athletic (although largely unexercised) frame. I was also sweaty, my dress was crumpled and hitched up so my stockings were showing — one of which was ripped. I was covered in dust. Goodness knows what I looked like. Müller, who had now run up to me, managed to add to my humiliation:

"Your hair, Milady?"

"Yes — well, what about it?" I snapped, after recovering my breath.

"Well, it's gone. I mean your wig, Milady, it's gone."

I raised my hand to my unclad head. So to add to everything else I also looked like a scarecrow.

Schneider came back from the railway telegraph office where he had been for the last couple of minutes. "Let's hope they get him in Karlsbad. There's nothing more we can do. Time to turn in, I guess. What a day!"

"No, there's just one thing more tonight," I said. "At Grand Duke Mikhailovich's castle there was only one light on. I think I know whose it is. I need to go out there now. If we go back to the Weimar and take that motor, can you drive, Inspector?"

"I think so. Not driven that particular marque, but one is much the same as another — I hope."

"Good. And Müller, you have had a very tiring day, I am sure. We'll be walking past the Continental where I understand you have a room."

"If I may, Milady, I would like to come too. I'll see this thing through to the end yet. And —"

"Yes, I know what you are going to say: and I may need rescuing again."

"Precisely, Milady!"

The estate wall was again bathed by the light of the moon which sailed, pure white and mystical, through its occasional veil of clouds. The lodgekeeper was asleep or gone and the gates were still wide open. Through the park we went again. There was no light and no sound from the Summer House now, and we kept to the right — up the carriage drive to the castle itself.

The castle was a neo-Gothic affair of a style popular in the first half of last century. Underneath its cloak of medieval romanticism and chivalry was probably the wretched — but genuine — stonework of some impoverished local Slavic tyrant's crudely fortified tower. How history graces the past with such poetic intentions.

Schneider stopped our motor under the *porte cochère*. After he had switched off the engine there was a sudden stillness. Indeed it was deathly quiet, even the owls had gone to their beds. Then there was a very faint sound. It was someone calling — calling for help, far off in the vast edifice.

The tall, studded, Baronial entrance doors were surprisingly unlocked. Müller pushed one of them open and we went into the empty entrance hall with its huge staircase rising at one end to a Gothic gallery. The grey-blue light of the night sky filtered dimly through the bogus heraldry of the painted roof windows. The balusters at the angles of the stairs were carved into fantastical beasts holding the shields of barons who had never lived.

Everywhere was evidence of a hurried evacuation — theatrical makeup, typewritten scripts, top-hats, trays and dishes, empty bottles, a scattering of hairpins. Schneider kicked a bottle. It rolled down the stairs, bumping on each echoing step before hitting the floor with a crash that shattered the eerie peace of the place.

That sound seemed to have given renewed hope to whoever was calling for help, and now knocking too, pounding on a door that was evidently locked against him.

That door was now at the end of a long corridor. The three of us approached it, not without some anxiety. We had already been shot at tonight — and that had given us all pause for thought. None of us was immortal. Death could be real — even in this peculiar world of make-believe in which we had found ourselves. The knocking and crying for help was interspersed with sobbing. At length we were on the other side of that door which had become as a cell door in a prison.

"Who's there?" Schneider shouted.

"Brodsky. Sir Emile Brodsky of Paris and London," came the reply. "Let me out, I beg you."

I turned to my companions. "I don't think he's dangerous, but by the time the police get involved or we take him back to Marienbad I may never get a chance to talk to this man quietly and sensibly. Can I do this, please? I'm quite determined to get to the bottom of this mystery and there are still a lot of unanswered questions."

"But let me actually open the door first," said Müller.

He had to push hard, as Brodsky was at first slumped against it on the other side. When it was open no more than a crack,

Brodsky pulled himself to his feet and stared at us. He looked nearly mad. "You see, if you hadn't come — then I could have starved to death in here. That's how he left me."

"Pilipenko or Jenks?"

"Jenks is not so bad as Pilipenko. Pilipenko is the monster."

"I want to talk to you before getting you to Marienbad. May I do that?"

"Yes, but not in this room, please. Mine is across the corridor. It has some air at least."

That was correct. They had locked him into little more than a housemaid's linen closet.

We walked over to what he called his room. It was a large bedroom with a good-sized writing desk and a glazed door leading onto what I presumed was a small balcony. The room's large windows must have had, in daylight, a fine view over the park. In other circumstances it must have been quite charming. Müller and Schneider retired to the corridor and shut the door behind them. I was alone with him — the key to all the mystery. I noticed he had suitcases and a *portmanteau* that hadn't even been unpacked. The castle cannot have been properly staffed by these ruffians.

"I've been a prisoner here — do you know that? And I was supposed to have entertained the King tonight. Do you know what happened?"

"Yes. I do. I will tell you later. Why were you planning this party for tonight?"

"It was to be my farewell to Society. They didn't know it, of course, but that's what it was meant to be."

He suddenly seemed to focus his eyes on me. Prior to that he had been looking into the vague distance.

"By the way, I remember you now. You called on me in London — in Albany, didn't you? I am so sorry I did not recognise you until now. You must have thought me very rude."

"It's of no consequence," I said. "Why was this to have been your 'farewell'? You can answer me truthfully. I know you knew Hammond in London, for example."

Brodsky looked more relieved than shocked by my knowledge. "The blackmail, you understand? I was to be named in the Cleveland Street business — and then with more recent matters."

"Jeseniova Street, for instance?"

However, at this Brodsky went white. "Yes. How do you know that?"

"Let's just say I'm making the correct assumption."

"I sold up in London. I found a cottage in some half-deserted fishing village in the south…in southern France, where I come from. An unknown little place called St. Tropez, on an empty stretch of the coast; out of the way. I would be happy there, I thought. I could find some affectionate boy from the region, or from North Africa. There are plenty of those in Marseilles. I could get on with the life I wanted, for once, but it would have meant a clean break from everything of my life before."

He looked at me, pleading for understanding. I let a faint flicker of it pass over my features. Nothing more. He went on:

"I wasn't going to be like Lord Arthur Somerset — he carried the can for Cleveland Street — living some half-life, exiled from his country but still yearning to be back in Society. Or Lord Euston, who for the rest of his life in London or the country, drew titters wherever he went, sniggers of 'Poses Plastiques', that sort of thing. But soon, I thought, the blackmailers could do their worst. I wouldn't care."

He was sitting down now, holding his head in his hands. But I wasn't going to be seduced into feeling too sorry for him — at least not yet.

"So tell me about the gas?"

"I invent things. Good with chemistry. I tried all kinds of mixes. I had started with carbon-monoxide, chlorine-trioxide, mercuric-oxide, conine, potassamide, potassium-carboxide, cynogen, but then I began to try simpler combinations like sulphuric and cyanide of potassium. Eventually, what I was looking for was to be found in ordinary vegetables — incredible as that may seem. One could buy all the ingredients at one's local greengrocer's. However, it took many months to find the way — then eventually I had it —"

"Had what?" I still didn't understand.

"A gas which could kill in thousands almost instantly. It could transform war. Soldiers wouldn't have to fight any more."

"You mean they could simply die instead — like poor sheep at the slaughter-house?"

"But with such power it could cause peace, don't you see? No-one would be prepared to use it, don't you understand? It would deter the warmonger, especially if both sides had it. That's how I began thinking of selling it to both sides at once — but a perfectly honest transaction. I had worked once for the German Government. They had asked me to perfect an idea they already had of an explosive which was to be smokeless, devoid of smell, and also of such a nature that it would be impossible for it to ignite except when placed in certain combinations."

"And was that possible?" I asked. I had never heard of such a thing.

"I did it. I succeeded. But it was such a dangerous weapon that would transform war into something anyone could do. War could be everywhere: on the tram, in the library, at a restaurant. No battlefield required. Children could blow up express trains, sink ocean liners. No parliament or court where the public was admitted would be safe. There could be no real peace. I withdrew the patent and destroyed my notes. Eventually I told Berlin it was impossible."

"But you did patent a gun with a rotating barrel — what did the patent say: 'capable of firing three hundred rounds a minute'?"

"Yes. Think of the Austrians mown down at the Battle of König-grätz — just because they still had muzzle-loading rifles. Governments should simply look out to get the best weapons in manufacture. It was not a fault of the inventors, but of the Austrian Government who didn't believe it would make any difference. And don't forget I've many patents for humanitarian inventions. I'm just the chef."

"Yes, I've heard that before tonight."

"So what do people want me to do? Turn guns into saucepans or explosives into fertiliser? Well, I suppose I did start to listen in the end. I was having second thoughts about the gas, in particular. Then the blackmail emerged."

"How did it start?"

"Firstly, by my own foolishness. Cleveland Street should have warned me off for good. But in sex there is desire, lust — and also an exciting element of danger, risk. You probably won't understand, as a woman."

"Risk doesn't appeal to me, but I do understand this is something men crave for — to take it to the very edge of the cliff — right to the abyss —"

"— and sometimes to fall. I was an idiot to get involved in Prague. I had first gone there sightseeing from Marienbad. But there were other clients, respectable people."

"A bishop? A Grand Duke? A reputable general?"

"I see you know. I got involved. There was this theatre — attractive and available young actors. Hammond, he was behind it all. He had a friend, Duvalier — ran the theatre, but got killed in an accident. It could have gone on. Hammond paid the police."

"And then the Pilipenkos came along?"

"They did." Here he buried his head in his hands once more. After a few moments he raised his sorrowful face: "Then came the blackmail."

"Money?"

"No, more than that. This Pilipenko decided to sell my gas to both sides by fraud — and to take most of the money for his silence."

"Jenks?"

"A legman. Merely an errand boy — first for Hammond, then Pilipenko took him over too. He was none too fussy about what he was asked to do."

I moved across the room and sat on the edge of the bed. I was tired.

"So how do we come to be here?" I asked.

"I was already having second thoughts about the gas, as I said. It was brought home to me that if something like that were to fall into the hands of even minor villains like Pilipenko, then all would be lost. I decided simply to destroy the formula and all my working papers, all stocks of chemicals — even the equipment in the laboratory. There would be nothing left to reconstruct it. I kept just three phials of the chemical. I suppose my pride wouldn't allow me to destroy it all, as if it had never existed — not after all that work."

"That didn't deter them?"

"No. It gave them the idea to sell nothing but lies to both sides — and for an even higher price. They produced this elaborate charade which I suppose they have acted out tonight. That you are here means it didn't work out, yes?"

"Shall we say, not quite?"

"I took the train to the Continent. I had given that Jenks the slip. But in a few days they found me and I was their prisoner this time. They forced me to help two actors to copy my mannerisms and to emulate my speech."

Now I was finally getting to the bit which really intrigued me:

"So what did you do in those missing days? You didn't go to Biarritz — but to where?"

Brodsky didn't answer, but I could see he was struggling with the question. He knew that I knew those days must hold some dark secret. I had guessed correctly.

"To Prague? One last visit there?"

"I know you know — so what's the use in denying it? It was that Olga Pilipenko. I went to confront her. She was the brains behind all the blackmail, all the extortion. She would have been quite content to ruin people utterly. She was quite indifferent to anyone else's life."

Yes, she had ruined Uncle Berty's life. I had been so shocked that night that I had forgotten to spit on her corpse.

"And so you ended hers?"

"We had a row. No, more than that — it was much more. I was blind with rage. I wanted her to hand over the book she kept — the names of all the clients. She got a knife from the kitchen. There was a struggle. She managed to get upstairs — tried to hold the door against me. I was wild and had a strength I never knew I possessed. I got into that room. She was shrinking away from me on the bed. I grabbed the knife and pushed it into her — again and again. A cut for every life she wanted to ruin — that's how it felt. Then I was overcome with fear, remorse, sheer terror. I tried to find her records, the book. In my confused state it was impossible to do anything. I was shaking. I just took the letters she was writing at the time and left. No doubt the book has been found by the police."

"No. I had it and I burnt it. I don't understand homosexuals, but I don't think they should be persecuted. In the same way I don't understand Baptists — or for that matter, people who grow giant marrows."

"I had become a murderer."

He was sobbing now. I could have told him that he could say it was self-defence after such a row, or that he was mentally disturbed, on the other hand, there were so many stab wounds: the work of a maniac. He was right, he was a murderer in the eyes of the law. Maybe under God there would be forgiveness, but there was still something cold about the man, something lacking in his passion.

"There's one last thing. The dog collars."

"How else was I to experiment with the gas?"

"You can buy laboratory monkeys — or even dogs, for that matter. These were people's pets, their friends —"

"But it was for a far greater good, don't you understand?"

Ever the excuse for any kind of mass slaughter, Acts of Barbarity, as I think they are properly called — even though this must rank as the smallest episode under such a term. I told him the situation without mincing my words:

"The British public may be able to forgive you for killing a blackmailer during a struggle. I wonder if they might be coaxed into forgiving an inoffensive homosexual. But kidnapping and killing people's pet dogs has made you — without doubt — permanently beyond the pale."

"My life is already ruined. This whole affair — tonight, everything. I am finished. Don't you understand? I've told you everything so that at least one person can know the truth. Now I have to end it all."

I could sense he might well be serious. I was alarmed. I stood up. "Well, I didn't mean it about the dogs, it was an image only

— to make a point. Once your story is properly told, then the public will understand."

Brodsky opened the drawer of his writing table — and took from it a small glass sphere. I advanced towards him.

"Stand back," he barked, "This is the gas. The only phial I have now. I crush it in my hand and you and I are both dead. You have been my confessor. I feel better now. Now is the time."

I did stand back. I began moving back, step by step.

The man was mad. I didn't want to shout for Müller and Schneider. He could simply squeeze his fingers and that would be it — if the gas worked as well as he claimed then they would be dead too. Behind me was the door to the balcony. I glanced round quickly. It had a key in the lock. In a second I had withdrawn the key, got to the other side of the door and locked it. My heart was thumping and I could see back through its glass panels into the room.

There was a small cloud issuing from his hand. The features of his face suddenly contorted and he fell to the floor. It was all over so quickly, just as he had said. I knew immediately that Sir Emile Brodsky was dead.

Chapter Thirteen
A Chance Encounter

I was now left in a peculiarly perilous position. I was on a high balcony and my only means of escape, short of climbing (or wasn't it that word "shimmying" which Northcott had used?) a vertical drainpipe — if only I could find one, for life is never as convenient as fiction — was through the door to a room filled with a deadly poison gas. Likewise, if I shouted for help, then Müller and Schneider would come rushing into the room from the corridor and suffer, perhaps, the same fate as Brodsky.

The longer I delayed finding a solution to this problem increased the likelihood of Müller and Schneider simply opening the fatal door to find out what was going on. I had to act fast, but I had no ideas of any use whatsoever. No magic solution. This was not a fairy tale, but real life — and with that decided lack of favouritism of a lottery, that cold impartiality of Fate. Perhaps I should take the risk of the gas — opening the balcony door might disperse it into the atmosphere and at least save my companions. All these thoughts were wasting crucial time. It could only be a matter of time. I had my hand on the door handle, my other hand on the key.

Tight-fitting evening gowns did not afford room for a hand-kerchief, which I would have liked to put over my mouth and nose at least. I was prepared for the worst. Then I heard a sound.

I looked down. The sound was coming from some way below me. A solitary figure was staggering along one of the winding paths of what must have been, in broad and sunlit daylight, a delightful garden of intrigue and romance to match the modern medieval battlements. The figure seemed misshapen, stumbling — a fearful figure like that of the hunchback of Notre Dame. Or was there a far simpler explanation: a man dead drunk?

"Reverend," I called, "Reverend Swinnerton?"

This fearful figure looked up. The white of his body linen was still showing through his unbuttoned trouser fly. The portly figure of the spitting image of King Emperor Edward VII, Monarch of Great Britain — and France (claim lost c. 1450) and Emperor of India and everywhere else, it seemed, looked up. His collar was undone; cravat lost. Bottle held onto.

"And who are you up there?"

"Now look, Reverend — I want you to understand what I am going to ask you to do. Concentrate. Don't argue. Turn to your right, find the main entrance to the castle — big doors. Step inside — make lots of noise. Shout. Two gentlemen will then join you. Bring them here. I need to speak to them urgently."

If this worked, then I would have to thank the real King. How wonderful to be monarch, I was thinking: "Press no charges," he had said — and Hey! Presto — there are no charges, and the hapless Reverend Gerald Swinnerton is a free, drunk man cast abroad in the midnight garden of a castle in Bohemia! That's power, I was thinking.

However, these thoughts did not occupy all the time it took for something to happen. I did have time to imagine all the alternatives — such as Müller and Schneider opening that door merely to see that I was all right before investigating the drunken commotion in the hall.

"Milady — are you locked out of the room?" It was Müller's reassuring voice. At last! There he was, down there with Schneider. The reverend had also managed to stagger round behind them.

"I will need a ladder — again. Brodsky has released a poisonous gas. He is dead. I don't want to be."

"As Milady wishes," Müller replied, unruffled as ever.

Colonel Northcott was sitting slumped in one of the comfortable chairs of the lounge of the Hotel Weimar. The electric lights had been switched off, and the room was lit indirectly from the bright glow — through an archway — of the reception hall beyond and by the first grey glimmering of dawn through the windows. I shook his shoulder.

"James," I said, "James. It's me." As the King had so rightly observed, such situations do breed intimacy.

He awoke, gradually focusing his eyes on me. He looked at me as if I had come back from the dead. "Beatrice?" he mumbled. I could see he noticed my hair, but then had the gentlemanly decency to ignore it.

"Would you like something more, sir?" Müller asked in his usual deadpan way.

He would still be asking this on a sinking iceberg. On the low table in front of Northcott was an assortment of finished drinks. Cocoa might have been the thing at this hour. Or maybe another stiff brandy. It was already past four in the morning.

"No, no thank you," he said. "I've tried whisky — and matchsticks — already."

"So tell me what happened. We left when the fun was just starting, I think." I asked.

He was fully awake now. He had been waiting up for us, dear thing.

"HRH wasn't to be put off by some equerry or hotel manager, the Emperor of India etc being told by some functionary he cannot speak to his nephew — especially as one of my men checked that a light was still on in his suite, of course not. HRH then brushes aside the hotel people and stalks into the bowels of the Klinger. We all follow. He tries every door, closet and cupboard until he finds the room with the hotel switchboard. A startled old man wearing makeup — you get the strange ones on night shift, so I was told — is half asleep there. The fellow is wearing pearl earrings! 'I'm the King of England', HRH shouts. Without looking up the operator says 'I know, Ducky, and I'm the Queen of Sheba...' but his words die in his throat as he turns and looks up — to see the real thing. His manner changes rather suddenly! 'Connect us to our nephew the Kaiser of Germany,' HRH roars. 'Willy,' he says, 'you've been had! It's all been an audacious swindle. You are lucky to be alive at the hands of these villains.' We can almost feel the silence at the other end. Then the Kaiser says something we don't hear properly and HRH concludes by saying, 'Then we'll talk about it in the morning' — and that's it. Home to bed. However, I was so worried about you all, I naturally waited up for your report."

"Nothing else happened?" I asked.

"Well, only that one of the Kaiser's equerries, von Alberdyll, admitted to us that they'd paid a million marks in cash — with a banker's draft for a second million. Oh, and another thing, someone from the railway station was looking for Inspector Schneider. No one knew where he was staying."

"He's out at the Grand Duke's. He's dealing with the corpse of Sir Emile Brodsky — the real one, that is…or was. That's another story, perhaps for tomorrow morning."

"Brodsky's dead?" Northcott looked shocked.

"Yes, I'm afraid so. But the people from the station? It might be very important."

"They left a note for him." Northcott continued, "They felt sure he would be bound to turn up here."

"And where is this note?" This could be news of Pilipenko — and of the two million marks.

"With the Hall Porter."

I hurried to the desk. After some persuasion, and with Northcott showing some official-looking paper, I was handed an envelope. Inside was a handwritten note. I have improved the punctuation and spelling, and even typed it out:

00.23 HRS: SPECIAL TRAIN DEPARTED MARIENBAD ON THE LINE TO KARLSBAD. DESTINATION KARLSBAD LOWER.

01.15 HRS: SIGNAL BOX AT KRÁSNY JEZ JUNCTION REPORTS NO SIGHTING OF SPECIAL. SIGNALMAN

Nevrklo sets out to investigate and finds points switched onto The Elbogen branch. Makes report of this irregularity.

02.05 hrs: Special stops at Loket Station and reports that passengers pulled alarm cord at 01.46 hrs and must have alighted in forests somewhere on down gradient between Horni Slavkov and Loket.

02.20 hrs: Special continues journey to Karlsbad, arriving 02.43 hrs.

03.00 hrs: Reports filed.

So Pilipenko and Jenks had made their getaway into the forests that cloak the hills above the town of Loket. If they had prepared a carriage in advance — or even a motor somewhere — then by dawn they would be over the border into Germany with a million marks in cash.

"Clean away!" sighed Northcott as he read it after me. "The buggers!"

I had been asked to solve a mystery, not to save money — and at least no one had been hurt last night. The only person shot at had been me! As for Sir Emile, then he had simply joined the list of what one might term the collateral casualties of this affair, which included my Uncle Berty — and the unfortunate Duvalier. Olga Pilipenko, I did not treat as a mere casualty but as an execution, possibly deservedly so. Her brother now had her blood money to spend.

⁌

The hotel maid was parting the curtains, drawing the net drapes, opening the shutters and finally rolling up the blind to let the innocent daylight in. I looked out over the vista of the counterpane. My bedroom seemed alive with activity. Sabine was laying out a new dress with the rest of my day's outfit. I watched her carefully arranging it all: shoes, stockings, intimate garments, corsets, hat, gloves — then she was busying herself at the dressing table, arranging the boxes of hairpins, the powders, rouge — all so that she could put her hand on just what she wanted, just when she wanted it. I was continuously envious of her neatness.

In the meantime, a breakfast tray was being set up on a butler's folding table, and the hotel's maid was plumping up cushions to prop me up in bed. Two hotel waiters in livery were clanging about with big silver chafing-dishes and lighting a spirit lamp under the coffee pot. And what time was all this?

"Seven-thirty!" I shrieked, "I've only had three and a half hours sleep."

"I know, Madame, but His Majesty the Duke has requested you to come to the New Baths at nine. He has requested you meet the Kaiser. Then there's church at eleven."

So I had better get to it, I thought. In my mind I still thought I had met the Kaiser, but of course I hadn't. Being with the King's party meant that they were serving me an English breakfast. The coffee did smell good, but I wasn't sure I was up to hot devilled kidneys at this hour.

Sabine was looking under the bed, behind the wardrobe, even under the tragic, crumpled remains of my tulle dress. Whatever she was seeking wasn't in the bathroom, either.

"For Heavens' sake, Sabine, what are you looking for?"

"She's not here. I have been looking high and low for her — and she's vanished."

"Who? Who should be hiding in here, behind the wardrobe?"

This game was intolerable. It had taken all the powers of concentration I possessed at this hour to lift the lid of the scrambled egg dish. I couldn't deal with brainteasers.

"Madame, she — you know — her…"

She looked at my dark expression. They used to call it in novels "a brown study."

"Madame — your wig!"

I had evidently been in the company of English people too long. How just a few days can make one forgetful! In sensible English, of course, an inanimate wig is an "it." In Czech, as well as in French, it was a "she." I had visions of this wig crawling back to the hotel on her own from the railway sidings or from wherever she had jumped ship last night, bedraggled and disconsolate.

"I'm afraid it has been lost. I really don't think we can find it."

"But Madame, that was the only one. Shall I send out for another?"

I couldn't imagine the hotel housekeeper's choice of wig being at all presentable. Perhaps they kept a couple of moth-eaten spares in a cupboard just in case. Maybe I should wear a hat, and pull it down a little. Or, maybe…

With the breakfast dealt with, I was sitting in front of the dressing table's triptych of mirrors and Sabine was just combing the hair I had attacked with nail scissors a few weeks ago when it had first dawned on me that females may have "wiles," but very few other advantages in the world, compared to men. As I was remembering this I was thinking of a labourer I had noticed from my window last summer. He was going to work, wearing one of those blue overall suits which are popular with working men. He had no socks to his shoes, no underwear I should have thought, carried no papers nor purse. All he had to do in the morning was to wake up, put on this one garment, two shoes, a belt to heave in his beer tummy a little, and leave his lodgings. He might pick up a discarded clay pipe somewhere and borrow some 'baccy from a workmate and he was happy all the day long. That's why I had cut my hair. It had been the first signs of my protest at being an incapable, helpless, overcomplicated female.

"Madame, I can cut a little 'ere — even these ragged ends. Maybe even shorten a little 'ere, too, and then we have a new cut."

If I could be brave enough, then I would at least be at the start of a fashion. In a month or two all the shopgirls would be sporting their "Countess Cuts." Or I would be laughed at. Hmm. A risk, but all it would take was nerve.

Thus, I braved it to the New Baths. I didn't know what to expect. In school in Switzerland the library had possessed such edifying classics as Gibbon's *Decline and Fall of the Roman Empire*. Out of twelve volumes, there were three or four which each had several sections of very well-thumbed pages. The Sabine Women, for example, had "lost their glorious crowns of virginity." We had to imagine how. The direct cause of the fall of that great empire was Emperors fooling about in bath-houses when they should have been out killing Goths. There had been a particularly vivid description of the carnal nature of the Roman Baths.

I therefore steeled myself so that I could ignore these rulers disporting themselves in their Birthday attire. No amount of persuasion would make me remove any garment, not even my gloves. Perhaps I had been foolish not to have questioned this invitation, which had, however, been in the form of a command. By now I had learned precisely what would happen when the King chose a new hat at a certain milliner's here, and this little Mizzi had to take it round to the Weimar personally — when the King's door would be locked for an hour. I, however, would defend my honour.

I was shown in through marble corridors. I was somewhat unnerved by the fact that the splendid baths, built less than ten years ago, were in Roman style. Very Gibbon. I glimpsed a large pool with many fat men wallowing. Another pair of doors was opened. There they were, in a small private chamber. My fears had been groundless.

In two wooden contraptions, side by side, sat the King of England and the Kaiser of Germany. They were up to their necks in steaming black mud. King Edward was smoking a cigar between phrases of his conversation:

"But how could you have been fooled for an instant, Willy? You know we would never have taken Caesar to a meeting with you. We know you hate small dogs — 'yappers' didn't you call them once?"

They had not noticed me. "Good morning," I said rather timidly.

Their two heads turned simultaneously.

"Good Heavens, Trixie! — what an admirable hair arrangement! Is this the latest thing in Prague? We really didn't notice it yesterday, otherwise we would have commented on it then. We wonder if Mrs. Keppel will be trying it?" Then he turned to his nephew: "Willy, this is the Countess von Falklenburg. She allows some men to call her Trixie."

"Charmed, Madame. I hope you will forgive the mud."

"Mud, Willy! It's 'Mineral Peat' and we heard Ponsonby complaining on the telephone to someone how much it cost per hour. So don't call it 'mud,' please. It devalues it, don't you think?"

The King stubbed out his cigar in some of the mineral peat — which made a sudden hissing sound. "Trixie's the detective who's spent the last however many weeks unravelling this whole damned business."

The King then asked me to turn away as four gentlemen attendants in smart white uniforms came and released their royal victims from the contraptions. In extremely large towels they were escorted to a shower room. As they were walking away, I heard the King saying to his nephew "In a few moments Trixie Falklenburg is going to explain to you exactly how the confidence trick was to have worked." I heard the Kaiser reply sourly, "And in my case, did."

I had to wait, not knowing quite what to do. I really do hate hanging around for people, however grand. Shortly, however, a gentleman in a dark suit asked me to follow him out onto a glazed verandah, where a circular table was set with three comfortable cane chairs. The table had an admirably thick white starched linen cloth and a small vase of gardenias. The warm sun was streaming through the glass, one tall pane of which was open just a chink. On a green slope below the verandah, four horses were tethered to nibble at the grass; they belonged to the hiring carriages which were on the street opposite, below the Catholic Church. After the horrors of the night before, all seemed well with the world again.

Soon chairs were being pulled back and the two rulers, this time in Lounge rather than Birthday Suits, were seating themselves beside me. "Now we want you to explain this whole thing to my nephew. He still believes he actually went to our dinner party last night."

"Before that, Uncle, there's something else."

The Kaiser's equerry with whom we had rowed last night appeared and handed his ruler a leather-bound book and a small circular glass phial. I froze at the sight of it. I felt the King's hand on my knee — to steady me. He must have seen me go as white as a sheet. I quickly recovered myself, although the hand remained even as the coffee was served.

"So tell me, this notebook here — full of formulas, results of experiments, calculations of all kinds — it means nothing?" The Kaiser began.

The notebook was similar to those we had found in Sir Emile's stove, although this one appeared new — and of course not signed.

"It's just gibberish, Willy. A fake. A nothing. The real formula's been destroyed."

"And I paid two million marks for it!"

"Only one million, Willy. They'll never get away with trying to encash that draft. The bank will see to that."

"And this phial…if we were to crush it in our hand, then it would be…what? Just coloured water or something?"

I could see he was about to do just that. Without a fraction of a second's hesitation I rose up, pushing my chair backwards, flung myself across the table scattering coffee cups, pot, saucers — flinging myself right at the Kaiser, and grabbing hold of the phial which I managed to hurl into the park outside just as it burst open. I tugged the glass pane back and shut it tight. The two men were astounded — and even more astounded by what they then saw on the grass outside.

For a couple of seconds, it can only have been, although the longest two seconds of my life, the horses there attempted to rear up — but they were held back by their tethers. Their expressions were dreadful to behold as their features were horribly contorted, their organs struggling to resist the effect of the deadly gas. The sounds they made were pitiful too. In such an open space, and with such a small quantity, the gas quickly dispersed, but not before it had killed all four of those beasts.

"Oh, our God!" cried the Kaiser. He helped me back to my feet. "You have saved all our lives."

Then both men fell silent for a moment. Eventually, the King spoke:

"We think it was a good thing that neither of us bought this formula — and from what Northcott has related to us, Brodsky himself destroyed his own monstrous work. Can you imagine that on the scale that the inventor first conceived? Whole cities annihilated in the space of a few minutes? It is too terrible to contemplate."

There was commotion in the park outside. Inside, waiters and even the plainclothes men were suddenly all over us cleaning up. One had a gun in his hand. Perhaps they thought it was some anarchist outrage.

The manager of the Baths was now with us, apologising profusely — but what for exactly, we didn't know. The King was saying he would pay for the horses and any other damage. New dress for me, of course. Coffee had ruined it — two gone in as many days. We had to move, for there was the ghastly spectacle outside of four dead horses and an animated crowd pointing to the verandah.

"Look, we'd like you to come to church with our party, if you would. We've all had a narrow escape from death — and it's only thanks to you. The party assembles at five minutes to eleven, downstairs in the hotel," the King said to me as we were walking back through the marble corridors. Then he said more quietly: "The fact that Brodsky did get rid of his invention deserves some credit, we think. We understand he was no saint in his non-scientific life, but he's dead now. He should have a proper funeral and the usual honours."

I simply nodded. I wasn't quite so sure. Nor was I of the Kaiser. That moment when the King had said how good it was that the formula hadn't been purchased — I was looking at his face. If anything, it was registering disappointment.

At eleven we were all seated in the red brick English church, uncompromisingly British and dully Protestant with its plain ritual. The priest intoned prayers which heavily stressed thanks to God for deliverance from perils for the Sovereign and members of his family. I could see the King smiling wryly. We had all three of us been a fraction of a second away from a ghastly death. After church there would be lunch and after that the two rulers would finally hold their political discussions, where the fate of Europe could hang in the balance of their words or their indigestion.

During the sermon I thought of the elaborate swindle enacted the night before. In fact, two swindles — how audacious and how brilliant it had all been! And how very nearly the whole scheme had come off! Only the German treasury was down by a million marks.

We had been taken in the motors to the church. I had been in the King's big Praga, and he invited me to sit beside him as we left the service.

"The station," he said to the chauffeur — and then to me: "We are going to pick up the owner of this motor from his train. He was kind enough to lend it to us for our visit. Giving him a ride in his own conveyance is the least we can do for him, don't you think?"

Isidor Pinkerstein — for he was the motor's owner I was just about to discover — was coming out of the station booking hall as we arrived. He looked amused to see me. After greetings, on the way to the Weimar, the King waxed enthusiastically about the fact that I had just saved the lives of his royal self and that of the Kaiser. I wondered, fancifully I'm sure, if he spoke of my saving the Kaiser's life with just a faint twinge of regret.

As we stepped down outside the hotel, the King told us that he would see us for drinks at one-fifteen, again later than normal, due to the circumstances. So I had time to rest a moment from this whirlwind of continual social — and dramatic — events.

A letter awaited me in my room. It was from Karel. I had almost forgotten I had a husband.

My Dearest Trixie,

The railway has lost my luggage again. It is so infu-riating. Since you have my butler, who was supposed to have been acting as my valet, as well as that maid of yours, I would be grateful if you would instruct Müller immediately upon his return to send my check shoot-ing clothes, coat and breeches, the new gaiters, the other cartridge bag and that thick white flannel shirt if it finally can be found and the stout brown shooting boots with nails. Have them packed in a cardboard or other box and tie my old shooting stick on. Forward by post to Schloss Sommerberg to which I am returning tomorrow.

Trust you are well. I am sending sixty krone — the halves of three twenties enclosed and the three other halves by separate post.

Hope all is well with you. Have you met His Majesty yet?

Ever your loving husband with sincerest felicitations,

Karel.

So it was back to the domestic round again. I could suddenly picture him standing by me in those very shooting clothes (minus the thick white flannel shirt, of course; I'd have to find something else), clouds of filthy tobacco smoke from that Triumf pipe of his. It would be no good explaining that I had saved the two most powerful monarchs in the world, that I had nearly been murdered by a mad scientist, that I had broken the most elaborate fraud — a double fraud, at that — so instead I got Sabine to ring for Müller who was waiting downstairs.

I told my loyal employees (as servants were now preferring to be called) that by the next post the other halves of these banknotes should arrive. There would be twenty krone for Müller, twenty krone for Sabine, and twenty krone to divide amongst the young men as bonuses for their invaluable assistance. Naturally, there was the packing to do for my husband, and I handed Müller the letter. At this I suddenly had a feeling of emptiness — the parade had gone by, I felt. There was nothing more to do. Tomorrow, probably, I should go back to Prague — with a yearning for another adventure in the pit of my stomach. I had a small supper party to organise, one which had been cancelled due to Uncle

Berty's death. How the trivial would soon begin to dominate my thoughts again.

It was Müller, as ever, who broke my mood — as always by speaking of the purely practical or the completely overlooked. "What about old Alois?" he asked.

My God — I had clean forgotten all about him and the Tontine, where this whole adventure had begun.

A good, jolly crowd. The awful events of the last days forgotten. The King and the Kaiser appearing to get on well together, '85 champagne, the King's favourite. Pinkerstein came straight up to me and drew me aside.

"I want a word," he said. "I wasn't very fair with you the other week when you called. In fact I was — shall we say? — something less than candid with you over that Tontine business."

"You weren't?" I said all innocently. I certainly hadn't been candid.

"It was started twenty years ago, as you know. I really had no idea then how it would all work out. My nominee was just a clerk in my office — a fit enough chap for his age. Naturally, for the first few years I kept my eyes on him, since he was — unbeknown to him — my future investment. I should have told him, of course. But I didn't want him to demand too much from me. So when the first great Klondike gold rush was on only seven years ago, he suddenly upped and left for the wilds of Canada. Older men than he got taken over by this fever, I can assure you. I was left paying for my meanness — there was gold at home if he had stayed, I should have said. The upshot of it is, I really don't know if he is alive or dead at this moment — and in all probability will never know. His elder sister kept in contact, and he had survived until last Christmas when he sent this sister a card. But even she has now died. And that's it."

"But what about the Tontine Financial Association? Haven't they checked up recently?"

"I said he had gone to live in the country. I pay a doctor there to say he's alive, and I have paid an old man to sit through the visits by the representative of the Association."

"So why are you confessing this to me?" He seemed to have been doing all right as things were — and it just seemed to be a contest, in actual fact, of whose impostor might last the longest.

"Because, Countess, it isn't fair. This bit of profit's just a drop in the bucket for me — and I've already had goodness knows how much interest out of it. So I am simply going to announce the death of my nominee, and the Tontine will be all yours."

This now posed a severe moral dilemma for me — a crisis even. In the New Year I had listened through a sermon on a priest's definition of honesty. "You take a train and just before the ticket barrier at your destination you find you have lost your ticket. Now you could say you came from only one or two stations back, and no one would be the wiser, but the honest man will declare his true point of departure." The priest seemed to know so much about avoiding paying the full fare I had my own opinion on his honesty. It had seemed trifling at the time, but here was the same dilemma, magnified several thousand times over, the essence of any parable.

The temptation was that I could get away with it. Maybe old Alois did outlive his last rival. But on the other hand, maybe he didn't. However no one would know. Added to that, Pinkerstein was rich, and we von Falklenburgs certainly weren't.

"Mr. Pinkerstein," I said firmly, "when we met I proposed a compromise. I still do. We split it down the middle — half each. My nominee also had his problems, that I admit. As you say, let's be fair and we will both walk away from this affair with honour."

To Karel and me, even half the Tontine would be a small fortune, one which would keep our heads held modesty high and the old Harrach Palace as our home.

"To say I am surprised is indeed an understatement. I accept with pleasure. Will you allow me to settle this theatre business for the best possible price?"

I hadn't considered it. In fact it was better having Pinkerstein as my partner than trying to deal with the matter alone. After all that had happened, I was pleased never to see or set foot in the Fenix Theatre ever again.

"Of course, Mr. Pinkerstein. I am sure you know best."

"In the meantime, I've taken enough of your time, Your Lady-ship. I promised the 'Duke' that I'd take no more than a minute. Come with me."

I took his arm as he led me through into the ballroom. There were balloons and streamers — was this for someone's party? There was the sound of more corks popping and the sudden blinding flashes of photographers' assistants igniting their powders. There stood His Majesty the King and the Kaiser Wilhelm — both resplendent in each other's uniforms. The mellifluous tones of a duet of two sopranos could be heard and I looked across to see not one but two Emmy Destinnovas singing it!

There, too, was James Northcott — and even Inspector Schneider back from his unpleasant duties. Over the heads of other guests, some of them familiar to me, I noticed Müller and Sabine. One of the ladies (and in such a fine silk dress too — all turquoise), I noticed, had already had her hair cut short. Such a compliment to me, or perhaps more to Sabine's scissors.

The King raised his glass first saying, "To our charming Countess from Prague," he declared, "who has saved our lives and solved an almost impenetrable mystery!"

The Kaiser raised his too: "Not *from* Prague, Uncle, we give you The Countess *von* Prag, or so she should be!"

A veritable forest of hands raised glasses: "To the Countess of Prague!"

Announcing

Sins of the Father

Book Two of
The Countess of Prague Mysteries

It is 1905, a year after The Countess' first case.

Beginning with the discovery of a headless corpse with a slip of paper bearing the Countess' phone number on the funicular railway which climbs Petrin Hill in Prague, the story moves swiftly into the arcane and often murky world of stage illusionists. The Countess identifies the body as that of the Great Orsini, whose spectacular invention — the illusion of levitation — is much coveted by his sinister rival from New York, Ira Devine. The Great Orsini's head is eventually found in his famous Disappearing Cabinet, then in pawn at Moses Reach's premises in the Prague Ghetto....

Thanks to her fame spreading in the highest circles, the Countess is also summoned to Vienna for a private audience with Emperor Franz-Josef, who sets her off on the second strand of the story: a strange and secret quest to resolve certain matters concerning his ill-fated son, Crown Prince Rudolf, who had committed suicide at Mayerling sixteen years before. In due course this will involve the clandestine opening of the Prince's coffin in the Habsburg vault in the crypt of the Capuchin monastery...and this is only the beginning of the story, which ranges from Prague and Vienna to Paris and the South of France, with its eventual climax in the wilds of the Austrian Alps.

As in the Countess' first case, the two strands of the story — that of the high life and its low life counterpart — come together in a complex and unusual conclusion.

Familiar characters come and go from the Countess' first adventure.

To see more Poisoned Pen Press titles:
Visit our website: poisonedpenpress.com/
Request a digital catalog: info@poisonedpenpress.com

CPSIA information can be obtained
at www.ICGtesting.com
Printed in the USA
BVOW09s1706270917
496100BV00002B/185/P